THE SEATTLE BARISTA KILLER

THE SEATTLE BARISTA KILLER

A HARLEY WOLF MYSTERY

MURDOCH HUGHES

Mundania Press

This book is dedicated to Orion,
and all those who dare to be different.

A Mundania Press Production
Mundania Press LLC
6470A Glenway Avenue, #109
Cincinnati, Ohio 45211-5222

To order additional copies of this book, contact:
books@mundania.com
www.mundania.com

Cover Art © 2007 by SkyeWolf
SkyeWolf Images (http://www.skyewolfimages.com)
Book Design, Production, and Layout by Daniel J. Reitz, Sr.
Marketing and Promotion by Bob Sanders
Edited by Heather Bollinger

Trade Paperback ISBN: 978-1-59426-486-3
eBook ISBN: 978-1-59426-485-6
First Edition • July 2007

Production by Mundania Press LLC
Printed in the United States of America
10   9   8   7   6   5   4   3   2   1

ONE

I sniffed the air, shook the excess moisture from my coat, looked up through the misting sky toward the moon hiding behind layers of cloud, and stifled the howl that tried to escape me. Then I stuck out my right arm, raised the yellow crime scene tape and ducked under it as a uniformed Seattle cop leaning against the old brick building hollered, "Hey you—" and started walking toward me.

Looking up, SPD Detective Larry Meyers waved him off. "It's okay, he's with me. How's it going Harley?"

I avoided his outstretched, meaty palm, keeping my hands jammed in my black windbreaker pockets, and nodded, hoping that would be enough. The greeting rituals of pureblooded humans were nauseous. Didn't they know they were passing germs? Of course, I'm half werewolf so prancing around and sniffing butts and genitals as a form of greeting also had a down side.

Detective Meyers, his hand hanging alone in space for an instant, tried to recover by clapping me on the back. He said, "About time we got some back-up. Good to see you again."

"In the alley?"

"Yeah, c'mon, I'll show you," he replied, leading the way. "But with this rain we're not going to get much from the scene."

I had a reputation to uphold. The SPD used me as a consultant on their tough cases. They hated to admit it, but they thought I was some kind of psychic Sherlock Holmes. I didn't discourage them. The truth would be a lot harder to accept and taxpayers might balk at paying a bill submitted by a werewolf.

As we approached the Dumpster I said, "This barista, she worked at the Second Cup espresso café, in the University District."

"Huh? Jeez Harley, how can you be sure of that already?"

The victim was in the Dumpster, on top of several full, black plastic garbage bags, her right arm hanging over the side. Her face had been beaten to a pulp, like someone holding onto her hair had smashed her head repeatedly into the concrete.

"She was killed over there," I said, pointing to a spot next to the building where I had picked up the strongest scent of her blood. "This makes the third barista murdered. About time you people called me in."

He took my gruff manner as a warning and didn't respond, but I could sense him watching me intently. Being a werewolf detective meant my extra senses came in handy at crime scenes. I had a forensics lab brain. My mutant genes gave me special powers, kind of like those comic book superheroes—although I tended to think of my human genes as the mutant ones, but that was me. I was not even your run of the woods werewolf, because my werewolf genes had jumped ahead by one mutation. Maybe it was all the Seattle rain. Things grew wild in it.

Unlike other werewolves, in times of extreme stress I could do the *change* without a full moon, thanks to the unique brain chemical cocktail my werewolf adrenalin sparked in me. I hadn't told the other werewolves I knew, because I was different enough as it was, even from them. It was scary too. I tried to avoid *changing* like that because it was unpredictable. It might be embarrassing and could be dangerous. If I wasn't careful, something like a citizen putting a scratch on my Harley-Davidson Night Rod motorcycle could set me off. Hell, scratching my helmet might do it. It might be fun, siccing my inner being on bad drivers, but I had so far resisted the urge to see the look on their faces.

I'd learned to control myself—to keep from *changing* at inopportune times—with mantras and meditation, which I'd practiced for years. It's like self-hypnosis. I needed that control now, because these barista murders felt like an attack on my own family.

Easy Harley, easy boy. I turned my head aside from the rank odors of death and the Dumpster, took a deep breath, held it for three beats, and exhaled. Then I pulled on a pair of latex gloves and approached the body. "Do you mind staying back, Larry?" I said, suppressing a growl while waving at him to get farther behind me.

The victim was a barista all right, and it was no hunch. I'd picked up the scent of coffee way back on the street. Mukilteo brand. Used by only one stand in Seattle. I lifted her arm and examined the nails so Detective Meyers would think I was using some actual police techniques.

Even without disturbing the body too much, I could see her badly beaten face, but I didn't think it was the cause of death. From the signs, I'd guess strangulation. It was sickening. Killing your own kind for pleasure violated one of the strongest taboos no matter the species. And they called us the monsters.

Sniffing lightly I picked up a different coffee scent. Carefully lifting the vic's right leg, I peered into the Dumpster. A spilled and crushed McBucks coffee cup was beneath the body, thrown into the Dumpster before the victim had been deposited there. It smelled older than the death, as did the beer-soaked garbage bags below. Did the killer sip his latte while waiting for the barista?

The smell of Chinese food was strong in her mouth. This area of downtown Seattle, called Pioneer Square—where Seattle's pioneer roots first took hold in muddy ground—was near the International District, so she might have come from there. For Larry's benefit I said, loudly, "She ate at a Chinese restaurant recently...in the International District...sweet and sour pork."

They could get the composition of her last meal from a

coroner's report, and it was no great revelation that she had likely eaten her last meal at a Chinese restaurant, but I always mixed mundane revelations with stuff I discovered using my extraordinary senses. That way they felt they were getting the taxpayer's money's worth, and Larry would have some magical flourishes to excite the higher-ups.

However, I needed to come up with something more, something better, some clue that might actually help me solve this case. She still had the smell of sweat and fear on her. She wasn't a smoker, but I could smell a faint aroma of cigarettes. I sniffed lightly again...a Marlboro Man. I had trained myself to distinguish cigarette brands, among countless other things. It came in handy in my business. A werewolf nose was a wonderful thing, in the open air. Shut up in a room with a smoker was torture though. Perfume was almost as bad.

I searched the alley, stooping to pick up a small piece of paper. It was a bus transfer ticket...the kind they give you when you switch buses. I held it up like I was looking it over, but I was smelling it. It wasn't the barista's. It had the Marlboro Man's scent all over it.

"What's that you found?" Meyers said.

"Bus transfer...the number seventy-three from the University route. It might have belonged to the killer. He could have followed her from work, on the bus. Maybe he took the transfer in case she got back on another one. And he smokes...Marlboros.

"She got off the bus, ate Chinese, and afterwards she walked over here. She was nervous, scared, hurrying. Maybe she spotted him, but I think it was something else. He surprised her, even though she was on the alert for something or someone...got her from behind and choked her so she couldn't cry out. Oh yeah, and she has a boyfriend."

I threw the boyfriend bit in because the chances were good I was right. Throw enough info at them like a magician does, they get overwhelmed. I laid the transfer back where I'd found it. Larry's CSI crew would come in after I was done. As a special favor he'd held them back, knowing I needed to go over the scene first.

"My gosh, Harley. How do you do it?"

"Just hunches, detective. They're worth nothing until you guys do the real police work." No sense pissing on his territory. "I get a feeling about stuff like this, but feelings won't even get me past the metal detectors at the front door of the courthouse. And I have been wrong a couple of times."

"You've already been a huge help. We needed to come up with something quick to feed the newshounds, so the Mayor and the brass agreed to call you in. These baristas are like princesses around here. We all have our favorites. I really appreciate your coming in. Did you know this one, Harley?"

"No," thank the Gods. "Am I on for the duration?"

"Yeah, but keep a low profile, okay? You know how they are about too much psychic stuff. That door swings both ways. And you're not the Captain's favorite—"

"Sure, but he's an idiot and his wife is a bitch in heat— not my fault." It had happened at a cop function I hadn't been able to get out of. Larry's boss, Captain White, had come into the hallway while I was trying to get his drunken wife's paws off me.

"Aw c'mon guy, take it easy. We've all got our weaknesses."

"All right, he's your headache anyway. Where's the press now?"

"We didn't put it out on the radio. Until some citizen calls them on a cell phone, they probably won't pick up on it."

"Great. I think I'll beat it before they do show up."

"Roger. Keep in touch, you know, if anything else strikes you."

"Okay. And let me know if your crew comes up with something more.

"Like always, Harley. Thanks for your help here."

"Sure. I'll probably start by talking to the owner of the Second Cup."

"Good idea. I can't believe how you figured that out."

He shook his head as I walked away feeling like a magician after a good show. I had learned to differentiate brands and blends of coffee in the same way I had learned brands of cigarettes. It's an easy thing for a werewolf, but in the matter of espresso it was my discerning palate as much as my nose. The Second Cup in the U-district was the only place in Seattle serving the Northwest Blend of the Mukilteo brand of espresso beans. They were the absolute best slow-roasted Arabica grade beans sold in the Northwest, by a small family group whose goal was the ultimate espresso—making it so that the espresso product, properly prepared, tastes as good as the beans smell when they're ground. Like fresh-baked bread tastes as good as it smells hot from the oven. It was far superior to the McBucks blends. There was no way the huge factory roasters could match the art of a small roaster dedicated to quality. When it was freshly ground I could smell the difference a mile away...maybe ten. I loved my espresso and I needed one now.

I slipped under the police tape and circled the area. I'd had a strong scent of the Marlboro Man at the scene and I hoped to be able to follow the trail. However, the misting rain had been falling for hours, and the scent faded within a few blocks. I felt frustrated and enraged over the murdered baristas and I needed to walk it off.

I looked up. Although I couldn't see the moon through the heavy clouds, I could feel its magical presence watching over me. With the moon in its first quarter, my werewolf senses were only about half-strength. Closer to the glorious full moon, I might have been able to follow the trail right to his den, although in this drizzle, maybe not.

Ordinarily I loved these late nights on the streets in the rain. It kept the mob inside, leaving the damp shadows to the loners—and the ghosts.

Yeah, ghosts. As I walked through Pioneer Square—built with bricks on top of the wood-framed ruins of the Great Seattle Fire—I kept to the alleys, where the occasional restless spirit drifted through the red brick side of a building, like a wisp of fog to ordinary senses. In this area they were mostly ancestors of local tribes, who could not rest at peace with a modern urban center weighing them down. Change doesn't ride easily on the remains of the dead.

They were my friends on these late night prowls. I could communicate with the stronger of them. Not like you converse with people. With the spirits it was more like shared feelings, usually of melancholy, but also anger, and even happiness at meeting a kindred spirit. They had helped me, in ways that were closer to intuition than actual conversations. But even the weakest could sense my presence, like the one drifting through just ahead, dressed in the cedar hat and shirt of his time. I let him drift past rather than walk through him like most ordinary pedestrians—who had no idea of the bad luck they were accruing. The streets at night were no place for the weak or the ignorant. I felt a sense of anger and contempt that radiated from the spirit as it passed, and I crept into the shadows to determine the source of its unease.

Unfortunately, it turned out not to be my Marlboro Man. With the bars letting out this time of night, there were a lot of the ignorant roaming the concrete trails, looking for trouble, like the three crossing the alley on the street ahead. They looked me over with their drunken eyes probing for weakness, and hurried on when they found none. I let them get ahead, and followed at a good distance. I didn't have to be close and didn't want to. The nauseous alcohol vapors trailing them and the mean tone of their raucous laughter marked them from afar, like they were wearing glow stick dunce caps blasting amplified prattle.

They kicked over a trashcan, sending it crashing into the street, and walked north under the Alaskan Way Viaduct, an elevated highway running along the Seattle waterfront. I crept closer, keeping in the shadows, struggling to control the primal urge to *change* surging within.

I sensed where they were headed as one snapped the antenna off an older model pickup, and another picked up a piece of broken two-by-four lying next to a building. The third finished off the bottle he was drinking from and held it by the neck like a club, as they switched to clumsy juvenile predator mode, searching the shadows for homeless people sheltering in doorways. Needing an outlet for the emotions that seeing the dead barista had released, I surrendered to the primal urge to change. *Mother Moon, take me.*

Wolf takes me fast, replacing human frustrations from the night's senseless violence with his predator's instincts, the sharp pain of reforming bone structure deadened by adrenalin rush. A low, throaty growl as red-tinged, light-brown fur and padded feet silence his/my approach.

"Hey, hey, hey, what do we have here?" one of them shouted. Two people were huddling beneath a huge piece of cardboard, which he grabbed up, flinging it away.

Wolf/I closing ground on the unaware trio now intent on their victims.

"Hey they've got a bottle of booze and they're not sharing. How about if I give you mine and you give me yours?" shouted one of the three. He grabbed their bottle from an outstretched hand, and raised his to strike down at his two victims.

Growling, snarling, leaping, taking the prey's arm in my canine teeth, I crunch down hard on the meaty flesh, the force of the leap knocking him to the ground.

Wolf senses another attacking from behind. Whirling, we face him, lips curled in warning as he raises the club over his head to strike us.

Teeth-bared, growling, crouching to spring, I can nearly taste his fear-stinking blood, but the coward cringes, drops the board to turn and run. Following the other around the corner, they abandon the third now scrambling to his feet and also running, screaming, dripping blood from the useless arm he holds with his other hand.

Wolf/I, letting them go while repeating the mantra...easy boy, easy boy, Mother Moon, easy.

This *change* was never like that of the full moon. It comes and goes quickly, and as I *changed* back I gathered up the clothes I'd strewn behind me. I'd barely managed to get my jacket and shoes off, but my short-sleeved, pullover shirt had stretched to accommodate my wolf body. I'd unfastened my jeans...but the zipper had ripped out. Luckily I never wore a belt just in case, and the jeans had slipped off me. My socks stayed on, however. I must have made some impression on my newfound playmates. *Changing* in public was not a good idea. I'd been lucky this time. Humans could accept seeing a wolf, but not in human clothing...that old saying about sheep I suppose.

As I gathered up my clothes and tried to make myself presentable enough to make it home, the two homeless guys stared at me. Their bottle hadn't broken and there was a bit left in it so I handed it back to them, and then replaced the cardboard shelter over their heads. Hey, maybe the shock of what they'd seen would make them swear off alcohol. Or they would keep drinking hoping to get back there.

Whatever. They were temporarily safe, they had their wine, and I needed a nice triple espresso. I loped toward my houseboat on Lake Union to get a change of clothes. Then I would ride my motorcycle up to Capitol Hill, where I knew a nice espresso stand serving a decent roast would still be open...at least for me. I could almost smell it. Well, okay, there was also the stored scent of redheaded Helene, sometimes called Hell for short, and not alone because she was a hell of a barista. Not by far. She could be hell in every way, but playing with fire does have its rewards, and I figured I deserved one.

Two

Hmm, one habanero or two? Two at least, I decided, chopping and scraping them into the green chilequile sauce, a recipe to combat one more rainy winter morning in a long, endless stretch of them. My mind mold was beginning to grow a second layer of fungus. I desperately needed a long run in the snowy woods.

It wasn't that I minded the Seattle rain. Looking out of my houseboat's window over the kitchen sink, the urban scene on the far shore of Lake Union was muted by the soft mist falling on the water. I could just make out Gas Works Park on the far shore, with its rusted pipe and steel tower remnants from the park's former incarnation as a gasification plant that had powered much of Seattle from 1907 to the mid 1950s. Now, it looked like an aging robot monster out of a Science Fiction scenario: The past haunting the present's dreams of the future.

Closer in, an armada of urban ducks patrolled, hoping for a handout of bread crumbs from the bored old lady or her visiting grandchildren who lived two houseboats to the north.

Living in Seattle sure as hell beat the suburbs, and the really nice part was that with the rain, people stayed home or kept their distance, cloaked in the rainproof Gore-Tex that had become as much a part of the Northwest as the eternal mist. The rain tended to insulate us from each other, not a bad thing in an urban environment. And it kept most of the Californicators away. They couldn't stand not being seen.

I rinsed off my cooking utensils. Breakfast was ready and it was time to wake the dead. "Helene," I shouted toward the bedroom. No answer. I bounded up the stairs and pushed open the door. She was lying with her back to me, her naked torso outlined all toasty under the comforter, curled into herself. "How about some breakfast?" I asked.

"Go away," she growled back, a warning from deep in her throat I knew not to take lightly.

"Chilequiles," I said. "How do you want your eggs?" Helene didn't share my vegan sensibilities, which I had accepted and prepared for to some degree.

The pause was heavy with suspense. Would she snarl a final warning or spring for my throat? "Fresh," she mumbled, resigned to the need for sustenance after a hard night doing the dog. I smiled and walked back to the kitchen, hungry myself and needing that second cup.

A couple of minutes later Helene padded into the kitchen in stocking feet and slumped into a chair at the table as I gave the thick green sauce a last stir, then poured it over the tortilla chips. She was wearing one of my tee shirts...very sensuously, not leaving much to my overactive imagination. I licked my chops. She looked good enough to—

"What time is it anyway?" she growled, though not very convincingly this time. Her bite was definitely worse than her bark, but I knew from much experience that her heart was all puppy-dog at times like this.

I slid the three fried chicken embryos on top of the chilequiles tortilla chips, and handed her the plate. "It's nearly one," I said, setting her double cappuccino on the table in front of her.

"It's early, but I guess I'll let you live," she murmured. "Mmmm, not bad shots for an amateur," she said, sucking into her full lips the wolf's paw I'd drawn on the foam. She smiled, and that was a heckuva compliment. She took her espresso very seriously. I smiled back, our eyes locked, and for a moment another primal urge fought for supremacy. But the phrase 'hungry as a wolf' had real meaning, and the scent of food won out.

I prepared my own plate and sat down—no eggs for me, just the chilequiles, rice and beans, V8 juice and a double soy latte. "I'm sorry to get you up early, but I knew you'd be hungry, and I have some work to do. There was another one last night."

She laid her fork down. "Oh no...why didn't you tell me?"

"Selfish reasons," I admitted. "I didn't want to upset you. Nothing you could do at that late hour. I shouldn't have ruined your breakfast either."

"No, I want to know. Who was it? Anyone I know?"

"No one I recognized, thank goodness. She's from the Second Cup, but she must be new. I haven't been in there as often, what with the special treatment I've been getting at your place."

"I'll give Sarah a call after breakfast. She'll be destroyed, losing one of her girls like that."

"Yeah. Will you tell her I'm going to stop by later?"

"They've got you on the trail?"

"Yes, finally. It took three deaths before they asked for help."

"Yeah, men and their precious egos."

We ate in silence for the rest of the meal. Helene had to wipe back the occasional tear, but we ate. It was in our blood to eat when we had the chance. For a wolf, survival is a very strong instinct. Oh yeah, Helene was a werewolf too, but much more than me. She's full-blooded. The real deal.

I made her a second cappuccino, and started clearing the table. "Thanks for breakfast," she said, the growl all gone from her voice. "Sorry I woke up grouchy...I'd be happy to do the dishes."

"No, I like doing them. Gives me some thinking time. Besides, you know I get all domesticated when I'm with you." I turned my back on her, filling the sink with soapy water. When I'm alone I usually run the dishwasher once a week or so, and it happened to be full. Besides, a woman once told me that it's a turn-on to see a guy up to his elbows in soapy water. Yes,

I've considered it might have been a manipulative lie, but at the least it gets you points.

"You're sweet, Harley, but let's not get carried away. We're both loners, in our own way. Too much domestication wouldn't be good for us."

"Yes, I know, but I can enjoy the moment can't I?"

"Sure, hon," she said. I heard her rise and felt her arms encircle my chest. She nibbled on my ear. "By the way, what do you think about when you're doing dishes?"

"Oh sure, like there is any doubt now?" One of her hands had worked its way down to my brain override mechanism. I was wearing a tee shirt and some black silk pajama bottoms that I wore around the house in the morning. If I'd been a cat, gods forbid, I'd have purred, but something between a growl and a moan escaped me, and my legs weakened.

"Why don't we let those dishes soak for a while?" she whispered in my ear. Her other hand found its way under my shirt and stroked the thick hair on my chest. Then she fondled my nipples, and I could feel hers pressing into my back as she pulled herself hard against me. I enjoyed the moment, and another, and another, and a few more, then gathered my strength to turn around.

As I turned she ripped off my shirt, her red polished nails barely scratching me. I pulled her close, with one arm around her back and the other hand supporting her butt while the words "mango juicy" flashed through my mind like some kind of subliminal overload.

We kissed and shared habañero hot tongues, futilely prolonging the launch sequence while pushing every available button. Luckily I'd cleared the table and only the condiments went flying as she wrapped her runner's legs around me and we found the leverage we needed.

Yes, I'm afraid we wolfed down our dessert, and then showered together. Afterwards, I tried to help her towel off, but she handed me another towel and pushed me out of the bathroom. "We'll never get anywhere unless we get dressed separately. Go finish the dishes or something."

"Now there's an idea," I said. "Want to help?"

"Go, Harley." She gave me a fake stern look.

I laughed, kissed her on the forehead, lingered for one last moment to impress in the folds of my brain like a rose in a favorite book. After putting on clean jeans and an unshredded tee shirt, I returned to my domestic duties.

I was finishing cleaning and polishing the espresso machine when Helene returned to the kitchen. Even fully dressed, the sight of her started me stirring.

"Thanks for the fantastic breakfast," she said, smiling.

"You too," I said. "You want me to fire up the Harley and give you a ride?" She had left her tricked-out, 4X, Toyota pickup at the stand.

"Another ride? Sure why not? I had intended to run, but that last tango definitely took the edge off. Riding the big bike with my arms around you will be the nuts and cherry on top of the whipped cream on the hot fudge sundae," she said, her dark chocolate eyes sparkling.

"You got it," I said. I went to the bedroom and pulled on some socks, my boots, and my black fake-leather moto jacket.

"You want a sweater or something?" I hollered from the bedroom.

"No, the rain has let up for the moment. I'll be fine." She met me in the hallway. "One last kiss?"

"Please don't say the words 'last kiss.' How about '—one for the road'?"

"Okay." She embraced me as our lips caressed, gently mouthing a long goodbye.

We walked up the dock from my houseboat to the little boathouse where I kept the bike. It had once been a shed for storing a boat, but I'd customized it with ramps and doors on both ends, and a workbench for the constant TLC a fine machine requires.

"Harley," Helene said, as I opened the doors. "You haven't told me yet if you're going."

Oh no, I thought, the one thing besides murder that would ruin my perfect mood. Well, there was plenty of murder about, so it had to end soon anyway. I threw my leg over the bike and slumped there, not wanting this conversation again. *The full moon dance.*

"Harley, I'm sorry, but I have to know. How can you not do the pack run when it's in the National Forrest connected to your Gram's farm? I'd really love to run with you."

"I love to run with you, Helene, you know that. But I can't handle all of that pack stuff, the stupid alpha wolf dance that always gets in the way. You know I've tried, and it didn't work out."

"It's who we are, Harley. It's our heritage. The pack needs you, and I think you need the pack."

"I don't think so, Hel," I said, using her nickname because that's how I felt, like hell. I would have killed him the last time, and he would love to kill me too. "I'm against unnecessary violence and I'm very much against murder. That is what it would be if I went there knowing what would happen."

"That's your human side spouting human rules, which *humans* violate every day. When we're under the moon, the call of the wild rules, and those are a lot fairer than the ones your fat-cat humans impose on us."

"You're right," I said, "for you and the rest of them, but not for me. I'd do anything else you asked, but I can't kill for you, you know that."

"I'm only asking you to run free with me, and accept who we are. What happens, happens."

I shook my head and fired up the bike—end of conversation, mercifully. We'd had this same argument many times. It always ended in the same place, with me offering to mate with her forever and create our own pack. And her reminding me angrily of who we are and how she could never perpetuate a hellish life like ours through her own offspring. In that sense I am a lot more accepting of who we are than she is. We love each other but we can never get past that bottomless gulf. I wanted more than anything to cross over to her side, to run free under the moon with her, and be like her, all wolf. I'd even fight to the death for her, but not for domination of her pack. It was their way, but it wasn't mine.

I handed her the extra helmet. She looked away from me as she pulled it on over her long red hair, but I saw the tears. She threw her leg over but sat up straight and rigid behind me, and I felt her wiping her eyes. Then she leaned forward, hugging me close, and my own eyes overflowed. Like wolves in a steel trap, we could gnaw our legs off, but then we'd never run free, at least not far and not for long.

I revved the bike a couple of times and eased it out of the shed. The mist had returned, and we rode through it, our inconsequential tears washed away by the indifferent rain, as always for the thousands of years our kind had endured the endless curse of neither here nor there. I wanted to hit the open road and go full throttle, but the pavement was slick and the highway would be clogged with traffic, so we rode along slowly, like two lost souls adrift on an endless black sea.

THREE

When I dropped her off, Helene dismounted and hung her helmet on the bike. I felt all of this without turning around. The warm place her thighs had wrapped around me, already growing cold in her absence. She patted my helmet, like saying 'good dog,' and I roared off without looking back. I could hear Gram saying, *"Don't be stubborn now,"* but it did no good. The macho rumble of the Harley said all the goodbyes I could handle at the moment.

I hit Broadway, the main north and south street through the Capitol Hill district, and headed north toward the University district. I gunned it a little hard taking off from a stoplight, and the back end tried to slide out from under me on the slick pavement. That bit of adrenalin surge rushed some sense back into my overloaded brain. It would be very stupid to lay this beautiful bike down over another rendition of an old country and western tune.

Throttling back, I reached the U-district in one piece. There was no such thing as an open parking space in that area, but I managed to squeeze into the alley parking behind an old apartment house my friend Greg lived in and managed for free rent. It was one of those big old houses subdivided into teeny apartments. For Greg the lure was free housing near a bus line, because he'd been nearly blind the last few years of his life and didn't drive. He was an old cowboy friend of my grandmother, from Idaho, and I'd known him all my life. He didn't have a horse anymore either, but he still kept his saddle.

I couldn't imagine not driving, especially a motorcycle. It would be like having your genitals drop off, and if I had to choose between the two I would be hard-pressed to decide. They went so well together.

I followed the irresistible scent of Mukilteo coffee the several blocks to the Second Cup. I could have found it with my eyes closed from miles away, but it got better the closer I came. Sarah was there, hanging new art on the walls that looked like it had been done by some loco local with the coffee jitters and a splash of schizoid high. I guess I don't have a taste for bad art, but hey, maybe it was free.

It matched the thrift store furniture feel of the place though, and maybe some starving artist got a free espresso out of the deal, to go with the bad publicity. There would be no other kind for that dude. Sarah looked around, waved and said, "Hi Harley," but without feeling or even a smile as I went to the end of the long line at the counter. I waved back.

I got my double cafe americano with soymilk, grabbed the front page of a leftover newspaper, and found a place with my back to the artwork. After a couple of minutes Sarah came over, and I folded the front page in as she sat down.

"Isn't it terrible?" she said, tears already welling in her eyes.

"You mean about the horrible painting?" I said, not wanting to start off with the dead barista.

She gave me that look of equal parts half-hearted smile, pity and disgust that people usually reserve for bad puns. "Okay," she said. "The painting is bad, but the artist is a young student with no money...practically a street person. Maybe it will impress some girl to see it up in our little gallery here. He was so happy when I said I'd put it up."

Sarah was nothing if not big-hearted. "Yeah, and maybe some blind person will see something in it and buy it," I said.

She kicked me under the table, but she did smile, for an instant.

I sipped my espresso to prolong the moment. When I looked up I could see in her eyes it was no use. "I'm working on the case, Sarah, but I don't even know her name."

"Sunny," she said. "Sunny Brown, of all things."

"Why do you say that?"

"Because she wasn't very sunny, personality-wise. She hadn't worked for us long, but she seemed to be weighed down, you know, like a street kid. I tried to get her to open up, but she played it close. She was pretty, in a sorta bluesy way. Like a lost waif you wanted to pick up and hug. She got good tips that way though. She made good drinks too so it wasn't just pity. The tips, I mean."

I nodded, taking another sip, letting Sarah get it out.

"She was actually very good. She had—"

Sarah stopped mid-sentence, cupping her head in her hands for a moment, then she dabbed her eyes with a napkin, sniffled and went on. "She had a great palate and she loved coffee. If another barista didn't pour her shots quickly enough, Sunny would be all over her. Or if someone left the bean bag open, she'd really go off. You know, timing the shots and having fresh beans is important with espresso. It's a simple fact, but some never get it. She set a good example, although she did come off a bit arrogant.

"Sunny is...was...different from most we get." Sarah grabbed another napkin and carefully soaked up a tear. "She cared. There are coffee tasters, like wine tasters, who can tell you where the beans came from, and even the types of beans in a blend, stuff like that, just from tasting. I told Sunny she could be a professional taster, but she got this hard look and mumbled something about how she wouldn't work with those phonies. You know these twenty-year-olds. They reinvent the world every day, like no one ever figured out anything before them. I put it down to that, you know, arrogance of youth."

"Yeah, I was one once," I said, at the same time thinking that arrogance was probably a big part of the reason I'd fought with Helene a while ago. "I was real sorry to find out she was one of yours."

"Well like I said, she was only here about three weeks, but she was becoming one of us."

Sarah treated her employees like family.

"Do you know...did she have a boyfriend?"

"Not that I know of. She was pretty serious, like I said—she didn't flirt for tips or anything like some of the girls do even if they have regular boyfriends. Are you and Helene still together?"

I was sipping my espresso and almost choked. I looked up and Sarah was eyeing me like a chicken hawk. "Uh, yeah, sort of," I said wiping my mouth on the napkin. "I saw her last night. She said she would give you a call. She felt real bad about your barista."

"Yes, I know. What affects one of us affects us all. Helene's a wonderful person...a very strong woman."

"Yes, she is," I said. "So you're sure Sunny had no steady boyfriend?"

"Well, I never saw anyone around. Do you have some reason for suspecting it was something like that, someone she knew?"

"No, but so far we don't have any connection with the other deaths, so we have to check everything out...most murders are committed by someone the victim knew. How about someone who smokes who might have been hanging around on her shift? Someone who smokes Marlboros?"

"You know smoking isn't allowed in the café so I really wouldn't—hey, there was a guy outside under the awning last night. It was raining and I hate people throwing their cigarette butts down out there. What are those people thinking anyway, that their mother is going to come along and pick up after them? Don't even get me started about how rude cigarette smokers are. It's just unbelievable how they think—"

"So the smoker guy threw his butt down out there?"

"I don't know. I remember noticing him because of the cigarettes. Then I got busy and the next time I looked he was gone."

"He didn't come in?"

"No. People stop out there under the awning, waiting for the bus or whatever. Just getting out of the rain. I've thought about getting rid of the awning, but then I'd feel bad about people getting wet. There's the loitering problem we have along the ave too. And drug stuff. Maybe I should put up a no smoking sign or–"

"Do you remember what the guy looked like?"

"Um, I don't know...he was big, I noticed that. He had a sweatshirt with the hood up...blue I think, or dark colored. He had his back to me, mostly. He was turned a little to the side...his right side, and he was looking the wrong way for the bus. That's something else I noticed. He wasn't looking up the street for the bus, like the ones who are usually out there. A lot of the bus people come in for an espresso to take on the bus with them, so that's another reason I don't mind them waiting under there...if they're not just loitering or something."

Sarah paused in her stream-of-consciousness conversational style. She'd be murder on the witness stand. Out of left field I heard her say, "Helene is like that isn't–"

"Huh," I said, trying to catch up. I'd drifted off thinking about the Marlboro Man. "Helene doesn't smoke."

"No, I mean the tasting thing. I was thinking about poor Sunny. Helene is really sharp about coffee, like Sunny. She does her own roasting, right?"

"Oh, yeah, sure." Helene's espresso was fantastic, although I preferred Mukilteo. I made the mistake of telling her that once. She went off on me, and I had to listen to a forty-minute lecture on roasting and beans and on and on. I like drinking the stuff, but I don't care *beans* to have endless conversations about the process and tasting like roasters get into. "Do you remember any more about him?"

"The smoking guy? Um...I think he was white...I mean, he had a light complexion. And he smoked with his cigarette between his thumb and forefinger. You know, like a joint."

"Did he wear glasses or anything?"

"Nope, no glasses. He did have a ball cap on."

"Any logo on it, like the Mariners or something?"

"Sorry, Harley. I didn't see it from the front and he had that hood up. It was dark too, and raining, like I said."

"Do you think he might have been waiting for Sunny to leave?"

"It was near the end of her shift, but I have no reason to think he was waiting for her. I only mentioned it because you asked about smokers and I remember seeing him out there. It's probably nothing. I can't remember if he was still there when she got off either."

"Do you know where Sunny worked before?"

"Java Time. That's where she trained."

"Java Time? Their espresso sucks."

She smiled. "Sunny knew someone there so that's where she started. It takes a special person to be a good barista. You have to care about what you're doing. It's an art. Then you have to be able to communicate with the customer. Sunny wasn't so good about that, but she was real good with the beans and she did a killer design. She could draw a coffee bush in the foam. Never saw anyone do that before. Four leaf clovers, leaves, sure, but a coffee bush? She was really talented like that. We have a regular customer who has a Chihuahua. Sunny drew the dog's face in the owner's cappuccino. She probably doesn't know about Sunny yet. Won't be in until tomorrow. I don't know how I'm going to tell her."

Sarah was welling up again. Time to wrap it up. "Sorry, Sarah. Just a couple more questions. Do you know how to get in touch with anyone who knew her? Relatives, maybe?"

"She has a sister up in Everett. I can get you her number. She also talked about a friend who worked for McBucks Coffee. She worked in the office over there before she got trained at Java Time. I think she mentioned her name, but I don't remember. Maybe it's on Sunny's application. Just a minute, I'll get you the sister's address too."

I finished my americano while she went to get the info. The smoker was a Lotto long shot. The random act, serial killer angle still seemed the likeliest, but I had to start somewhere and the police had a blank sheet so far.

"Here's her sister's number," Sarah said, handing me one of her cards. She'd written the name on the back.

"Lovely? Her name is Lovely?"

Sarah nodded her head yes. "Sunny said her grandmother was one of the originals in the Love family commune, and her mother was raised on their farm out near Arlington."

"For her sake, I hope she is lovely. Is she older, younger...?"

"Older, I think. Harley, I'm so glad you're doing this. I know you'll catch him."

"We don't even know it is a him yet. You're probably right though. I'll do my best. Are the girls spooked?"

"Yes. Me too. You know we have the one guy-barista. Young college student...and artist." She looked at the painting. "He is spooked too, I could tell."

"You know, I may come back and talk to him. What time does he work?"

"Harley, I know he wouldn't–"

"I'm sure you're right, Sarah, but I'll probably talk to everyone who had contact with her. Like you said, the killer is most likely a guy, so I need to at least check him out."

"Okay, I understand. I'm not worried about him...it's just that this is so hard on everyone, so go easy on him will you? He works mornings."

"Great. Did you get the friend's name?"

"Arlene Fisher. The phone number is her work. I remember I called her there, when I checked Sunny's references. I wrote it down for you, too."

"All right, thanks Sarah. You've been a big help. I'll keep in touch...let you know how things are going."

"I'd appreciate that, Harley. Say 'hi' to Helene for me."

I didn't say anything. How do you explain to a citizen the whole pack thing? Love was too easy for humans. They'd never understand. And if you tried to explain about being a werewolf? First thing they'd think of was doing it doggy style. Not that there is anything wrong with doggy style if you're an unimaginative pooch. Werewolves? We invent our own styles, all called 'woofin.' What's so great about the missionary position, anyway? Is it in the Bible or something?

Don't be rude, Harley. Gram's voice in my head again.

How'd I get off on that tangent, anyway? Aw hell. As I got up to leave, Sarah joined me. She was welling up again so I stopped and gave her a big hug. "I'll find the killer," I said. She nodded. I turned and left.

I got to the bike and backed it out. I should have gone in to say hi to Greg, but I was in a foul mood and would not be good company. He'd understand. He's a bachelor and he has a cowboy temperament, taking life as it comes.

The eternal mist was still falling so I headed for home. By the time I got the bike polished up, it would be late enough for me to head downtown to the cop shop and check out the files on the two preceding victims of the Barista Basher, as the Seattle paper had tagged the killer. I hadn't had time to read much of the article while I was in the Second Cup, but it looked like they rehashed the earlier murders and had already connected the dots to the Sunny Brown murder.

It was hard enough for baristas before these apparent serial killings, dealing with the occasional weird customers, tip thieves, flashers and armed robbers. Now they had to look over their shoulders for a murderer as well. New customers were not going to get the sunshine smiles the regulars got with their cup of java. The espresso ritual had a new boogeyman giving every barista the jitters. It was too bad, and I wanted to make him pay.

❧ ❦

It was seven p.m. and dark before I left home for the copshop. I walked along Lake Union, taking Eastlake Avenue to Fairview. It was an area long in transition from a working waterfront and low-end apartments to biotech research complexes, office buildings and high-end condominiums...with the help of Paul Allen's Microsoft billions. They called it progress.

I checked in at the downtown police headquarters to see Detective Meyers. Wanting to bypass the ritual formality of the rule-oriented eight-to-five day-shifters, I'd waited until after the bureaucrats turned things over to the nightshift.

Detective Meyers was in his cubicle, surrounded by boxes

and stacks of unfinished stuff that reminded me of those elderly obsessive-compulsive types they sometimes find dead in apartments or old rundown houses, amidst a maze of newspapers and other paperwork stacked to the ceilings. Okay, it was an exaggeration, but in spite of the transition to outdated computers, police-work still generated a certain amount of stuff. And someone has to enter all that data.

"Hi Larry," I said, searching for a space for the coffee I was carrying and to sit down.

"Huh?" He looked up owlishly. "Oh, Harley, hey, clear that chair off and sit down. I'm just catching up on some paperwork." He pushed some papers aside to make room for the coffee.

"Looks to me like you've got a long way to go. Here's a latte." I'd stopped by an espresso cart on the way over.

"Wowee, thanks Harley," he said, taking the cup. "I was about to resort to the department mud."

"A fate worse than death," I said, smiling as I sat down. Detective Meyers said things like 'wowee' when excited. He was a Sunday school teacher and didn't believe in swearing. I wondered if he'd make the sign of the cross at me if he knew I was a werewolf. Maybe not. He was a nice guy.

"I can't seem to ever get this place caught up," he said. "But the thing is I always intended to. Now, with the Barista Basher, I'm really getting buried. So, how goes it, Harley?" He picked up his coffee and sipped it.

"Thought I'd stop by to look over the files on the earlier victims. Anything new?"

"Got the coroner's report. We're getting everything quickly with all the publicity."

"Does it match the others?"

"Pretty much. There are some differences, but there usually are. The big difference is the first two died of trauma to the head after being repeatedly bashed to the ground, although there was some bruising to the neck. The last one died of strangulation, like you said. She'd been severely beaten, too...but after death."

"Whoa, Larry, that's a huge difference."

"Well, maybe not. I figure he had a harder time controlling the third victim and ended up choking her to death. But he still had the rage thing going so he bashed her good anyway. Maybe he didn't even realize he'd already strangled her to death. Maybe he thought she was just unconscious. Maybe he doesn't care much as long as he can beat the hell out of them."

"Yeah, maybe. Seems the important element is the violent rage he's releasing by smashing their heads on the ground, with considerable damage to their faces. This guy might have a history of anger management problems. Hopefully he has a record."

"We're going over the records to find anyone with a rap sheet of violence against women. That's a lot of suspects, considering all the domestic violence calls we get. Maybe something will match or stand out though. It's a long shot, but it's about all we've got this far. You come up with anything, Sherlock?"

He was laughing so I let him get away with it. Some people around the department called me that, but it was a derisive term from those who envied my success and unusual methods. I discouraged it, although if Sherlock Holmes had been a real person he would most likely have been a werewolf. I frowned and said, "Watch it, Watson."

"Just kidding, Harley. Sorry."

"No problem...goes with the territory."

"Thanks for the latte. You can use the computer at that cubicle over there. You know my password." He stood up and pointed the way. "I sure feel sorry for all those young women out there right now. Glad I don't have daughters to worry about."

"Yeah, that's for sure. Thanks for the help." I carried my coffee to the cubicle, thinking about daughters and Helene and the what-ifs. I imagined a twenty-year-old werewolf female barista going off on an attacker during the *change*, and I had to smile. Maybe a daughter wouldn't be so bad after all.

I didn't find anything new or helpful in the reports. They had the phone number and address of Sunny's older sister. She'd been listed as next of kin on the victim's work records and probably lots of other places. She didn't seem a likely suspect, but most murders were committed by someone the victim knew, so police always started there, questioning everyone who knew her. As far as the sister went, she might know someone else who knew the victim well, like a boyfriend. I was anxious to talk to her, but I didn't want to "interfere in police business" so I'd have to get permission. I was technically a part of the team on this case, working as a consultant, but I was the bottom of the chain the brass might yank.

I logged off. "I'm up to speed Larry," I said, leaning into his cubicle.

"Great Harley. Find anything?"

"Not really. I'd picked up on the sister earlier, when I talked to the owner of the espresso café, where the vic worked. You remember? It's the Second Cup, up on University Avenue."

"Yes, I talked to her. She said you'd been there. I sent a squad car by to contact the sister last night, and she agreed to come down and identify the body. She broke down badly, poor girl, but we needed the ID. I didn't bother her with a lot of other stuff. There's no way she's the perp."

"Yeah, it doesn't seem likely. The owner of the Second Cup said she didn't know of any boyfriends or other close friends, but the victim hadn't worked there long. Before the Second Cup, she had worked at Java Time. I'm planning to talk to the sister and anybody at Java Time who knew her, if that's okay with you?"

"Sure, Harley, you're working for us...detailed reports though, like always."

"Of course. It's nice working with you. Some of the detectives in this department get touchy about working with an outside consultant."

"In most cases, I'd agree with them, but you've been a huge help to us in the past and you're not out to get a bunch of press."

"That kind of attention is the last thing I want. You can have that job."

"You'd make a heckuva cop."

"Couldn't stand the bureaucracy, so probably not."

"You'd get used to it—eventually."

"Okay, Larry, I'm going to hit the streets. I'll get back to you soon and we can compare notes." I picked up my copy of the coroner's report I'd printed out, and the others Larry had copied for me. He was terrific about stuff like that and it made my job easier. Any other SPD detective would go all twitchy about sharing files. "See ya,"

"Thanks for the coffee," Larry said, "and watch yourself out there."

≈≈≈

Nine minutes after nine, and the rain continued to hang in the air nearly as fine as fog. I walked a few blocks toward uptown trying to decide what to do next. I was having a hard time concentrating on the case—the argument with Helene kept creeping into my thoughts. It wasn't all my fault, but enough of it was that it wouldn't kill me to make the first move. This particular disagreement was nothing new so we had to get past it if...no...there could be no if. I cared about her too much to let such an insignificant word come between us.

I found a sidewalk awning, got my cell phone out and stared at it. I hated the damn thing, so only a few people had my number, including Helene and Lieutenant Larry Meyers. I didn't make calls if I could avoid doing so, but there were times I needed the phone for work. Trouble was the battery was always running down because I didn't use it enough to remember to charge it regularly.

I was definitely born in the wrong period, although cell phones were probably better than torch-lit mobs with pitch-forks. To be honest, I didn't really care much when it did go dead. It was one of the small things that bugged Helene though. She was all over the cell phone, social as she was.

After hitting a few buttons and getting nothing, I figured

the battery was dead again. Then I remembered to turn it on and sure enough the stupid little jingle played. Helene had told me I could pick any tune I wanted, but to me that seemed too much like being co-opted.

I punched in her cell phone number, and while it rang I could hear her voice saying, *you know, you could put my number on your speed dial.*

"Hello?"

"Oh, ah...Hi, Helene?"

"Hi Harley. What's up?"

"Nothing really, I...ah...I want to—"

"You call up to apologize?"

"Okay, sure, I apologize. You're way too important to me to let a stupid argument come between us."

"Stupid argument?"

"No, you know what I mean. It's not like we have to decide this today."

"I'm going to be twenty-nine."

"You mean in dog years?"

"Not funny, Harley."

"Okay, but can't we lighten up and discuss this some other time?"

There was a long pause, and I was afraid we'd lost the connection. "Helene, you there?"

"Yes," she said, "I was thinking about it...what did you mean when you said I'm way too important to you?"

It was my turn for a long pause.

"Harley?"

"Yeah, I'm here. I meant...I love you too much..."

"Hmmm...all right, we'll talk about it later."

"Later tonight?"

"That would be great. I'm going over to The Den after work. You want to meet me there?"

"Sure...were you going alone?"

"No, some pack members are going. Does that make a difference?"

I sensed the steel trap and backed off. "No, of course not.

I'll meet you there."

"Cool. See you there. And Harley...?"

"Yeah?"

"I love you too. Most nights..."

She hung up. I flipped my phone shut and nearly howled at the soggy, cloud-covered moon. Then I remembered my promise to meet her at The Den. "Damn," I said. The Den was a sort of club frequented by werewolves and other creatures of the night like the occasional vampire from New Orleans, out slumming. We tolerated each other around the watering hole, but otherwise we kept our distance.

If a citizen wandered in they didn't stay long after picking up the decidedly unfriendly vibe. If they still didn't catch on that they weren't welcome someone would pick a fight and they'd be shown the door for troublemakers. It was bad enough we had to put up with their attitudes in our working lives. At least that's the way most felt. I didn't have much patience for the attitudes of my own kind either.

The Den was not my late night preference, but I had to show Helene that I could compromise. The real problem was that it was owned and run by a werewolf in Helene's pack, named Silver. I guess it was because of his silver hair...I'd never asked. I didn't like the guy and he didn't like me. He wore a silver bullet on a big chain around his neck as both a challenge and a boast. It was strange, but even his pale gray eyes looked silver at times. He was smart, in a cunning, street-smart way——I had to give him that.

I pulled up my collar and started walking, thinking back to how it had all started. Silver had been running with Helene's pack when I first met her and he had expected to become both pack leader and her mate, although he hadn't consulted Helene about his plans. He was a dominator type in everything he did, alpha male all the way. When she brought me along on that run, he had called me out with fangs bared. I stood my ground, all full of Helene's scent and quite willing to fight to the death. I knew from instinct that Silver was no innocent. This was a mortal enemy.

He started to circle me, looking for an opening, but suddenly Helene lit into him like heat lightning, all fangs and fury, and he slunk off growling, knowing if he challenged Helene he'd have the majority of the pack to deal with. Individually he could handle any of them, maybe any two, or he thought he could. But no one, not even Silver, believed he could defeat Helene in a fair fight, not with the pack behind her.

It wasn't easy, letting Helene answer Silver's challenge for me, even though she had a right. She had brought me into the pack, so a challenge to me was a challenge to her. Everyone knew that our confrontation that night wasn't the end of it. The pack was Helene's, and no one, including me, could take the lead without her okay. But Silver didn't see it that way. He was threatened by my relationship with Helene so he had to take me out, one way or another, and he'd worry about Helene later. They had a history going back to their teenage days on the streets together, back to their first change.

Helene and I never talked pack politics much. I didn't want anything to do with leading the pack. Oh, it was fun running with them, right up to the kill. As we closed in though, I'd drop back or I'd try to lead them off the scent, which never worked for long.

Although Silver continued to run with them, after our confrontation an undercurrent of tension remained. Helene told me he seemed to be biding his time, waiting for an opening, a weakness. Instead of challenging her outright, he had managed to influence some of the fringe members, mostly young males and a couple of females who behaved like renegades. They participated in hunts, responding to Helene's call, but otherwise they hung out by themselves. The pack usually numbered from twenty to twenty-five, making it large by wolf standards, but being werewolves, the pack didn't have to hunt to eat. The kill was more of a ritual, like some club initiation held once a month on the full moon, and afterwards everyone went back to their city jobs or businesses.

Usually the pack would form up in the foothills of the Cascades twenty miles east of Seattle, to keep the travel time down. Occasionally, for the last couple of years, they'd started going to Eastern Washington, near the Idaho border, where deer and other prey were more plentiful and there were more wide-open areas to run. It was some kind of weird mystical convergence of our lives—that territory bordered on my Gram's farm and it had always been my territory...mine alone.

Helene's pack had invaded it. One day I would have to join them...or fight them.

FOUR

A car horn blared and I stepped back to the curb as the driver splashed past, flashing the universal sign of the arrogant idiot. He was right though. In the city you needed to keep your senses attuned at all times, despite sensory overload. Werewolves are an endangered species, but no one knows that except us, and no one would mourn us if we died out. Look how they treat wolves, shooting them from helicopters. And the guy in the car would run down his own species to save a few seconds.

Might as well howl at your reflection in a puddle than worry about what you can do nothing about. I had work to do before the Barista Basher struck again, and I needed to focus for a while. My nose pointed toward a McBucks Espresso Café cornerwise across the street. This time I crossed with the lights. I was repulsed by McBucks' multinationally marketed brand— they were probably opening a couple of new ones at that very moment in Tibet—but I was too far from any of my regular espresso refuges, so I'd have to go slumming. McBucks had once been the best, but that was many years ago when they'd still been in tune with their original goal of serving the finest espresso possible. Now they'd become another multinational conglomerate, glomming up the world with overpriced hype. I hoped no one saw me there.

I walked in, ordered a triple soy grande, and hunched with my back to the windows, looking in my wallet for the number I'd jotted down. Sunny's sister.

I found the number, punched it into my cell before I lost it, pressed save and then entered the name. L-o-v-e-l-y. What kind of mother would hang those two names on her daughters? All that naïve optimism had ended with Sunny dead and draped over a Dumpster. No happy ending. No sunshine. And not lovely at all.

I picked up my soy latte and sat down in a corner away from the windows. It was a stupid thing to worry about, but I was always ranting about McBucks, and if someone saw me in here I'd never hear the end of it. I hit the number to ring up the sister.

Three rings...four rings...a couple more and I'd hang up. Six——

"Hello." A woman's voice.

"Uh, hello, I uh..." I had a hard time saying it. "Is this...Lovely?"

"No. I'm her friend, Heidi. Who is this?" She had resisted the pun, which a friend would.

"She doesn't know me. I'm calling about her sister."

"I'll see if she feels like talking to anybody right now. Are you with the newspapers? Because I don't think she wants to——"

"My name is Harley Wolf. I'm working with the Seattle Police investigating her sister's death."

"Okay, hold on, I'll see."

Sunny. Lovely. Harley Wolf. Who was I to talk about weird names? At least I'd chosen mine.

"Hello?"

"Hi, is this Lovely? I mean, Lovely Brown?"

"Yes."

"Ms. Brown, my name is Harley Wolf. I work as a consultant for the Seattle Police Department. If you wish, before talking to me you can call them for confirmation."

"No, Mr. Wolf, that's not necessary. The detective said you would get in touch with me. And please, call me Lovely. It's not so bad once you get used to it."

"Oh, great. I'm sorry to call you so late——"

"No that's okay. It's not even nine yet. I'm staying with a friend for a few days while I...well you know, it's easier for..."

"Of course, sure...was that your cell phone I called?"

"Yes. I left it in the kitchen so my friend answered it for me."

"Oh, good. I'm always getting numbers mixed up. I wonder if we could get together, maybe tomorrow or sometime...so I can get some information from you? I'm sorry to bother you, but with a case like this we need to do everything we can as soon as possible...like they say, while the trail is warm."

"Sure, I want to help in any way possible to catch the..." Her voice trailed off, unable to say it. "What do you want to know?"

"We'll have a conversation and see what we can come up with. You might know more than you think you do, and you surely know more about your sister than we do. You've probably heard that most murders are committed by someone the victim knows. Not likely in this case, but there could have been a stalker someone might have seen...things like that. And I'd like to see your sister's apartment, if you don't mind?"

"Sure, I understand. Do you want to see it tonight?"

"Um...that's not necessary. I just wanted to make contact."

"I don't mind, really. I need to get some of her stuff...personal things...like that. I haven't been able to do it yet, but that's one of the reasons I'm staying in Seattle. One of the things I need to do. I think I'll feel better going with someone like you. You know, if it will help catch the killer. It will feel like I'm doing something to..."

Her voice broke up so I jumped in to give her a moment. "That would be great...it would help us a lot. Do you want me to pick you up? I'm downtown now. I don't have a vehicle with me at the moment, but I can get—"

"No, that's okay, I'll drive down." She sniffled. "I'm on Queen Ann Hill. I can be there in thirty minutes...oh, let's make it forty-five?"

"That would be great. Are you sure you want to do this? Tomorrow would be fine—or another day when you feel up to it."

"No, I'd prefer to do it tonight. I'm not afraid of the dark, Mr. Wolf. I've had some training—marshal arts stuff—and the way I feel...losing Sunny and everything...I would love to have some jerk try something."

"I understand how you...well, I probably don't, but I want to catch this guy very badly. I have a lot of friends in the espresso business."

"You know how to get there? Her apartment I mean. Of course it's not really an apartment...it's an artist's loft. She was an artist, among other things."

"Yes, I have the address. I'll meet you there." I paused. "Thank you for being so cooperative."

"Sure. See you in a few."

"Bye."

I sat back, sipping my soy latte. She seemed in control for someone whose sister had just been murdered, but not in a bad way. I heard anger in her voice. Like an older sibling who was used to looking after her sister. She sounded stronger and more organized than the description Sarah had given me of Sunny. I was an only pup so I didn't know much about sibling stuff. But my intuition was reliable.

Even the sister was a suspect. Something didn't feel right about these Barista Basher killings. It would have been nice to be called in earlier. The other two cases were cold, and although the Seattle Police Department was a fine organization, I should've been called in to those crime scenes. It would have given me a better feel for the killer—or killers. These cases were tied together mainly because the victims were baristas, and the press loved serial killers. They could sell a lot of newspapers with a case like this. It sounded harsh, but that's the way it was. Life in the big city was like living—or dying—in an urban wilderness, full of prey and predators.

I wasn't far away from Sunny Brown's loft. The old brick building was just off Yesler Street, down by the Alaskan Way Viaduct, which ran beside and above the Elliot Bay waterfront. The building had once been a piecework-sewing sweatshop in the days before the garment industry took advantage of modern transportation to move their sweatshops to sweatier climates, where they could pay even lower wages while charging higher prices for the finished products. The means of production were very mean, indeed.

I meandered, but still got to the building early. The loft was on the third floor and I could see a light on in the corner, which I guessed to be the dead girl's space. Maybe her sister got here early, too.

A piece of cardboard had been folded and placed in the latch of the front door. Probably someone in the building expected friends and had left the door ajar to save a trip downstairs. The place was rustic without any fancy call boxes. I knew another artist who had lived there once, and the means of communicating from the street was to toss pebbles against the windows or to scream your head off.

Since the stairs were at the other end of the building, I decided to take the rickety old freight elevator up to the third floor. The elevator wheezed and rattled and lurched its way slowly upward, like a very old man with emphysema. It stopped six inches short, but close was better than not at all. I pulled back the heavy gate and stepped up and out.

A twenty-watt light lit the small space outside the elevator. A place for a padlock existed on the door to the loft hallway, but Lovely had probably taken it inside with her so some joker couldn't lock her in.

I pulled the heavy fire door and it slid easily, helped along by the attached rope and counterweight. She had originally said half-an-hour and she sounded like the prompt type. She had probably added the extra fifteen minutes because she hated being late. It seemed weird, but that was how my mind worked, constantly analyzing people and their actions. I wasn't always right, but practice nearly made perfect.

The hallway was dark, but a light shone from a doorway at the end of the hall to the right, and I saw the yellow police tape, which wouldn't keep anyone out except the law-abiding.

"Ms. Brown," I hollered, turning that way.

I smelled it, but the journey through synapses forming the thought, *sweat-fear-Marlboro tobacco-danger*, was a fraction of an instant too late. Like a wolf in a trap my muscles tensed in the ancient fight or flight response, as something hard hit me up side the head and I fell into a deep, black hole.

FIVE

"Mr. Wolf...Mr. Wolf! Are you all right?"

I moaned as I felt someone lean over me to lift my head. I tried to react, but the light at the end of the tunnel rushed toward me like a freight train load of pain. I mentally ducked and closed my eyes again as a boxcar of nausea swept through me. Something was wrong. I rolled onto my side trying the classic PLF defensive move, but barely achieved a helpless womb curl.

"Are you all right? It looks like you've been hit over the head." A distant woman's voice. "Do you want me to call an ambulance? You are Harley Wolf, aren't you?"

Sometimes people say the dumbest things in emergencies. *Am I all right?* I felt like I'd been knocked halfway to Safeco Field, and someone asks if I'm okay.

"No," I groaned..."

"You're not the detective?"

"Yes, I'm Harley. I meant I'll...I'll be all right. Give me a couple of minutes," I mumbled. "No need to call anyone." I tried opening my eyes again but my sight was blurry and I felt dizzy. I closed them and watched the fireworks display going off behind my eyelids. I wasn't sure I wouldn't puke all over myself so I tried to wave her away.

"Okay, I'll be right back," she said. "I'll get a cold washcloth...maybe there's ice."

I heard her leave and I swallowed as nausea swept through me again. I was sweating now. And the recriminations started.

How in the hell did I get ambushed? I was a wolf, for crying out loud...a dead wolf if I'd been in the wild. Oh, it hurt to think, but I had to before that person came back and panicked. It would not be good for my reputation if—

"Here you are. Lay on your back if you can."

I summoned wolf reserves and did as instructed, rolling over like a good boy. The nausea lessened. I felt her hand under my head and wet coolness on my forehead.

"Mmmm, thanks," I said.

"Are you sure I shouldn't call someone?"

I opened my eyes. "Lovely," I said with what I hoped was a smile. Even through my blurry eyes I could see she was lovely. Her soft brown hair fell down over her shoulders and her big brown eyes were lovely, too. Hey, I'm a detective. I'm supposed to notice things and I'm especially good at recognizing beautiful women. In this case, even being half-cocked I didn't need any superhero senses.

"What happened?" she said with concern, ignoring my bad manners. She would be used to the reaction to her name as well as her beauty. That got me zero points for originality to go with my no-score for defense. I had a lot of ground to make up.

"The door was unlocked," I said, thinking back with difficulty. "So I thought you were here ahead of me. I walked in and...I guess someone hit me."

"He slipped into the elevator after I got off," she said. "When the elevator door opened I saw you lying just inside here. Your foot was holding the door open. I was shocked to see you lying there like that, not moving. He must have been standing next to the elevator, but I was focused on you. Something caught my eye and I turned around just as the elevator door was closing."

"Lucky he didn't..." I left the sentence hanging. No use scaring her.

"Yes," she said. "He must have heard the elevator coming."

"Did..." I winced as my head throbbed. It hurt to talk.

"Did you get a look at him?"

"It's dark and he had his face covered up. I barely caught a glimpse of him. I saw the bill of a baseball cap, but he had a hood up over that—some kind of sweatshirt."

"Did the cap or the shirt have any markings?"

"I think maybe the sweat shirt was gray, and he might've been wearing jeans, but I didn't see his face."

"Anything else? Was he fat, thin, short or tall?"

"I was concerned about you and that distracted me from paying more attention to him. I thought you might be dead or dying so to be honest I was glad he was gone."

I tried to get up, but only managed to sit up, resting with my hands behind me. I had to go slow, because if I passed out or something she might feel obligated to call someone. "Can you help me get up...maybe into your...help me inside?"

"Okay. What can I do?"

"Steady me. I still feel shaky."

"Sure."

I rolled over and pushed myself to my knees. Although my head throbbed like a Haida tribe ceremonial drum, I was feeling better. Looking around for the first time I saw a three foot long piece of two-by-four lying on the floor not far away.

I reached up and put one hand on Lovely's shoulder and got to feet. She moved in under my arm so that my arm was around her shoulders and her right arm was around my waist. We stood there a minute, with me swaying with the rolling deck, but then my equilibrium steadied and I felt able to walk.

We went under the police tape and got inside all right. She helped me to a futon sofa-bed. She slid around half-facing me, but with her arm still around me. For a moment we stood there like that, and then another moment too long as animal attraction passed between us. I don't mean a werewolf thing—she wasn't one of us. You always knew that right away. No, it was the human animal spark. She felt warm and nice, and she was Lovely after all and her hair smelled good.

Hey I'm part human, but it was getting to an awkward

place and I was trying to think. She saved the moment.

"Do you want to sit down here?" she asked, in a husky whisper, looking up at me like it was okay if I didn't feel up to moving just yet.

"Yes, okay, I'm still a little woozy."

She opened a little space between us to see if I could stand on my own, and the spell was broken. I sat down. What in the hell was I doing? The whack on the head, I told myself, blaming it for the sexual chemistry with Lovely. I wasn't myself yet—or worse, maybe I was.

She sat down on the futon beside me, but left space between us. "Can I get you anything, Mr. Wolf?"

I smiled. "Since you may have saved my life a few minutes ago, I think you can call me Harley."

"Harley, then. That was some introduction, but I really didn't do much."

"Timing is everything. If you hadn't scared him off he might have finished me. That could have been the guy who murdered your sister. On the other hand maybe it was just a burglar surprised in the act. Except I don't remember seeing any signs of forced entry."

"Yes, the lock is over there on the counter. Sunny kept a key hidden out by the elevator. He could have found it. She was always losing things like keys so she kept an extra hidden out there."

"Do you know where she hid it?"

"Yes. She kept it under that big floor-stand ashtray out by the elevator, where she made people go when they smoked."

I didn't mention the Marlboro Man. "Do you want to go check to see if it's there?"

"Okay."

She popped up and went out. With my fingers I gingerly explored the bump on the side of my skull. It was near the top, on the left side, but it wasn't bleeding. Maybe I'd ducked away after all, making it a glancing blow. The club had hit me hard enough that if it had landed square he might have killed me. I was sure it wasn't a burglar. A sneak thief like a burglar would have waited until I was inside and then snuck out. I'd already had my back to him. Besides, I had recognized the scent of Marlboros. He'd spent some time in here, but without lighting up. Strange for a burglar to honor a no smoking sign. Lovely came back in, but I'd already decided not to tell her I'd sniffed out the Marlboro Man. It would be hard to explain, and she had enough to worry about for the moment.

"The key is gone," she said.

"Well, that's it then——probably a burglar. Maybe he read about the murder and thought he could break in and go through her stuff. That happens sometimes when deaths make the papers."

"I hope so," she said with a shudder. "I'd hate to think the one who...that he'd come back here after what he did to her and go through her things or something."

"Not likely," I said, hoping to ease her fears.

"I'm going to move in here."

"Huh?" I said, surprised.

"I know it sounds strange, with my sister being murdered and everything. But it didn't happen here, and until tonight I didn't think...I mean I thought it was random. This was her home, such as it is, and I can still feel her presence. Even with what happened I still feel comfortable here."

"I understand, but——"

"See, we had been talking about me moving in here with her. I've been managing three espresso stands up in Everett and working a shift at one of them besides. It's too much. I needed a change."

"You're a barista too?"

"Oh sure. That's how Sunny got started in the business, because of me."

"Boy, sometimes it seems like everybody in Seattle has an espresso connection."

"Yes, like that Kevin Bacon, six degrees of separation thing."

"Yeah, but only once removed. Now that she's not here...?"

"Well, the thing is, places like these are hard to find. And they make you pay first and last, plus a deposit...and Sunny had paid her rent for the month. We had even discussed it with the manager so I know he would let me move in and take it over."

"It still doesn't sound like a great idea to me, especially after tonight."

"So you do think there is some connection? I suspected you might be trying to reassure me. Being a barista you get used to reading people, and that's a typical male reaction."

Okay, guilty as charged, although I'm not your typical male of the human kind and I liked a lot of wolf in a female.

"If that was him I'm not going to let the bastard who killed my little sister scare me off. In fact I hope it was and that he does come back. He deserves to die. I've got a gun and a permit. I got it after I was held up a couple of years ago. With being manager and closing and picking up the money all the time, I took shooting lessons and went out and bought the gun. Martial arts are good, but you can't beat a gun in certain situations. It wasn't so much losing the money. It's letting the little rat finks get away with doing that to you...making you afraid."

"Wow." I said, shaking my head. I had to smile. "Why the heck didn't you shoot the guy who whacked me?" I was kidding, but interested in her answer, too.

"Because I saw you lying there and didn't know how bad you were hurt. And the other thing was that I had left the gun locked in the glove compartment of my car. I figured that with you being with the police and everything—and I can take care of myself okay without a gun—that I didn't need to bring it up here with me."

"Maybe that was a good decision," I said. She sounded impulsive.

"I'll keep it with me from now on though. I'd love to come across the guy who did that to my sister. I'd empty the gun in him without thinking twice."

This gal was something else. "I understand how you feel, but it's best to leave stuff like that to the police. In the first place, you would have to know for certain he was the person who killed her. That's why you have a court system. Even then they get the wrong guy sometimes. They're having to free a few innocent people now that they're checking back on cases...with DNA tests."

"I guess you're right, but if someone attacked me and I knew——"

"But only to protect yourself."

"You're right," she said, but I wasn't convinced from her tone that she meant it. Probably shining on the typical male she had mistaken me for.

"Did your sister have a boyfriend?" The whack on the head had knocked the reason I was here right out of my mind. Maybe the concussion was worse than I thought. Here we were chatting like a couple on a first date. She was supposed to be all weepy and I was supposed to be trying to solve a murder or two or three. If I didn't get a move on it could be *four* soon.

"No boyfriend," said Lovely, after thinking it over a while. "Not per se. She told me someone looked after her...sort of."

"What do you mean?"

"Well, a few weeks back I mentioned that she should be careful, working the night shift and coming down here on the bus. I'd been trying to get her to enroll in a martial arts class. She got smart with me. She said she had taken lots of art classes and could handle a brush pretty damn well, and the pointy ends were sharp."

I laughed and she smiled at the memory. It was nice to see her smile, but in a state of mourning and grief, sadness and even laughter were never far apart, like manic-depressive.

"We had our smart-alecky routines like any siblings, but I didn't let her off that easy. I told her I was serious, and if she didn't want to learn to protect herself she should at least get a gun. Then I actually went out and bought her one. She went off on that...she was very anti-gun. But to appease me, she said she had a friend, a very big friend, who looked out for her. I asked her if there was sex involved, but she told me to fuck off." Lovely smiled again. It looked good on her, especially under these conditions.

"That was more of our sister act routine," she went on. "I was always into her personal affairs, being the big sister. She didn't like that—too independent for her own good. We were close, but she would never let me read her diary or anything like that."

"She kept a diary?"

"No, no...I don't know...I just meant..."

She started to well up. "What else did she tell you about this guy?" I said, trying to keep her on track.

She wiped away the tears and shook her head, angry at letting her emotions show. Lovely wasn't as tough as she was trying to be, but she got herself under control again.

"She didn't tell me anything else. In fact I'm not sure there was any big friend. She was probably making him up to get me off her back. She tried to act like she wasn't interested in men and I'm sure she didn't date much, but basically she was waiting for some comic book superhero to sweep her off into the night.

"One of the reasons I wanted to move in here with her is that I worried about her being alone. I thought I could get her to do some self-defense work. That's also probably the reason she had put me off, not wanting to be the little sister."

She got up and went over to the windows, looking out, fighting the tears. I decided to give her a couple of minutes so I went to the cupboards over the sink. Half of my brain still seemed to be missing.

"Think she had any kind of painkillers around here?" I said, opening a cupboard. Ordinarily I avoided the stuff, relying on the extra body chemistry a werewolf had for wounds and things.

"In the far one," she said, pointing behind her in the general direction of where I was standing. "She got headaches sometimes."

I looked where she said, opening the far cupboard door, and a couple of plastic pill bottles tumbled out. On the shelf

inside there was every kind of non-prescription pain medi-
cine available over the counter...those and half a bottle of
Vicodin, along with some stuff I didn't recognize. "Wow, she
had those headaches covered."

"She had sinus problems, like migraines," Lovely said
defensively. "Help yourself. That is if you're sure you don't
want to go get checked out. Concussions can be serious you
know."

"I know, but I have a hard head. Thanks though." I took
three Vicodin and a couple of Tylenols. In spite of what I said,
the drums were still beating and the ceremony would probably go on way into the night.

I walked around the loft, looking at Sunny's paintings. A
weird one on an easel could have been a giant coffee bean, or
a pair of brown lips, but turned vertical it might've been a
chocolate vagina...but that was probably just me, loving chocolate like I do.

Lovely came over as I was looking at it, and stood there
with me studying it. An awkward moment came and went.
"Sunny's paintings are all like that. No matter what she painted
it turned into something sensual. She was like that...I wish she
had found love before she died. That would have been one
lucky dude. She had a lot to give, but only to the right guy...in
spite of how she acted." Her voice choked and she looked away,
trying to get her emotions under control again.

"Did Sunny smoke?" I asked, changing the subject.

"No, why? You mean because of all the butts out in the
big ashtray?"

"Just curious. Do you think there is any chance she wrote
something down about the mysterious 'big guy'?"

"I doubt it, but I'll keep an eye out when I go through her
stuff. I don't feel like doing it tonight, if that's okay?"

"Sure," I said. "Did she have any other friends, maybe
girlfriends she might have been more open with?"

"She was a loner. She wasn't interested in the same things
most women her age are into. Painting is a lonely thing to do.
She never minded being alone, but that's not to say she didn't

want companionship. We talked a lot on the phone and like I said, she was thinking seriously about me moving in, under certain guidelines she had already outlined for me." She sniffled and laughed.

"But there was one gal she worked with before, over at McBucks. Anna...no...Arlene...yes, that's her name. She talked about her some...for a while. I was sort of jealous, you know, that I might be losing my little sister and best friend. I knew it had to happen sometime. One or the other of us was bound to hook up with a guy for good, maybe even a good guy, and then...well, things change."

"Do you know any more about this Arlene person—your sister's friend?"

"Not much...nothing important. They weren't as close as they had been. Sunny hated that McBucks place with a passion. As far as I know, that Arlene still works there. I think Sunny saw it as a betrayal that her friend kept working there after my sister left. If Arlene's not there, I'm sure they can tell you how to find her."

I wandered over to the windows, and Lovely followed, leaving a few feet between us. The outer two walls of the 1,200 square foot loft consisted mostly of windows, reaching from a couple of feet off the floor to the ceiling. We stood there looking out, lost in our own thoughts, watching the occasional night wanderer on the wet streets below, passing by in the misting rain. The red neon of an old tavern's rusting sign reflected back at us, like blood on the street. The bond we'd woven had fallen away some. Sharing a traumatic event had swept us past the usual awkwardness of strangers. But then you realize you don't really know this person you've gotten all familiar with, so you pull back from each other's private space.

I decided we'd done enough for one night.

"Hey, thanks for helping me out back there," I said, awkwardly. "If I ever get whacked again there is no one I'd rather have come along. I appreciate that you didn't call anyone or panic. It's kind of embarrassing for someone like me to get bushwhacked." I didn't mention how hard it was to explain the embarrassment to my werewolf side. Like having your voice crack in the middle of a full moon howl.

"You're welcome, Harley," she said, turning to me and flashing a half-smile, like she shared the secret with the Mona Lisa, "but I really didn't do anything. And I wouldn't worry about being caught off guard. I bet it doesn't happen to you often."

"Let's hope not or I'd soon be out of business."

"I'm glad I was here—I've enjoyed meeting you—you seem like a really nice guy," she said, suddenly turning the smile up to high-beam. She paused for a moment, like she was deciding something. "I hope you don't mind my asking...do you have a wife or a girlfriend?"

I was embarrassed and unprepared by the sudden turn of the conversation to more personal matters, but I was relieved to mark off my boundaries. In spite of her bravado she was facing being alone in her murdered sister's place and I was a handy soft shoulder.

"Yes, I have a girlfriend, but no, I'm not married."

"Well, thank goodness it's not both," she said laughing. "I had to ask. I like to know right away what the odds are. I'm more forward than Sunny...well...a lot more forward."

A lot of women seemed to be like that with me. I've never been able to figure out why. But I certainly wasn't shocked. She was beautiful and easy to be around, considering the situation. I might have blushed. I had to admit I was...um...affected, in a big-bad-wolf-meets-the-grown-up-Red-Riding-Hood way.

"How about you?" I asked, smiling. "Do you have anyone?"

"Not at the moment. After meeting you, it's going to be difficult," she said, smiling back at me now with invitational eyes.

Whoa, boy. Let's not give the wrong impression while she is feeling vulnerable. I looked at my watch, backtracking quickly.

"It's getting late," I said. "And speaking of my longtime girlfriend, I'm supposed to be meeting her about now." It was unsettling to witness Lovely's demeanor jumping from sorrow to flirty, but unstable emotions weren't unusual for someone going through the dark trauma of a murdered relative. Like the ocean crashing against the shore, feelings of guilt clashed with the absurdity of life moving onward.

"Okay, if you wait a minute, I'll lock up and walk out with you," she said. "I had been thinking of staying here tonight, but I don't think I want to be here *alone* this soon." She flashed me that very pretty, dimpled smile and emphasized the *alone* part. Lovely didn't give up easily.

"You're right not to stay here tonight," I said, thankful for that at least. I wouldn't have felt comfortable leaving her there by herself. "I'd appreciate it if you'd walk me out. After getting hit over the head, I'll feel better with someone like you to protect me."

She laughed and gave up the chase, at least for now.

After we'd locked up the place and made our way to the street, I said, "Thanks again for your help tonight."

"My pleasure," she said. "Is your car nearby?"

"I didn't drive. I live up by Lake Union so I usually walk or jog downtown. I like being in the open air, even with all the car exhaust. I don't like adding to the pollution unnecessarily."

"But you said you were going to meet your girlfriend?"

"Yes, up on Capitol Hill. It's not far."

"Look Harley, I'm sure you know if you're all right, but I wouldn't feel comfortable leaving you on the street like this. I insist on taking you to where you're going. That's my car over there." She pointed to a new-looking blue Beetle—one of those cute Volkswagens women seem to like.

"It's not necessary, but if it will make you feel better, okay." I still felt woozy, but I didn't want to admit it and cause more concern.

"It will," she said. We crossed the street to her car. She clicked the alarm off and the locks open, and we got in. "Where to?"

"Get over to Pine Street," I said. "Then up past Broadway. It's a club called The Den. Do you know it?"

"No, I haven't been around the Seattle club scene for about three years," she said as we drove off. "Those places come and go quickly."

"I'd be surprised if you had heard of it. It caters to a limited clientele, but Helene's friends hang out there."

"That's your girlfriend's name, Helene?"

"Oh, yeah, sorry."

"Pretty name," she said, sounding like she meant it.

"Yes," I said, feeling uneasy, even guilty, although I wasn't sure why. Probably emotional leftovers from the argument with Helene. "She's a barista too. She owns her own espresso stand."

"You're kidding," she said, excitedly. "It's like Bacon bits all over the place...that six degrees removed thing again."

"It feels like a big family sometimes," I said, realizing I didn't know what it was like to be in a large family. Not many people do these days, with all the dysfunctional families and limited extended family situations. So we make them up out of the people we do have around us.

"Where is her stand? What's it called?"

I felt uncomfortable discussing Helene's affairs with Lovely. It seemed too personal, somehow, partly because we werewolves try to keep a low profile. We have to. Mobs with pitchforks and torches played a big part in our past, and like muscle-memory, the wariness existed under the surface, in our subconscious, in our instinct, in our genes.

We'd arrived, so I avoided answering Lovely's questions by pointing out the club. "That's The Den's entrance, over there." It was unlikely to be noticed by casual passersby if someone didn't point it out. It was in an old brick building that had once been REI's headquarters—Seattle's famous hiking and mountain climbing coop—although The Den only occupied a small below-ground part of the building.

She started to back into a parking spot so I said, "You can drop me off here. You don't have to park."

"Oh no," she said, "it's early for me and besides, now I have to meet Helene. Since I'm moving back to Seattle, I might want to work for her. At least she would know who needs baristas, wouldn't she?"

"I don't know...I guess she might, but—"

"You don't want me to meet her, Harley?"

"No, no...I mean, yes, sure, she'd like meeting you. I just thought—"

"Thanks. It would be nice to meet some new people in the business before moving back here."

I couldn't come up with any excuse that might change her mind, and she had already parked the blue bug by that time, so we got out and crossed the street. My mind went woozy again, but this time from an overload of complicated emotions and the infinite crossing of possible outcomes, none of them good. I was bringing a beautiful stranger into The Den, the hangout of a matriarchal pack of protective werewolves, and other creatures of the night—on top of my barely resolved argument with Helene. A headache was going to be the least of my problems.

Then, to make matters even worse, I stumbled as we entered the club.

"Are you all right Harley?" Lovely said, putting her arm around my waist and looking up at me with concern. At that moment, everyone, including those dancing, turned to check out the newcomers. They had probably sensed us before we even opened the door.

"I'm great, just great," I said pulling away to give us some degree of Bacon separation. That only made things worse of course. Lovely dropped her hands from my arm, looking hurt. It was definitely not my night.

I glanced at the crowd and could see the cogs turning like some slow torture apparatus that pulls the arms and legs off anyone strapped to it. And that was probably the milder of the slow deaths some were contemplating.

Wouldn't you know it? The first person to get to us was Silver. He was dressed in his usual all-black, with an expensive lambskin jacket. His silver hair was combed straight back, and a silver wolf's head earring dangled from his right ear. As if that weren't enough the guy wore a .44 magnum silver bullet on a heavy silver chain that hung in a mat of black chest hair framed by an open-neck silk shirt. To me he looked like the winning entrant in a dog show.

"Hello...Harley," he said with sarcastic emphasis and a toothy grin. Hopefully, Lovely didn't notice him sniffing me aggressively. "Have you been out stalking the wild asparagus for dinner?" He looked like he couldn't have been happier if the Three Little Pigs had just wandered into his club unawares. "Who is your ravenous chick?" he said, pulling her into his embrace and doing the two-cheek kiss thing while holding the embrace an extra two beats longer than protocol required. "Has Helene met this sumptuous creature yet? Probably not," he said with a sly wink, finally releasing her. "My name is, Silver," he said, stepping back with a slight bow. "Welcome to The Den. Such beauty is always a welcome sight to the beast."

I groaned. "This is Lovely," I said. "And her——"

"Yes, isn't she?" he asked, the slimy innuendo sliding off his long, slick tongue.

"No...I meant...she's *Lovely*," I stammered like some unsuspecting person face-to-face with a werewolf for the first time.

At that moment Helene stepped to the forefront of the pack encircling us. "We're not blind, Harley," she said in a sarcastic tone that had teeth. "If you won't introduce your friend I'll have to do it for you. "I'm Helene," she said. "And you are?"

"That's what I was trying to tell——"

"My name *is* Lovely," she said, smiling as she took Helene's hand in the mature and gentle way women have of greeting. If they were men in this same situation one of them might have walked away with broken fingers. "It's always awkward being introduced for the first time," Lovely said, without showing any hint of impatience at having to explain her name once again. "It's an unusual name, but I've become ever more stubborn about not caring. Some names you grow into, right Harley? I'm so happy to meet you, Helene. Harley's been telling me about you."

"Oh, has he?" she said, giving me *the Look*. "He's muddle-headed at times. He hasn't told me a thing about you."

Lovely laughed, and gave me a different kind of look, which was immediately followed by another, more piercing *Look* from Helene while I stood there helpless, like the next guest at the guillotine. "Harley and I just met tonight. He's working on the case of my sister's murder. She's one of the baristas who—"

"Oh, I'm so sorry," Helene said, moving in to embrace Lovely, who returned the long hug.

When Helene pulled back there were tears in her eyes, and tears welled in Lovely's eyes also. "C'mon," Helene said. She put her arm around Lovely's waist and pulled her with her into the room toward the pack's usual huge round booth. The other pack gals closed in behind them, following and at the same time making it obvious with disdainful looks that I wasn't welcome. I stood there frozen, like a deer with no place to jump to, surrounded by hungry wolves.

"That was exciting," Silver said. "For a moment there I thought you were done for, but you may have squeaked by once again. Too bad. Still, I haven't had so much fun since...why I don't think ever. Come on," he said motioning me to the bar. "You look like you could use a drink, and for the first time since I first smelled your ugly ass, I feel like buying you one. The look on your face..." He laughed. "Bringing a beautiful citizen whose name happens to be, Lovely, into Helene's den...why, there's still hope that one day she will rip you from ear to asshole."

What could I say? It had been a rough night and there was nothing I'd like better than a snifter of Silver's finest cognac, so I followed him to a stool at the bar and let the grinning idiot pour me a stiff one.

I sat there for a long time, sniffing the heady bouquet and sipping the nectar, and then ordered another, ignoring Silver, who smirked as he prowled his territory playing host. I contemplated leaving even before I noticed Helene and Lovely dancing in hair-tossing abandon to some fast song I didn't recognize. At one point, Helene looked my way and motioned for me to join them. I shook my head no, and she bounced away. Triangles were the very farthest geometric formation from my mind at the moment. Walking a meandering line in the dark to the sanctuary of a soft rectangular bed beckoned me, and I finished my drink and slipped out the door. Morning would be a much better time for unraveling the tangled ball of my complicated relationship with Helene. I'd had enough battering for one night.

As I walked through the shadows, the falling mist enveloping me in its cool cocoon of life-sustaining liquid, I thought about the case. It calmed me to turn my mind from the unfathomable depths of personal relationships.

Walking down the hill on Denny Way, with the Space Needle pointing up through the mist to hidden stars above, like some giant compass needle showing the way to infinity, my own small problems became insignificant. Stopping this murderer was the one thing I could do to separate myself from the dark side of the kill and be killed world I existed in. Protecting the innocent lessened the rage I sometimes felt. A lot of good existed in the world, blooming like fragile flowers in the wilderness, and I wanted to be a part of it, to know it was a part of me, to reaffirm over and over that I was not some monster of childhood horror.

My instinct told me that Sunny's friend, Arlene, the one Lovely had told me about, might point me in the right direction. I felt that Sunny's rage against the McBucks coffee company might be more than the usual twenty-something's railing against the corporate machine grinding away on the world. It had sounded personal. If the barista's death was more than a random encounter with a serial killer on Seattle's damp streets, then Arlene could be Sunny's finger from the grave pointing the way. On the other hand, if her death was random after all, there wasn't much hope of a quick solution, and the police, with their resources, were more apt to find that killer than me.

At least now there was a trail, and the big guy in the sweatshirt, my Marlboro Man phantom, was a viable suspect. Tomorrow the hunt would begin in earnest.

Six

Near dawn I felt Helene's warm, naked body slip in next to mine, spooning against my backside, with her arm draped over to pull me close. Was it a ploy to get inside my defenses? I hoped so. If I had to die this was the way I wanted to go.

"Mmmm" I said.

"How's your head, hon?" she murmured, twirling my chest hair in her fingers.

"Uhm, which one?" I asked with a sly smile.

Her hand slid down past my stomach. "I don't need to ask about this one, I can find that out for myself...hmmm...seems to be in good shape."

"Ummm...what was it you wanted to know? Like they say, there's not enough blood to run both that and my brain at the same time."

"Okay," she said as I turned over, "let's take care of this one first..."

✍✍

Sometime later, as we lay happily satiated with Helene cuddled inside my arm, we resumed our earlier, premature attempt at conversation.

"You seem to be functioning okay, Harley. Lovely told me what happened. She said you said you were fine, but she wasn't so sure. Are you positive you've recovered from the concussion?"

"Thanks to you, I'm feeling fantastic."

"C'mon Harley, I'm being serious now. Concussions can cause complications."

"Hey, I'm okay. I don't even have a headache, thank goodness. So you're not still mad at me?"

"Not at the moment. I'm sorry about last night. I jumped to conclusions. Lovely seems like a nice gal, and I'm glad she was there to help you. I really felt ashamed when I found out it was her sister who was murdered. We had a nice talk and then danced it off. Did you leave because you were upset?"

"Well, we did have that fight, but no, I wasn't upset. I was tired, my head thumped like those gazillion watt bass car speakers, and I needed to get out on the prowl and do some thinking about the case. I thought it best to leave you two alone to get acquainted."

"Silver said you looked upset when you left."

"Consider the source. What did he want, a kiss goodnight? Usually he does everything he can to get rid of me, but last night he was enjoying my perceived predicament."

"Yes I'm sorry about that. It's my fault really. You know he's jealous of you. He doesn't get that he wouldn't have a chance even with you out of the picture. On the other hand, in that situation he probably would lose interest."

"Silver and I wouldn't get along under any circumstances. He doesn't have friends, he has followers. I'm not including you. I know your relationship is more like that of siblings, from being kids on the streets together. But he acts like a jealous lover and he'd like nothing more than to be rid of me."

"Well, be careful, Harley. Silver can be very dangerous. He has you marked for an enemy. I hope you know though, that while I may not be able to get along with you at times, I couldn't get along without you...or at least I don't want to."

She threw her leg over, hugging me, and we lay there quietly embracing for a long time. I stroked her fiery hair, and after a while I said, "We'll work it out some way. You and I will always be soul mates."

After another pause, I said, "Lovely was worried about my head and insisted on giving me a ride. Then she wanted to go in the club and meet you. I couldn't very well tell her no."

"That's okay, I was happy to meet her, although I was a whisker from ripping into you both when you walked in. Like I said, it was horrible to find out her sister was one of the barista's who was murdered. I should have known you would have a reason for bringing a beautiful woman with you to The Den. Can you forgive me for getting all jealous and not trusting you?"

"I would have reacted the same way. I would have called to warn you, but I didn't know she was coming in until we were outside, and then I didn't think of it. I'm sure she did it on purpose."

" Well it was funny—you looked so helpless, like a lost puppy."

"Hey!"

"Okay, you're no puppy," she said, laughing. "Lovely probably needed the diversion after all she has gone through. I like her. I'm going to try to help her find a job. It sounds like she really knows what she's doing. I hope you find her sister's killer soon."

"I will." I sounded more certain than I felt, but if I failed it wouldn't be because I didn't do everything I could. "Lovely gave me some good leads last night. In fact, I should get up and get going."

"Do you mind if I stay here and get some sleep? It was a long night."

"Of course. You can move in here if you like. You know that."

"I know, but I don't think this is a good time to make any changes. Thanks for asking though."

"Any time you're ready, we'll make it work."

"Thanks for being so understanding, Harley."

She kissed me sweetly, and then I eased out of the bed as she closed her eyes, hugging the pillow in my absence.

❧

I showered, shaved, and made myself some espresso. I

microwaved oatmeal, tossed in cranberries and sliced bananas, then poured some honey and soymilk on it.

After breakfast I called Larry Meyers on his cell phone to bring him up to date.

"Hello, Detective Meyers here."

"Hi, Larry, this is Harley."

"Oh, hi Harley. How are you today."

"Fine. I'm sorry about calling so early."

"No problem, glad you called in. What's up Harley?"

"I went over to Sunny Brown's artist's loft last night—where she lived before she was murdered—to meet with her sister, Lovely."

"Who would name a kid like that, huh Harley? She called me this morning...said she'd met with you."

"Well, she probably told you then, about me getting cold-cocked?"

"Hmmm...nope she didn't tell me about that. What happened?"

"She knew I was embarrassed...that's probably why she didn't mention it."

"Could be, but it's awful close to withholding information, although I guess we wouldn't make a big deal of it, considering." He paused. "The thing is, she said she was taking over her sister's place and wanted to know if it was all right. I told her we'd finished there so it's all hers. I said she could go ahead and take down the police tape. Now I'm thinking maybe that's not such a good idea. What happened last night anyway? We need to get the crew over there to check for prints."

"Well, when I got there the door was unlocked. No sign of forced entry. I thought she'd arrived before me, and when I started to walk in, somebody hit me over the head with a two-by-four."

"Are you okay?"

"Got a bump on the head and I had a massive headache last night, but I feel better today.."

"Is the weapon still there, Harley?"

"Yes, it's still laying there. We didn't touch it. We did go inside though. I was woozy for a while. There were some pain pills in a cupboard—"

"Jeez Harley, you should have called me last night."

"I know. That's why I called first thing when I got up. I wasn't thinking clearly last night after getting whacked on the head."

"For crying out loud, Harley. You've put me in a pickle."

"Sorry Larry."

"Well, what do you think? How'd the perp get in?"

"He probably used a key. Lovely said her sister hid one outside the door, and it wasn't there. It could have been a B and E job, but I don't think so. I think it was our Marlboro Man."

"Aw gee whiz, Harley. We've *really* got to check for prints again. What am I going to tell the brass? If I tell them the whole story, you'll be off the case for not reporting it immediately, and I don't want to lose you."

"To be honest, Larry, when I realized how badly I'd messed you up, I thought about leaving out the part about me being whacked, and saying that Lovely discovered the door unlocked and that someone unauthorized had been there. Then you could have filed it that way in good conscience. But I decided I should give you the whole story."

"Hmmm," he said, "that's an idea. I can leave out the assault part, but get the crime scene crew in there on the chance the unauthorized entry might be related to the murder. I can say she noticed the two-by-four lying there out of place, so they'll check that too. Was there any blood from your injury?"

"No, just a big bump on my head."

"Harley, if it was the Barista Basher, why do you think he went there? Even if he knew her, it doesn't make sense he would take that kind of chance. These serial guys are usually real cunning. If it is him, he must have known her. We'll check up on the other vics...see if there is any indication he did the same with others...maybe he did, maybe he found out where they lived and went there. We can check for any recent unauthorized entries where they lived before they were killed."

"Thanks a lot, Larry, for covering for me."

"It's not just for you. We need your help to get this guy. A lot of people don't understand how good you are. Besides, police work is messy sometimes. We do what we have to do. And no harm, no foul, right? I'll make out a report, which I took over the telephone from you, okay? That should do it."

"There is a guy who keeps turning up in conversations...a friend of Sunny Brown's...not necessarily a boyfriend...all I know so far is that he is a big guy who wears a hooded sweatshirt and maybe smokes Marlboro cigarettes."

"Thanks Harley, I'll pass that on."

"I'm going up to the McBucks roasting plant in Everett. Lovely Brown told me her sister worked there and had a woman friend who might know more about the victim's other friends. The sister said their friendship—the McBucks woman and the vic, I mean—had ended some time ago, so I'll try to find out why they had a falling out, too."

"Great. I've got that woman down to be questioned also, so that will save us some work. We're looking more at the typical serial killer MO, which as you know is usually a crime of opportunity. If you can follow up on anyone who knew the last vic, that would be great."

"Sure. I have a lot of contacts in the espresso business. Can I charge my espressos to the City?"

"Not unless you bring me one," Larry chuckled, a high-pitched little sound he made when he laughed. "We've questioned the bus drivers and regulars on her route. Some remember the vic as a relatively new rider on that route...since she started taking that bus home from work. But so far no one remembers anything unusual on the night in question."

"Okay."

"We'll keep working the other angles—look for a lurker someone might remember. It's tough though because there is no vehicle involved. We do have some possibilities with battered-women perps that we're checking out, but nothing solid yet. I'll send a couple of detectives out to canvass baristas too...see if anyone has noticed a big guy lurking around, or if they do notice someone like that in the future, to let us know. If it's a pervert with an addiction for baristas he probably likes coffee too. And that narrows it down to about half of the millions of caffeine fiends in the area." He sighed. "We don't have a lot to go on so far," I agreed.

"Say, what do you think about the sister moving into that loft after what happened to you there? I'll call and tell her that she can't move in until after we go over it again, but that will be done today and after that I can't legally stop her. Do you think this guy might come back again? With the recent budget cutbacks we're too short-handed to put a watch on the place. We're lucky they let us have you, but that comes out of some special contingency fund."

"I don't know, Larry, anything is possible with a psycho like this. It might be good if he did come back. He's the only good lead we've got. I wouldn't think he'd do that after his close call with us, but anyway, I don't think anyone can talk Lovely Brown out of moving in if she makes up her mind. She can take care of herself...she has a permitted gun and knows martial arts. Maybe if we both tell her it's a bad idea...at least for a while."

"I guess that's all we can do. Harley, I'm counting on you...if anything more happens you let me know. And be careful with this Lovely gal, she seems a bit too much, if you know what I mean?"

"Yes, I know. She somehow got me to introduce her to my girlfriend last night."

"Wowee, that sounds dangerous. Hey, I didn't even know you had a girlfriend."

"That's what I mean."

"Watch yourself out there. Let me know what you find out about the vic's friend at McBucks."

"I will. Thanks again."

"Bye, Harley."

I felt bad knowing I should have called Larry last night. I didn't feel any closer to finding the Basher, and the Marlboro Man had come close to finishing me off too. But why? If he was the killer why did he go back there? It didn't make sense, but nothing did at this point, except my strong feeling that this wasn't an ordinary, random, serial killer case. Intuition is the twin sibling of instinct, strong in women and vital to a werewolf detective.

I went in to check on Helene. She looked so beautiful. I gave her a kiss on the cheek and she reached out for me, sleepily. "Mmmm...Harley, coming back to bed?" she said without opening her eyes.

"No hon, got to run," I said. "I'll see you later...maybe I'll stop by for an espresso and a kiss."

"All right, be careful, Harley."

I brushed her hair back and kissed her cheek again, fighting a huge urge to go back to bed...another curse on the Barista Basher. "See you later."

"Mmmmm..."

A strange celestial phenomenon had occurred on this unusually bright winter day. The sun was shining in Seattle. Not unheard of, but if I'd wanted to be dried out and burnt up by ultraviolet rays I'd have moved to one of those desert regions where herds of retired people go for pre-cremation rituals, stumbling from baked-on golf courses to freeze-dried air conditioning, using up the planet's resources with a passion. It wasn't my kind of weather.

I'm a creature of the night so I don't often greet people with, "Isn't it a beautiful day?" We are ninety-nine percent water and we only exist because of those molecules, and yes, a bit of sun to keep it all from crystallizing, but we really should worship the rain and the oceans we came from. Wasting water on golf courses in the desert should be a crime.

I got the bike out, keeping it at low idle to let Helene sleep. A few blocks away from home, I revved it up to let the citizens know we were coming. I rode down Eastlake Avenue to the Mercer street interchange, entering the freeway going north. The changeable express lanes weren't open yet. They switched from south to add lanes running north in the afternoon, so I wove my way through traffic to the far left lane, biding my time there until I could get to the Northgate area where the lane reserved for car pools, buses and motorcycles began.

Bundled up in my fleece and pseudo-leathers I stayed warm in the winter sun, enjoying the ride thirty-five miles or so north to Everett, where the McBucks roasting plant is located.

The City of Everett is a blue-collar town that seems unaware of its spectacular location overlooking Puget Sound, with the snow-capped Olympic Mountains to the west and Cascade Mountains to the east. It's most proud of its connection to the huge Boeing plant. Everett has an underdeveloped working waterfront with a Navy base and a marina that had once been home to a fishing fleet now aging ungracefully. The Snohomish River circles around its north end and empties into the bay in shallow tide flats to the west of the waterfront, which is protected by a dike and marked by the remnant pilings where log booms once were tied waiting to service the defunct lumber mill.

Everett has so far been by-passed by most of the Microsoft-fueled techno boom of Seattle and its Eastside extended family of cities, Redmond and Bellevue. Still in love with its Boeing image, it remained a one-horse, blue-collar town tied to the cyclic swings of the aircraft industry—which is okay if you aren't looking for a job.

I leaned the growling Harley-Davidson VRSCD Night Rod through the Pacific Street traffic and took a right on Marine View Drive, enjoying the spectacular view of Puget Sound and the Olympic Mountains, which were usually hidden from view by low-flying cloud cover.

I located the McBucks' roasting plant in an area where once had stood warehouses and small businesses supporting a working waterfront. Times were changing after all, if slowly and a bit backwards, like a derelict fishing boat dragging its anchor. It was a shame to see an era die, but everything changes. Either you manage it or it manages you.

My rumbling ride through streets, and philosophical meanderings at an end, I parked the Harley in the safest space

I could find and went inside. Despite not being a McBucks fan, the aroma of roasting coffee beans momentarily overcame my prejudice against the multinational coffee monolith.

Entering a lobby that was remarkably unassuming considering McBucks premiere place in the upscale coffee universe, I asked at the desk for Arlene Fisher and was pointed up some carpeted stairs. "Down the hall at the end," she said, "in the offices of George Rodriguez."

I passed doors marked "Lab, McBucks Personnel Only" that had keycard locks, and found Arlene Fisher sitting behind a desk fronting a corner office with an exterior view looking north and west, and an interior bank of windows overlooking the plant's roasting operations below. Nice setup for a coffee lover. The door to the big inner office was open, but I couldn't see if anyone was at the desk. Just as well if George Rodriguez wasn't there. I'd have some time with Arlene Fisher first, before I talked to her boss.

Arlene was on the phone as I walked in, but a modest nameplate on her desk told me I was in the right place. I was surprised. She was pretty in a subdued librarian kind of way...of medium height, with a very athletic-looking body. I had been thinking more of a shorter purple-haired gal with multiple piercings, like Sunny. Arlene Fisher was neat and business-like, with short, light-brown, highlighted hair, and she looked like a tennis pro. After a few moments, which I spent looking at picturesque coffee plantation scenes from Latin America that were hung on the wall, Ms. Fisher hung up the phone and said, "How can I help you? Mister——"

"Wolf," I said. "Harley Wolf." I paused, waiting, but there was no smirk at the name, just a very serious, slightly superior demeanor, as if I'd barged in, interrupting a busy office.

"Mr. Wolf, how can we help you?"

"I'm a consultant with the Seattle Police Department, working with them investigating a murder case. Being in the coffee business, I'm sure you are aware of the recent murders of baristas in Seattle?"

Her face went pale and she stammered, "Uh...er...um...of

course, I've heard about...um...but why are you asking me...?"

A scent of fear emanated from her and she became visibly nervous.

"You were a friend of the last victim. Her name was Sunny Brown."

"She worked here for a while, that's true, but we were more co-workers than friends. I don't see how I could be of any help."

"Let me be the judge of that. It's a murder investigation. If you don't wish to cooperate, the police might have to take you in for questioning," I said to shake her up. She was being defensive for some reason and didn't have the scent of sincerity.

"Of course I'll cooperate in any way I can...I didn't mean that...I just meant that I don't think I'll be much help."

"When was the last time you saw or heard from Sunny?"

"I don't know...a long time...maybe we talked on the phone a couple of times after she left."

"I understand she was upset with you for not being more supportive after she left? What was that all about?"

"Oh...I don't know, Sunny was moody. I don't think she liked working here, because...well I mean...it's a wonderful place to work. I love my job and the benefits are the best. I didn't agree with her opinions. You know how it is sometimes...we wanted different things, I guess. It wasn't any big deal."

"Why did she leave, anyway?"

"Um, like I said, she didn't... I'm not sure I'm supposed to talk about things like that. It's confidential ..."

"There is nothing confidential in a murder investigation. I need to talk to your boss and get copies of any files that apply."

"Mr. Rodriguez?" she asked, shocked. "There's nothing he can...I mean, he's very busy. Do you really need to bother him with this?"

"Either I or the police will talk to the CEO of McBucks and his grandmother if we think it will help find the killer.

Young women are being murdered on the streets of Seattle, and if we don't find the killer there are liable to be more deaths. Everyone should want to cooperate to stop the killer. It seems suspicious for someone, especially a woman in the coffee business like yourself, to act like they don't want to help with the investigation. Now, answer the questions. Why did Sunny leave? Was she fired? Or did she quit? And why?"

She looked around like a trapped animal. I'd come down on her hard, but I wanted some answers before we got into company lawyer territory. Her scent told me she was hiding information.

"I think she quit...I mean, she did quit," she blurted out. "She didn't like working here. She was upset about the coffee beans or something. She didn't think they were good enough, and she got into it with our boss, once...Mr. Rodriguez. He's an expert, after all, and she was trying to tell him all these things were wrong. Honestly, I was surprised he didn't fire her immediately, but he is such a nice guy, and he let it go. He told her she had a lot to learn about the coffee business, and that if she stayed around long enough she could go a long way. I heard him tell her that...and...I was upset. I mean, I work very hard and no one says stuff like that to me. It didn't seem fair, but that was Sunny. She could come on all super-bitch and everyone would let her get away with it. They always felt sorry for her."

"What was her job?"

"She was an assistant taster. I guess she was good, because she got promoted from down on the floor...working in the warehouse and on the production line. That's a big jump, and she didn't have any college degree or anything. I guess it's a question of palate, and they said she had a good one."

"Were others upset about that?"

"Oh, I suppose, maybe...but if you mean...like, you know...if you mean would they hurt her like that? Jeez, I don't think so. People here are all nice. We're like a family, really."

I didn't mention that most murders occurred between families and friends. "Is there anyone specifically that you know of, who might have wanted to hurt her?"

"No, no way. This was all office politics. She was difficult and thought she knew more than anyone else, but we all just...you know...shined her on...pretended to agree so she would shut up."

"Did she know how much you disliked her?"

"Hey, I didn't really dislike her. We were friends, but you know, just work friends. I got along with her. I mean she was good with coffee beans. Mr. Rodriguez said she was a natural. My job is different and doesn't really have anything to do with the...you know...the quality control side of things...so she liked me. She treated me like a kid sister...that's what she used to tell me...even though I'm a year older than her. Really, she was the immature one, but I played along because sometimes I could calm her down when she got all mad at the world."

"It sounds like you really were a good friend to her."

She smiled, "Yes, I tried to be...to everyone."

"Did Sunny have a boyfriend?"

She blinked, and hesitated before she answered, so I knew there was more than she would tell me. "Uh, er...not that I know of. She always dressed sexy...uh...you know...low rider pants and little tops. She had a tattoo on her butt of a snake coming up out of there. You know, come on stuff, and guys would hit on her all the time, but it was all just a tease. She didn't go out with even one guy. The guys all called her a lesbian behind her back. She was the kind of gal you thought might get into trouble some day...you know, upset the wrong guy. It's too bad...I hate to think about what happened to her. How horrible."

"Yes, it was. And we have to stop the murderer before he kills again."

"But if this is a serial killer, like that Ted Bundy guy, why are you asking about Sunny...about people who knew her?"

"We have to pursue every angle, Ms. Fisher—"

"Please, call me Arlene," she said, in an obvious attempt to change the mostly confrontational conversation we'd had up until then. It was a good sign.

"Okay. Arlene, it's possible someone knew all of the girls, or none of them. The killings haven't been entirely random. Right now we're gathering as much information as possible. We need the help of people like you, but if someone feeds us misinformation—that makes the job tougher. And it could mean an obstruction of justice charge if someone doesn't tell us the truth and we find out later."

"I've told you everything I know, as best I can remember. It's been a while."

She was giving me the ol' "I cannot recall" bit the politicians used. "If you think of anything more, you call me." I handed her my card. "When is your boss returning to the office?"

She got nervous again. "Um...why do you have to talk to him? He didn't know her very well...at least not as well as I did. I'm sure he wouldn't be able to help."

"Where is he and when do you expect him back?"

She did a big sigh. "He is in Switzerland, meeting with the coffee buyers. As of now, he will be in the office on Monday, but his schedule often changes."

"You'll let me know if it does, right?"

"He is a very busy man, and I'm sure interviewing him will be a waste of your time as well as his."

"It's worth a little wasted time if we catch the killer, Ms. Fisher. Thanks for your help. By the way, how does a guy get a cup of coffee around here?"

"I'm sorry, I should have asked. I don't drink coffee that often. Mr. Rodriguez has a machine in his office, and there is one in the kitchen down by the lobby, and on the floor of course—"

"You don't drink coffee?" I asked, incredulous. "Isn't that like a sacrilege in a place like this?"

"Oh, I don't mean I never drink it," she said with an embarrassed smile. "But I don't have any freshly roasted right now. We have it brought up, fresh, every day, when we want some. Do you want me to call down?"

"No, that's okay. It just seems weird to work here and not

drink the java."

She shrugged. "I can get you some for the trip home."

"I'm on a motorcycle and I couldn't——"

"Was that you on the Harley?"

I nodded, wary.

"Oh wow, I heard you come in! I love Harley-Davidson motorcycles."

Suddenly, she warmed up to me. Funny the effect Harleys have on people. "You want to see it?"

"I'd love to," she said, nearly jumping out of her chair. She had lost her fear of me.

We went down and she told the gal at the front desk about my Harley, and she called someone to answer the phone and came out too. I apologized that I couldn't give them a ride because I hadn't brought an extra helmet.

"When you come back, okay?"

"It's a deal."

"Some day I'm going to have my own." Arlene Fisher stared dreamily at the bike.

I'd bet she would. Some people couldn't resist a Harley's primal call.

❧❦

I stopped out on the street and plugged my cell phone into my built-in helmet speaker and microphone. I didn't like to talk on the phone when riding, but I needed to let Detective Meyers know about the interview. I punched in the redial with my thumb.

He answered on the second ring.

"Seattle Police Department, Detective Meyers here."

"Hi, Larry, this is Harley. I'm on my motorcycle so it might be a bit noisy."

"Go ahead, Harley. I can hear you all right."

I decided to hang there for the conversation so I shut down the bike. Harleys are built to be heard over most anything. You might hate them, but you sure noticed them. "I talked to Arlene Fisher, the woman Sunny Brown worked with at McBucks.

She claims they were just work friends, that Sunny was hard to get along with and nobody liked her much."

"Enough to kill her?"

"No, no specific beef as far as Fisher knows. I didn't mention that people get murdered over some pretty mundane things. She didn't tell me much that is new...nothing about Sunny Brown and boyfriends or anything, although she described her as a tease, wearing suggestive clothing, even at work. She said the victim did have a disagreement with their boss, George Rodriguez, but she really downplayed that, making it sound like a disgruntled employee thing. Fisher says he is a great boss, but she thought he let Sunny get away with a lot."

"That's interesting."

"Fisher says Brown quit because she didn't like the product. Other than that I didn't get a lot out of her, but I had a feeling she was holding back. The boss, Rodriguez, is out of town and won't be back until next week, so I didn't get a chance to talk to him, and she didn't seem to want me to."

"Okay, Harley, you following up with him?"

"Next week. Can you get Sunny Brown's records from McBucks' Human Resources? It may be nothing, but I have a strong feeling something was going on that Fisher didn't want me to know about. She didn't seem to want me to talk to her boss."

"Okay, we need to check everything out. I doubt if Sunny's murder was work-related, because of the other two vics, but you never know. They may have been connected in some way. There are a lot of espresso stands, but in spite of that the espresso business is a small world. Those girls get around, working at one place and another." He paused. "We've got some mugshots of known batterers and I've got a couple of detectives taking them around to the espresso places to see if anyone recognizes any of them. At the same time they're checking with the girls for other lurkers and stuff like that.

"We got one guy that's interesting. He beat up a girlfriend, who happened to be a barista. This gal worked up in Everett at a coffee stand. A friend of mine, a detective up there with Emeritt PD, tipped me off about this guy. It happened a year ago and the woman decided she didn't want to press charges. These days, in this kind of assault case, we prosecute anyway. Trouble is, the case got dropped eventually, because the prosecutor didn't think they had enough evidence to go to trial."

"Great lead though, Larry...could be a real break. Where does the guy live? Are you picking him up?"

"Yeah, we'll talk to him. The guy lives here in Seattle. He's well-known around here, but no convictions and no battery...runs a club up on Capitol Hill, called The——"

"Den?" I said, instinctively. "Is your guy named Silver?"

"Gee whiz, there you go again, Harley. How do you do it?"

"I know the guy, Larry."

"It's a small, small world, like that song down in Disneyland when we took the kids. His real name is Anthony Scappini?"

I'd never heard his given name before. I was shocked. Silver? A suspect?

"Hey, Harley, you still there?"

"Yeah, Larry. Can I be there when you talk to him?"

"Sure thing. We can do it together."

"Maybe it would be best if we show his picture at the places where the victims worked?"

"Good idea, Harley. If we get a positive hit we can haul the guy in, get a search warrant. I'll get the guys right on it. They have a mug shot in Everett, which my friend is sending down. At the least we have some eyewash for the brass upstairs. Give me a call later; I can never get you on that cell phone. You need a new one with better——"

Right on cue, I lost signal...or my battery went dead. I stuffed the phone into my pocket without looking, fired up the V-Rod and pulled away from the curve, cutting in front of a car, but with plenty of room. The guy blew his horn anyway. Drivers in SUVs seemed to have a thing about sharing the road, especially with motorcycles. Cranking the throttle, I roared away from the angry road hog.

"Silver," I said. Weird. Could he really be the one? As much as I disliked the guy, I couldn't believe it...too much co-incidence. Could the Barista Basher really be Silver? It could get complicated, with Helene, the pack and...with everything.

Seven

I decided to check in with Sarah at the Second Cup to see if Silver had ever been a customer there, so I got off I-5 at the Forty-fifth Street exit, working my way through traffic until finally parking behind Greg McKinley's place again.

This time I decided to stop and see if my Gram's old cow-poke friend was home. I knocked and he hollered, "C'mon in pardner. Wha'cha waitin' fer, some damn butler to come runnin'?"

Greg didn't lock his door when he was home, even at night. He had an old .44 revolver, but punks would get off lucky if Greg only shot 'em. He said he might not be able to take down a full-grown steer off a horse anymore, but he could handle any sneaky varmint that might crawl in there on its belly in the middle of the night.'

"How are you, Greg?" I said, closing the door behind me.

"Well, I'll be darned...Harley," he said, getting up from the well-worn leather recliner he called, 'Señor Saddle', his little joke meaning he was a senior citizen and that was the closest thing he had to riding a horse these days.

He took my hand to shake, pulled me in and hugged me at the same time. At eighty-three he still had a strong grip. "Good to see you, Greg. I'm on my way over to see Sarah, at the Second Cup, and thought maybe you would walk over with me."

"Why sure, long's yer buyin'," he said. Let me shut down the Ebay and get my new Stetson. Take a gander at this beauty, he said, tossing me a black Stetson that looked brand new.

"You got this off Ebay? Is it new?"

"Well son, newer'n me, but older'n you by quite a bit. That hat is fifty-seven years old. It must'a not belonged to a reglar Sunday-go-to-meetin' cowpoke. Saved it for good. I don't think it's been worn more'n a few times. A few weddings an' funerals most likely. Some kid in Montana put 'er up on the auction box, an' I damn near stol' it for 31 bucks. It came in the 'riginal box 'n everthin'. Fits me perfect too, although that kid's granddad's more 'n likely spinnin' in his boots."

"I imagine he's happy it found a home that appreciates it," I said.

"Yer probably right there. I got this here belt on Ebay too," he said proudly, tipping the buckle up at me with his thick, gnarled hands.

The buckle was big enough it could have served for a hubcap on a sports car, and had a big hunk of turquoise in the center.

"You know, Greg, a lot of people your age think the Internet is a sacrilege and won't go near a computer."

"Heck son, there are fools at any age. Believe me, there's nuthin' much folks do that ain't been done before. Why auctions are probly old as the human race, and the fact it's on some new gadget that looks a lot like a typewriter hooked up to a telyvision, shouldn't stop no one. Flushin' turds to the sea ain't so old neither, but you'll find most old folks usin' indoor toilets these days, thank goodness. Them old outhouses'd freeze yer balls off."

We left his house and headed to the café.

"Say, how's yer beautiful Gram, anyhoo?"

"She's great. I may get over to see her in a couple of days, around the full moon."

"For the *change?*"

"Yes." Greg and my Gram were the only two straight citizens who knew I was a werewolf. He'd sorta helped raise me. Him and my Gram went way back. He felt there should be a bounty on bankers and lawyers instead of wolves—after all, a wolf will only take what it needs.

"That lady friend of yours...she's one too, right?"

"Yes."

"How's that workin' out?"

"Great, most of the time. We've got some issues that come with the territory, some not that different than citizen couples."

"You mean about getting hitched an' raisin' young 'uns? That kind of troubles?"

"Yes, stuff like that. Helene had a rough childhood and doesn't want to bring kids into this world."

"Well, there's nuthin' 'bout raisin' a family that's easy, tha's fer sure, pardner."

"There's that and running with the pack. Helene is the leader and they're her family. She feels a responsibility to them. I like doing the *change*, running free, by myself or with her, but I'm too much of a loner to run with a pack."

"Hmmm, sounds like outlaw gang stuff. I don't blame you wantin' to hold back from all that. You're a good person, Harley...a damn good one, an' if you love this Helene, she must be too."

"She is."

"It seems like a law of life, that for every few good people, there's got to be a couple'a bad 'uns. My pa used to say, 'Boy, you sleep with someone, you gonna get what they got.' And a pack of wolves is a pack of wolves. When you *change*, the call of the wild is strong an' the rules o' life change too."

"I don't trust some of them, but it's more than that. It's like politics or something. Running with a pack...isn't me."

"I don' know 'bout you, but I ain't entirely at ease with a bunch of wild predators runnin' aroun' out by yer Gram's place. You be careful, son. You're a tough, honorable kid, but make sure yer not getting' in over yer head. I don' understan' everythin' 'bout being a werewolf, 'cept what you an yer Gram's tol' me. I know she wants more'n anythin' to see you happy an' settled down, but I'm livin' proof that there life ain't fer ever'one, no matter how much you might wan' it to be."

We walked into the Second Cup. I noticed the artwork

had changed. No one was ordering so we went up to the counter. "Hi Cherene. Is Sarah around?"

"Hi ya, Harley. Sarah's in back. Want me to get her for you?"

"No, I'll go back. Do you know Greg?"

"Handsome cowboy like him? Sure. How you doing, Greg? Picked up your bag of beans yet?"

"Yep, got 'em two days ago. Thanks fer askin'."

"What are you gonna have, guys?"

"Well, since my pardner, Harley's buyin', I'll have one o' them fancy la-te-da drinks. The ten-gallon hat size."

"And I'll have a double americano," I said, laughing. "With about an inch of soy milk. Make them both grandes." In Europe a café americano is actually a disparaging term for a drink that is like regular coffee American style. It's basically adding hot water to espresso, diluting its essence. A straight shot of espresso is meant to be gulped quickly, before the flavor oils dissipate, while coffee is a more social drink, to be sipped slowly. Adding steamed milk or soymilk, like for a latte or cappuccino, helps retain more of the flavor essence of the roasted coffee bean than water, but it's all good when prepared properly. Different strokes for different folks.

The barista rang up the sale and I added a buck to her tip jar. "Thanks," she said with a flip of her long dark hair." She bent over to get the milk out of the refrigerator and her low-rider pants flashed some 'barista crack' at us before we could turn away. I guess it's better than plumber's crack, but I still felt embarrassed. Greg smiled and shook his head.

"I'll be right back, Greg. I'm going to see if Sarah's got a couple of minutes to chat."

I walked back to the office, knocking and peering around the open door. "Hey, Sarah, you got a minute?"

"Huh? Oh hi, Harley. Just a second, so I don't forget where I'm at."

I waited.

"Do you want to come in and sit down?"

"My friend Greg is with me...out front."

"Oh, the old cowboy. I love that guy. He gets his coffee beans from us, but almost never buys a latte or anything." She laughed. "He says his cowboy coffee style is good enough for him. He doesn't grind the beans—he smashes them with a hammer. Then he dumps them in a pot of boiling water along with a raw egg."

"That's Greg, all right."

"I think you said he is a friend of your Gram's? Did they ever go together or anything?"

"There might have been something in the early days, before me. They grew up together. They're both too stubborn and independent for a lasting romantic relationship with each other, but they're the best of friends. I don't think it's too strong to say they'd die for each other."

"Wow, that's close. Yeah, I always mess up my relationships with sex."

"I know what you mean."

"Let's go out front," she said, putting her paperwork aside. Sarah rounded her desk and I followed her out.

"Hey, cowboy," she said, sneaking up behind Greg and throwing her arms around his neck and kissing him on the cheek. He blushed as we sat down.

I noticed the artwork had changed. "Sarah, what happened to the paintings?"

"Yes, someone bought the kid's stuff."

"You're kidding," I said. "Those paintings were horrible. How much did they sell for?"

"One hundred dollars for the pair," she said, and it was her turn to blush.

"You didn't?"

"Shhhh," she said, looking around with her finger to her lips. Whispering, she went on, "They're up in the attic. I couldn't stand them any more, but I couldn't break his heart."

"Geez, that is way more than they were worth."

"To be honest, it was partly in self defense. You were right. Those paintings were awful."

Greg said, "You're a good woman, Sarah. When are you

gonna come over and try out my cowboy coffee?"

"Cowboys have always been my weak spot. I might decide I like it," she said, winking at him.

"Hmmm, maybe you're right. Señior Saddle is getting' a mite old for carryin' two, but we could always go bareback."

We all laughed.

"Greg," she said, "does anyone ever give you grief about your western style? This isn't exactly cowboy country, especially here in the University District." The University of Washington was only a block away.

He made a fist, saying, "Nobody gives me a hard time about anythin'." Then he laughed. "Yeh, I get asked all the time if I'm a cowboy. I say, this is just a hat I'm wearing, which don't make me a cowboy." They'll maybe be wearing a baseball cap, so I say, "Are you a professional baseball player? That usually shuts them up."

We laughed, but Sarah's smile faded quickly.

"Any luck catching the bastard who's murdering baristas?" Sarah asked.

"That's why I stopped in."

"You came to ask about Silver, too?"

"How did you know?" I asked, surprised.

"Two detectives were here not long before you arrived."

"You know Silver?"

"Sure. He owns a couple of stands in Ballard."

"He *what?*"

"You didn't know? He's got his hands in all kinds of stuff and I don't think it's all on the up and up. I'm surprised you don't know, since he financed Helene's place—"

"Helene's Espresso Passion? Silver? You can't be...are you sure...?"

"Oh, gosh, I'm sorry Harley, I thought you knew."

"No...I...I...it never came up, I guess...but man...Silver? Why...?"

"He has the money. He always comes on like he wants to help people out...get them a start, but it's not charity. He has been coming by for months, trying to buy this place. But this building has been in the family for a long time and I'd never sell—especially not to someone like Silver. I told him that, and he...he actually *growled* at me. It was weird, and he hasn't been back since."

"Did you tell the cops about that?"

"Sure, they were——"

"Damn excited? Good. It looks like Silver is going to have a lot of questions to answer." I shook my head.

"Harley, you don't think Silver...?"

"I don't know, Sarah. This case is getting weirder and weirder."

"I don't like the guy, but I can't believe he'd..."

"To tell the truth, neither do I, but then it's hard to believe anyone would murder innocents like that."

"Harley," Greg said, "are you all right? You look kinda peaked."

"I don't know, Greg...I don't feel——"

A cell phone rang and I looked around to see what the ringing was...

"Harley, it's yours," Sarah said.

"Oh." I said, patting myself all over looking for the darned thing. "I thought the battery was dead." I finally located it in the first place I should have looked...my right hand coat pocket. After about a half-dozen rings, I fumbled it open. "Harley here."

"Harley, thank goodness I got hold of you. Listen guy——"

"Silver frequented the stands of the baristas, right Larry?"

"How'd you know?"

"Not important. You going to pick him up?"

"Yeah. This could be it. You coming?"

"Larry, I wouldn't miss this for Helene and the Wolf Moon."

"Huh?"

"Never mind. Not important."

"Okay, good. You want to meet me up at his place on Capital Hill...that place called The Den?"

"Yup. I'll take the shortcut through the woods."

"Huh?"

"I'll be waiting when you get there."

I snapped the phone shut and jumped up. "Greg, Sarah, sorry. I've got to run."

"Sure," Sarah said.

"Be careful, Harley," Greg said, with a strong grip on my arm.

I pulled away, sprinting for the door, happy to have an outlet for the sickening primal rage I felt inside. Unfortunately, my need for vengeance didn't have much to do with dead baristas. I felt betrayed—finding out he was in business with Helene and she hadn't told me. That's not something that would slip someone's mind. It was going to take all of my willpower to keep from making the *change* and ripping into Silver.

EIGHT

I ran to Greg's place, slapped on my helmet and fired up the bike. I was parked in the back, but there was a steep driveway with access to Brooklyn Avenue.

I squeezed the clutch, stomped into first gear, twisted the throttle hard and let out the clutch, spraying gravel across the alley behind me. As I peeled onto Brooklyn Avenue heading south, I hit the Brembo brakes, and then throttled hard looking for cars and pedestrians.

I rode fast, weaving through traffic as if my life depended on it—maybe Helene's too. Reckless abandon might be a mild description, with the Harley's V-Rod roar scaring citizens. A few pulled over to the side of the road, perhaps to check their pulses.

Luckily I didn't encounter cop cars, and I arrived at The Den first. I slid to a stop, shutting down and dismounting the Harley, leaving my helmet on the seat.

Halfway to the door I paused for a beat, mumbling my mantra, trying to bring myself down from boil to simmer, and then I walked into The Den with a burning smile on my face. I had to control my rage. *Easy Harley, easy boy, easy.* This was no time to be slipping into werewolf mode. Silver was behind the bar, leaning on it, with three of his minions seated on stools around him. They were in intense conversation, which it appeared I'd interrupted.

Irritation crossed Silver's face, and then recognition and a sleazy smile. "Well boys, look-it here. Mr. Harley Wolf himself is paying us a visit. He's getting to be a regular customer, but I never expected him to wander in here without his bodyguard." The sycophants slid off their stools and started to spread out, facing me.

"I want you to stay away from Helene," I said between grinding teeth. "Whatever money she owes you, I'll pay back."

He laughed as recognition lit up his face. He was smart and street-sly. "So, you didn't know about our little arrangement? She didn't tell you? I wonder who did, then? Nice of you to offer to run Helene's life for her, but I wonder how she'll feel when she finds out...having you bossing her around? You came here without talking to her, didn't you? Yeah. All in a self-righteous rage."

I moved a step closer. "Stay away from her, Mr. Anthony Scappini."

The name wiped away the sly grin. "Fuck you, Harley, my investment is with Helene and has nothing to do with you. Now why don't you put your tail between your legs and get out of my establishment——or I'll have the boys throw you out into the street."

However, the boys didn't seem quite as sure as Silver that throwing me out would be a job they'd get much enjoyment from. They were types who would nip in when your back was turned or you were otherwise distracted with something like a real opponent. They were street punks who'd been educated in juvenile detention and flunked even that lowly school.

"These boys couldn't handle my Gram on her worst day. If you want me out of here you'll have to come out from behind there and try to do it yourself."

"All right Harley, maybe it is time I put you in your place—— at the bottom of the pack." He stepped out from behind the bar, shoving his nearest minion hard out of the way. He was reaching into an inner pocket of his suit coat, when the door burst open behind me, filling the room with police.

"Harley, you did beat us here, I see," said Larry, stopping behind me.

"What the hell is this all about?" Silver yelled. "You have

no right busting in here like this."

"Is this guy Silver, Harley?"

"Yes, that's him."

"Okay, Silver, we didn't bust in here, since the door was open. But if need be, we can get a search warrant for this place."

"Burt, call my lawyer," Silver said to one of his three assistants. Turning back to Larry, he said, "You've made a huge mistake. I'm a respected businessman. What are the charges?"

"So far there are none; we'd like you to accompany us downtown for questioning in a murder investigation."

"Murder investigation? Are you crazy?" Silver looked around, obviously stunned, and then focused on me. He thought for a moment. "So Harley, this is all your doing? You've made a huge mistake, pal. They've got nothing on me."

He turned his attention to Larry. "Go ahead, arrest me. I'll sue you for more than you can make in a lifetime."

"Well, Silver, if you want to do it the hard way, fine. Read him his rights," Larry said, motioning to a detective.

"Wait a minute," Silver said, nervously. "I'm a respected citizen and I have nothing to hide. I'll be happy to accompany you and answer any questions, as long as my lawyer is present." He was smart, and knew the process would be a lot easier for his lawyer to handle if he pretended to cooperate.

"If you're an innocent, concerned citizen, I don't know why you would think you need a lawyer, but all right, great," Larry shrugged. "Bring him along."

Silver stepped up to me and said in a low voice. "This is all your doing. When I get out of this I'm going to get that bitch of yours—"

I hadn't meant to...I knew better, but suddenly all of the rage I'd fought to control spilled over, and needing an outlet for it to keep myself from the *change*, I unleashed my human side, thinking *easy boy easy*, and landed a punch square to Silver's nose before I realized what I'd done.

"Harley!" yelled Larry, as I was wrestled to the floor by the uniforms with him.

NINE

"Let him up," Larry said. He then turned to check on Silver, whose nose was bleeding into a bar rag one of his men had handed him. "Are you okay, Silver?"

"Noh ahm not hokay," he mumbled. "Hi thin my nothe ith broken."

"Do you want to see a doctor?" Larry asked.

"Yeth," Silver said, furiously nodding his head up and down for emphasis.

"Okay." Larry heaved a huge sigh of resignation. "Take Mr. Silver to Harborview Hospital, and inform his lawyer to meet us there."

Larry turned to me and escorted me off to a corner. I could see Silver over Larry's shoulder. As he was being helped out he took the bar rag away from his face for an instant and flashed me a huge grin.

"I'm sorry, Larry," I said. "He called my girlfriend a bitch and swore he would get her."

"Unfortunately, I didn't hear that, and I was the closest one to you. Gosh darn it, Harley, you've blown whatever chance we had with this guy, which wasn't real strong to begin with. We have the battery arrest that was never prosecuted, and the fact he frequented the establishments where the vics worked...along with hundreds of others. That's it. You should have warned me that you had personal issues with this guy."

"Yes, I know," I sighed, the jealous fury gone out of me as I realized how badly I'd screwed up.

"I have to write up a report on this. It's real bad, you know. He can sue us as well as you. If it was you and me and Silver, it would be different, but there are too many witnesses. I'm going to have to play this one straight as an arrow. If he wants to file an official assault and battery charge, which his lawyer will certainly insist on if he doesn't, then I'll have to arrest you. I should do it now. What is your connection with this guy anyway?"

"He's a friend of my girlfriend, Helene, and thinks he's my rival. And before I came over here I found out he had financed her espresso business. That's what we were talking about when you came in."

"You picked a heckuva time to settle a personal grudge. She hadn't told you?"

"Nope."

"I'm sorry, Harley, but as of right now you're off this case."

"*What?* Larry..."

"You're too personally involved and you're not thinking straight. I have to cover my butt on this one, but it doesn't matter. You know how the Captain feels about you, and the Chief would take you off anyway. With civil liability issues like we have now, you might as well have hit them with a stun gun in their privates. You're off the case. I'll try to get your pay for you, but now they're going to quibble about every cent we owe you."

He was right, and I'd known it as soon as I'd thrown the punch. "All right, Larry, do what you have to. Stopping the killer is the important thing. Let me know if I can help, unofficially, in any way."

"Thanks, Harley," he said, giving me a fatherly pat on the back as he walked out, while Silver's three stooges grinned at me like Halloween jack-o'-lanterns. I made a quick motion as if I was going for them, and blew their candles out as they scrambled over each other to get behind the bar to relative safety.

I left and walked in a daze to the bike, noticing how badly

it was parked and remembering with shame my reckless ride, which would have been barely justifiable if it had been a matter of life and death.

Larry was right. I was too personally involved in this case and had let myself become distracted by my roller coaster relationship with Helene. What about all of the other baristas who were at risk? With Silver now a suspect I had jeopardized that lead in the case and left Larry with a mess to straighten out with his superiors. I couldn't blame him for having kicked me off the case. And he didn't know the half of it. What would he think if he knew we were all werewolves?

He'd probably clutch that cross he wore around his neck, reacting like most citizens, who, if they believed we existed would think we were spawn of the devil and that symbols of the church would burn us. We weren't demons from hell and a cross wouldn't hurt us, of course. That was all mob myth. Now, blazing torches—that was another matter. Even our human forms wouldn't do well being burned at the stake.

Still, I felt a bit like a monster as I started up the bike and rode to the Espresso Passion to see Helene. I wanted to get on I-90 and head east for Gram's house, the only place I desired to be for the coming full moon run, now that I was off the case in disgrace. But I knew I should have talked to Helene before confronting Silver about their partnership, even though she had kept it from me. Silver would be eager to gloat. I wanted her to hear the news of my downfall directly from me. I owed her that much.

The fire had gone out of me though. While I loved Helene, I'd been resisting my instincts and compromising my true nature. I was a lone wolf with a human heart beating strong with my Gram's goodness. A dualist impulse drove me, but not a schizophrenic one. The snarling beast within, always lurking in the shadows of our inner selves—whether wolves or humans or creatures lower on the food chain—had leapt for Silver's throat. He had played me like a puppet in a shadow dance, winning with ease, pulling my strings and then pushing me aside with cunning manipulation.

I was no longer angry. I didn't like Silver, but I didn't hate him either. Sensing his dark depths was to pity him, and if it turned out he was a killer too, I'd fight him on the higher plane of justice. I had seriously damaged my career, but I could still fight for innocents.

When I walked into the Espresso Passion, I knew what I had to do, but Helene didn't make it easy. She was in the back doing the endless paperwork the government crushes truly small businesses with. She saw me, and before I could speak, she jumped up, throwing her arms around my neck in a passionate embrace still hot from our dawn engagement.

"Oh Harley," she said, "I didn't want you to leave this morning. What do you say we make up, sneak away and take up where we left off?"

"We have to talk," I said, sounding colder than I meant to, or felt.

She looked into my eyes, stunned by my tone and studying me with all her senses, probably scenting my distress. "What is it, Harley? What's happened? Is Gram okay?"

Not, 'your Gram', but just 'Gram'. "No, Helene, she's okay. It's me. Please, just listen."

"Okay Harley," she said, just above a worried whisper, backing off and sitting on the edge of her paper-strewn desk. "Go ahead."

"I did something really stupid today. Larry Meyers, the detective I work with in the Seattle Police Department, called me to say that Silver might be a suspect in the barista murders."

"What? That's crazy Harley. I've known him a long time and he has his bad side, but murder? I can't——"

"Let me finish," I said interrupting with a bit of the edginess I'd been determined to control. "The police found out he'd once been arrested for battering a barista in Everett——"

"What?"

"It happened, but the barista dropped the charges later and the prosecutor didn't have enough evidence to go to trial."

"So he wasn't convicted of anything?"

"No," I said, "he wasn't. But the police checked the espresso stands—including Sarah's café—where the victims worked, showing Silver's picture, and they recognized him at every place."

"That doesn't mean anything," Helene said defensively. "He owns a couple of espresso stands in Ballard, and he even..." Her voice trailed off as she began to understand something of my coldness.

"Yes. I talked to Sarah at the Second Cup, earlier, about Silver. She was surprised I didn't know about his involvement in the espresso business, or that he'd financed this place for you."

"Harley, it wasn't like...I mean, it never came up at first, and then after you two...well it didn't seem that important to me. It was before you and I had met and it's just a business arrangement."

"I know," I said with a sigh. "But finding out he'd beaten up a barista, and then finding out you were more involved with him than I thought, and not knowing if there had been more between you—"

"Harley, you know how I feel about you."

"Yes, but I lost it, thinking you were in danger too...but truthfully, I was jealous and angry. I was supposed to meet Detective Meyers at The Den, to interrogate Silver, but I beat the police there. I confronted Silver and told him I would pay off what you owed him."

"Harley, you had no right to—"

"Yes, I know. It was stupid and wrong. I was in a rage. Silver taunted me and we were about to have it out when the police arrived." I looked away, ashamed, but I had to get it out. "Silver agreed to go with them downtown to answer any questions. He seemed really upset, and he whispered to me that it was my fault. He called you a bitch and said he would get you."

"Oh Harley..." Tears welled. I realized she knew Silver had played me.

"Yeah," I said. "I punched him out, which I don't regret.

But of course it's what he wanted me to do. It wrecked any chance the police might have had to get anything out of him. I may be arrested for assault and battery, and he will probably sue the police department as well as me."

"Maybe I can talk to—"

"I'm off the case, obviously," I said, cutting her off. "They'll probably never hire me again for anything. I couldn't get a job with the city as a parking meter."

"I'm sorry, Harley. Silver is a devious guy, but he had a hard life growing up on the streets, and he helped me to—"

"It doesn't matter, Helene. Being a suspect in a murder doesn't make him guilty. They don't really have anything on him. This is not about him. It's about me...and us. I don't like what I did today. It's not a side of me that I like to acknowledge, but it's there. I feel right now, that I've lost touch with who I am and who I want to be."

"Harley, please don't..."

"I'm sorry Helene, but I need some time alone...to figure out where the hate is coming from. This is my problem and I have to deal with it. Loving you is one of the best things I've known, but if I don't trust you...even worse, if I don't trust myself..."

That's when the dam broke and the tears I'd been trying to hold back welled up. I wiped them away angrily. Crying wasn't the wolf way and I'd had enough of my too human emotions for one day. "I've got to go, Helene."

"Harley, don't—"

I turned and walked out the door, knowing there was really nothing more I could say—not understanding it myself. I got on the bike, took a deep breath, fired it up and rode off into the foggy night.

I felt the moon tugging at me. It was nearly full, although I couldn't see it through the fog. Tomorrow was the February full moon, known as the Wolf Moon. Helene had wanted me to run it with her and the pack, but that was out of the question. Especially now.

I felt bad knowing I'd hurt Helene. I didn't doubt her feelings for me, but I was no good to anyone in this emotional maelstrom. I didn't know if we could work out all of our complications and contradictions. We would always be friends...of that I was sure. It was the most I could hope for.

I rode home and the first thing I did was put my cell phone on the charger. I wouldn't need it or want it until I got back. Then I packed some things in my saddlebags, changed into my cold weather riding gear, filled a thermos with coffee, soymilk and a bit of Myers Dark Rum, and headed for Eastern Washington, with the Harley gobbling up the first of the five hundred ice-cold miles to my grandmother's ranch.

It was cloudy and damp riding in the beginning, on the Western side, but the highway had been cleared of snow as I reached the higher elevations and all the way over Snoqualmie Pass through the Cascade Mountains. Once I crossed the Columbia and hit the flats near Moses Lake, the sky was clear and mother moon lit the landscape, calming me with her call. I loved the silvered light of the moonlit night, which was most like that of my dreams.

I howled and the Harley rumbled, the miles rolling by with the galaxy tumbling sideways through the universe overhead, and the troubles that had seemed so huge back in Puget Sound's people-packed bowl, now seemed small under the twinkling light of a million suns so far away, knowing that the time-span of all life on Earth wouldn't fill a star-blink.

Whether wolf or human, we crawled together from the primordial ooze with a higher purpose, and though the muck still sucks at our toes at times, the stardust we are evolved from sings a consciousness of one, if we will but listen to the song.

The moon had sung me east, and I rode on beneath it, temporarily at peace, thinking of my Gram's warm embrace, the log fire, and the fresh-baked apple pie I knew would be waiting.

I had never missed a Wolf Moon run on the ranch since my first *change* running free. Gram knew I would be there, as she had always been for me. My heart skipped as I thought of her age, knowing that one day she wouldn't be there. But she was in good health and as tough as they come, so that time wouldn't be soon.

I adjusted my boots on the pegs and opened the throttle a bit more, relaxing to the rumble, letting the ride take me on through the night.

～～

I arrived at Gram's at nearly four-thirty in the morning, with the recent snowfall glistening in the moonlight. The snow must have fallen the day before, because Gram's long drive-way was clear of any deep snow. Gram's hired man, an old guy named Jorge who had worked for her for years, kept the lane clear. He lived down the road a mile and came when he felt Gram needed help—if it were up to her that wouldn't be often—or to do other things like clearing snow whenever he felt it was needed. Gram felt he did too much, often telling him, "I'm not helpless, you know." His reply was always, "*Si, mi amor,*" and he went on doing exactly what he thought was needed.

Jorge couldn't be categorized as a hired man, although that was how the relationship had started out, and they had kept their old habits. He was really a partner in the business of the ranch, which was mostly grazing cattle. Besides the 520 acres of the ranch, Gram had some grazing rights on the neigh-boring U.S. Forest Service land.

Gram had sold Jorge some acreage down the road, and he and his family worked the ranch out of their place. He paid her a small percentage of the profits. Gram wanted the ranch to go on functioning, and was happy to see them prosper. She didn't need money. She'd inherited the ranch and enough money to live comfortably, and knowing I wasn't interested in ranching, we all agreed the relationship would continue in the same way as long as Jorge and his three grown boys and two daughters wished it to.

I parked the bike in the garage, grabbed my saddlebags and tiptoed into the house, although Gram slept soundly, blessed even at her age. I pulled my boots off at the door and slipped into the fleece-lined moccasins she had left for me there. The wood in the fireplace had burned down and I could see she had waited up for me, with a down comforter in a heap in the recliner she called her cloud. I was sorry I hadn't arrived earlier...she was obviously expecting me. She also knew how unreliable I was when it came to phone calls or planning the details of these trips very far ahead.

A fresh apple pie made without animal products sat on the counter, and there was probably another, uncooked but ready in the refrigerator. I got out the five one-pound bags of Mukilteo coffee I'd brought Gram as a gift, and the fifth of Blue Bombay gin she used in her evening martini. I put the gin in the freezer where she kept it always ready.

I cut a quarter piece out of the pie and poured the last of the rum coffee out of my thermos. It was barely warm, but that was okay. I sat down at the three-bedroom log cabin's dining room table, carefully pushing aside the books and paperwork that had accumulated there.

Eating my pie and gazing through the eight-foot high windows overlooking the snowy fields and backdrop of small, tree-covered mountains, I was transported back to my youth, and it felt as good as ever. *Why do I leave this place?* The habitual question passed through my mind. *Because it is too perfect and I don't believe I deserve it?* Perhaps, in part, but I knew the answer was much more complicated—an unfathomable mixture of genes weighted too much on my grandfather's portion of the DNA helix I'd inherited.

Life here was too complete. I needed to be out in the cruel world fighting to prove, if only to myself, that being a werewolf wasn't a bad thing, a monstrous thing—trying to prove it was a matter of choice even for us, whether to be good or succumb to evil, or maybe worse yet, to be neutral, blaming pureblood humans for not being like us, for not accepting us, for not allowing us to be fallible like them.

I'd been sheltered for most of my youth. My mother hadn't loved me, but my Gram did, and I suppose because of Gram I felt it was more my mother's problem than mine.

The monster mythos permeated the culture too much for me to stay ignorant of the dangers to those who are different. The talk most parents are supposed to have, but avoid, with their children approaching pubescence, was different for me. How do you tell a child he or she is a werewolf? Most of the werewolves I know were taught—if they were taught any-thing—that our wolf natures were a dirty unmentionable thing—far, far worse than sexual thoughts, or masturbation. Is it any wonder werewolves were confused? Hey, at a certain time of the month we could lick our own genitals.

But it wasn't like that for me. Gram talked about the *change* with me in a natural way, like it was okay. She made it seem like I was the special one, like a comic book superhero with powers that I had a responsibility to use to help others. In fact she bought me comics for that very reason, and the Marvel superheroes were like family to me.

"Those comics are about you," she used to say, "and now you know why you have to keep your true identity secret. Never ever talk to anyone about the *change*. It would be dangerous for them as well as you." And Gram never lied. She truly believed in me, and therefore so did I.

Then, in my teenage years, I secretly devoured everything in the culture about werewolves, from fairy tales to old mov-ies, and I was horrified, finally breaking down in tears when Gram questioned my developing bout of depression.

"I'm evil, Gram," I told her angrily. "You lied to me. Werewolves are horrible creatures who do horrible things and don't even remember. Why didn't you tell me the truth? I might hurt you sometime and not even know it until it was too late."

"Son, look at me," she said, lifting my head from where I'd buried it in her lap. "I've never lied to you. Think about it. You remember every minute of your changes, don't you? I have even shown you what you look like in a mirror. You are that beautiful blond wolf...the most wonderful and good crea-ture I have ever known. Do any of those silly monkey-like jumping around things with mangy dog heads in the movies,

look like you? Of course not.

"People fear and deny what they don't understand, making up stories to scare themselves and their children. In the end they convince themselves the creatures they've fantasized don't exist, and in reality they don't, at least not in the horrible way they've imagined them."

"But Gram, I think they'd want to kill me if they knew."

"Some would, darling. It's a hard world out there sometimes. But the people who think like that are small people who will never grow to appreciate the special beauty in the world, the amazing miracle that we are all so alike, but always different."

"Are there many others like me?" I asked.

"I'm afraid not many, Harley, but I've done some research and I suspect, with all the so-called bigfoot sightings, the Northwest may be a favorite gathering place for those of your kind. Someday, you will find them, summoned by an inner call of the wild, like when you howl during your change."

Suddenly it was as if I was really back there, a confused boy, with Gram stroking my hair, reassuring—

"Morning, Harley."

"Jeez!" I said, nearly jumping out of my skin. "Gram! You scared the heck out of me!"

"My what big teeth you have," she said, laughing at the opportunity to use the old Red Riding Hood routine we'd done as far back as I could remember. "You're slipping, letting me sneak up on you like that."

"It's those darn sheepskin slippers, and this place is full of your scent." I started laughing too. "Jeez, Gram, I was thinking about when you and I had the talk..."

"You mean about not sniffing butts in public?"

"Gram! No, of course not." I peered at her. " I mean when you explained about werewolves and the *change*."

"Oh, those talks," she said laughing at me. "Took months, as I recall."

"What are you doing up anyway? Aren't you sleeping well? Are you okay?"

"I'm fine, Harley." She grabbed the comforter off her chair and joined me on the sofa, throwing it over our laps and feet. "I was excited that you were coming, and it is almost dawn. Past the time I get up anyway. I'm so happy you're here. You found the pie?"

"Yes, thanks," I said, hugging her close, realizing again how much she'd diminished in size. She had always been an athletic, tall woman, but she had shrunk, although she wasn't frail by any means.

Looking out the windows I noticed the moon was sinking behind the mountains.

"Tomorrow night," she said, following my eyes to gaze upon the moon. "Well tonight really...it's the Wolf Moon. Helene isn't coming out to run with you?"

All I could do was sigh.

"What's the matter, Harley? Trouble between you two?"

I sighed again and told her all that had happened in the last few days.

"I'm sorry, dear," she said when I'd finished. "She's a wonderful girl and I can tell you still love her. But don't blame yourself. Relationships are never easy, and there are so many extra complications for you two. You have to be true to yourself or you can't be true to anyone."

I remembered thinking a similar idea about trust. "We've been having troubles off and on, mostly about the pack thing. I don't know if I want to have my own kids, let alone adopting Helene's pack. She's the matriarch, not by blood but by choice, and they are like family to her. And some of them, like Silver and his crowd, are not good for her. I've got a feeling Silver's crowd are into some bad stuff, but then if I say anything, it feels like I'm trying to run her life...like I'm being overprotective. She took care of herself growing up and she has done well. She's a natural leader. And she wants me to be a part of that."

"I like her independence, but you're both that way." Gram said.

"I suppose. Anyway, I had a run in with him back in Seattle."

"That Silver? The one who runs with Helene's pack?"

"Yes."

I told her what had happened back in Seattle.

"I admit I was acting pretty irrational, and I shouldn't have let Silver goad me into hitting him. I've been kicked off the serial killer investigation, and now, if the Barista Basher kills again, it will be partly my fault. I've wrecked the two things I feel good about."

"Well hon, it's good you came over. Maybe you can sort some things out. The Wolf Moon run has always been your best."

"I hope so, Gram. Trouble is, Helene and the whole pack will also be over in this area. They'd already made plans. She was trying to get me to run with them."

"Maybe she will stop by tomorrow, before the run."

"I don't think so, Gram. She loves you, but I made it very clear we should take a break."

"That was rash."

"It's done now, so I might as well make use of the time to get my head back on straight."

"Perhaps you should listen more to your wolf side."

"I am."

"No son, you're sounding very human right now. That's not always a bad thing, but you're confused by the complications of human life in a city. I think life in the wild is a lot simpler. I don't know how anyone can live in a city."

"You're right Gram—as usual. Maybe the wolf will know what I should do." It wasn't going to be easy having Helene and the pack within howling distance. "I guess I'd better get some rest. It's been a long day...and night. It feels so good to be with you, Gram. I love you so." I hugged her and fought back tears that the boy in me wanted to let go, and the wolf in me wanted to howl away.

~ ~

I awoke in mid-afternoon, panicked, sweating and scared

to death of the horrible dream I'd been having. I sat up quickly, the flight or fight reflex chemistry surging through my veins. Wanting to forget while also trying to remember details, I sat there, my sweaty head in my clammy hands, the horrible scene replaying in a loop...remembering the smell of blood everywhere...Gram's blood.

The beginning of the dream had already faded beyond recall, wiped out by the horror of the last scene. I had returned to Gram's house after running the Wolf Moon, still in wolf form. From far away I could scent there were dead and dying animals everywhere, ripped apart with ferocious, senseless fury. The stench of blood, entrails, and bodily fluids was nauseating even to a wolf, and I nearly vomited as I bounded past a trail of mangled animals—racing toward the house I was whimpering with foreboding.

I'd rounded the barn, and saw another bloodied form lying near the back door to the house. I denied the horrible truth of Gram's scent overwhelming me as I raced to her mutilated body, pushed at her with my muzzle...pawed at her with my useless, five-toed appendages, frustrated at my helplessness to do anything to save her, while sensing she was already dead.

I looked around, growling, hackles stiff, picking up the scent of the crazed killers and recognizing that wolves like me that had done this, but their scent was as cold as my Gram's own, and revenge would have to wait while sorrow seared my heart. I could do nothing, nothing, nothing...I sat back on my haunches, soaked in the stench of my Gram's horrible death at the hands...no, not hands...the teeth and claws of werewolves like me. Werewolves Gram had trusted, accepted, loved. We had killed one of the few humans that loved, even revered our kind, and I howled my hatred of my wolfishness, wanting to tear myself to pieces...

And then I'd awakened full of horror of the dream while momentarily relieved that it had been a dream, and then recoiling with self-loathing that I'd been able to imagine such horror...that this wretched blood-drenched mangling of my beloved Gram, had arisen within myself.

I don't know how long I sat there on my bedside trying to rationalize the nightmare. I felt the pull of the full moon, and as the dream faded, as most dreams do, I convinced myself that it was just a dream, which grew from the seeds of fear and subconscious guilt we all feel as we go about our busy modern lives, too busy for those we love most. Those seeds of fear and guilt, I rationalized, fell on the fertile soil of murdered innocent victims past and still to come if the barista murders were not soon solved. My complex relationship with Helene and the dark shadow of Silver fed the black depths, the growling monster this gruesome dream had birthed.

Yes, I told myself it was that and nothing more...it was a dream, or so I fervently hoped. Being a werewolf, I struggled to push down and back the thought that nightmares can come alive, our worst fears leaping and snarling out of the night to devour us. I had fought desperately against my own nature, becoming vegan to protect the innocent and keep the beast at bay.

I shook off the dream and showered, luxuriating in the man-made hot water loosening taut muscles while washing away my fears. I dried off, and skipped shaving, glancing in the mirror at my nearly full beard. Shaving the day of a full moon was a waste of time since it grew back in so fast. By dusk I'd have a full luxurious coat to keep me warm.

Gram was at her table, playing poker on her computer, and the last of the nightmare fears evaporated, like morning fog. "Morning, Gram."

"Afternoon, son," she said, smiling. She had long since gotten used to my late hours, but she still kidded me about them. She had always been up at the crack of dawn, and earlier in winter. "I'll fix you some breakfast."

"No, don't bother, Gram. I can take care of myself." I kissed her cheek, hugged her over the back of her chair, and found it hard to let her go.

"I know you can, Harley. But I want to do it. It's nice to have someone else to do for, for a change. Besides, with what you eat, it's just getting stuff out. I put in a supply of that soy milk and cereal you like, got some bananas and vegetarian muffins and some strawberry jam I put up last summer. The coffee is ready to turn on. I found the gin...thanks for bringing me over some more of the good stuff, by the by."

"You're welcome, Gram. Thanks for looking after me."

"My pleasure. I know you like to fill up before a full moon, and there's three quarters of that apple pie left. Let's eat it up so I can bake the other one and have it fresh for in the morning."

Gram joined me for my breakfast, her lunch, having a piece of pie and cheese. "Tell me how the old cowpoke is doing, son. You mentioned him but I didn't want to interrupt the story to ask."

"He's doing great, as far as I could tell. Funny as ever and he keeps on flirting with the ladies, young or old."

"He was always a flirt, although he didn't have to try hard."

"You know, I don't think you've told me if you and Greg were ever, you know, romantically inclined?"

"Romantically reclined, don'cha mean?" She said with a grin. "Well, yes, we did go together for a bit back in high school. It was mostly because we had a small school and the choices were slim. He had a roving eye, even then...well, especially then. We've always been good friends, but I wasn't head over heels or anything.

"We kind of went our separate ways. I went off to school and he cowboyed up...like they say now, with no idea what it means. We didn't have the same interests beyond ranch stuff and rodeos. His idea of showing a gal a good time was to have her help him muck out the horse stalls and then do a tussle in the straw." She laughed so I knew it was at least a slight exaggeration. "I've always loved ranch life but I never wanted to be a ranch wife. I'm too independent, I guess, to ever play the little wife part.

"I might of though, coming back to the ranch after graduating college. But then your Grandad came along and I was ruined for any lesser man. We packed more love and romance into that short time than most folks get in a lifetime. He never said he'd stay, and I never expected it. He was straight with me from the very beginning. That first full moon we shared was the most amazing night of my life, traipsing around the summer meadows with a full on wolf...watching him howl at the moon.

"We spent our last day together, late in August in those same meadows, picnicking, drinking wine and making love. I knew he was leaving, although we didn't talk about it directly. Finally, as the moon came up, he *changed*, and I hugged him good and long. Then he bounded off up that mountain, making his way out on that rock bluff there, where you go to howl sometimes. His howl was like the sweetest sad song I have ever heard, and then he was gone.

"I thought he might come back some time, but he never did. I suspect he was killed. Ranchers back then killed every wolf they saw, whether it bothered them or not. Crazy bloody bastards. I think he would have come by sometime if he were alive. That hope has kept me going in hard times. I still have that hope deep in my heart."

"Did he say where he was going, Gram?" I'd often thought about him, like some mythological character, and I'd wanted to go looking for him, or at least to follow his trail and find out more about him. He seemed more God to me than flesh and blood werewolf.

"Well, not exactly. He talked about Alaska a lot. He said he wanted to run with wolves across the tundra, to chase caribou and smell the freedom of a wide-open land. Of course, even in that huge wilderness, they shoot and trap wolves for sport. They hunt them relentlessly from airplanes. How sporting is that? It's like genocide."

"Yes," I said, "and with helicopters...some fatcat from Texas or Pennsylvania or somewhere spending big bucks to kill a wolf. That's like somebody with a spear gun at Sea World bragging about being a fisherman.

"Remember that Toklat wolf pack in the Denali National Park?" I said, my werewolf blood running hot. "The alpha female was trapped and the alpha male was shot, leaving the young with no guidance and the pack decimated? Those were wolves millions of people had read about, seen photos of, and cared about, worldwide, and they were still killed for nothing but money and the lust to kill something wild. It's sick. There is no doubt in my mind they would kill me as quickly, without remorse."

We sat there in silence a while. I wished my grandpa would come back, like I had so many times in the past. I tried to imagine an old gray-haired man, or the gray, long-of-tooth wolf he'd be now.

"How're the Mustangs, Gram?" I asked, breaking the silence and changing the subject. Wild horses was my Gram's other favorite topic and maybe as close to her heart.

She had adopted wild horses that had been rounded up by the Federal Bureau of Land Mismanagement, to trim the herds on public lands, supposedly to prevent overgrazing. There are only 37,000 wild Mustangs in the United States, which the BLM says are 9,000 too many, but there are four million cattle grazing on those same lands. You'd think they could cut back a few thousand cattle instead.

"They're doing great. We have eighty-seven right now," Gram said proudly. "Most are out on the range, but we have a mare and her colt out here in the corral. It was a hard birth and the mare wasn't doing so well, so Jorge brought them in. I need to go out and check on them if you want to come along."

At the corral behind the barn, the Pinto mother seemed to be doing better, with the bandy-legged colt nursing. I threw a little more hay in for the mother, and we leaned on the fence watching them.

"It's hard to believe anyone could slaughter horses for meat," I said.

"Yes, it is, Harley. Any they round up that they can't find homes for, they butcher and send to other countries for meat. We're the fifth-largest exporter of horsemeat in the world, most of which goes to France, Belgium, Switzerland, Mexico and Japan.

"We took three more wild ones two weeks ago. Jorge breaks some to ride and sell, but most of them are running free out on the range. The ones we sell, we make the owners sign an agreement that they keep them for the life of the animal, or return them to us. We don't sell them for much, but we learned people don't seem to value them as much if we just give them away. We do give some away in special cases, to kids we're sure will take care of them."

We watched them a while longer, then wandered over to another corral where Gram had three old sheep and an aging potbellied pig she'd adopted, and we fed them. "Your home for aged and homeless critters is filling up." There were a bunch of chickens that ran free, too old to lay eggs, as well as a bunch of multi-colored rabbits.

"I like having animals around. Lots of people get animals for pets and then tire of them, so there are always more to take in. I'd do more if I weren't getting so old myself. You sure you're not ready to give up the city life and come on back here?"

"If I was smart, that's what I'd do," I said.

"I was kidding, Harley. You're doing good work over there, catching killers. I wouldn't want you to stop what you're doing. I'm proud of you. The small ranching life is a thing of the past. It was a community at one time, but there are fewer and fewer of us holdouts. Most have been bought out by corporate monoliths as a place to bury their unholy profits. Tax shelters, they call them. They gobble up the BLM leases and lock out the little guys' way of life...like they do the Mustangs. Don't get me started, Harley."

I laughed. It didn't take much to get Gram started on her beloved Mustangs.

By the time we'd finished the chores the sun was sinking in the west, and we headed for the house. The pull of the moon was strengthening, and my senses were overwhelming me, as they always did before the *change*. The warm sweet scent of Gram calmed me as I turned my head from side to side to catch the individual sounds of animals and other things, like a leaf long-dead but still attached, fluttering in the light breeze, and a woodpecker far away.

Then the memory of the dream hit me, and for the first time in my memory, I felt an uneasy fear of the *change* soon to come.

I tried to put the foreboding out of mind. "Are you okay, son?" Gram asked.

"Huh? Sure," I said, startled that she had noticed my odd mood.

"You seem distracted. Usually you're leaping off the furniture, all excited about the *change*."

"I don't know, Gram. I am feeling down."

"Helene?" she asked.

"Yeah, probably," I said, without feeling I was lying. I was sure that was what lay beneath the dream. Knowing she was out there, feeling the *change* too. Gram was right. I'd always looked forward to the *change*, like a kid at Christmas, or riding a Harley on the open road. Or a new romance and multiple orgasms and the smell of gourmet coffee and the taste of the best chocolate all rolled into one. Running free as a wolf with all my senses tuned like the finest violin in the hands of a maestro...even those words don't do it justice.

I did feel it though. I was excited, even with the undercurrent of fear, and I shook off the uneasiness. "I'm okay, Gram," I said, wanting to reassure her, but I could see she didn't believe it. We both let it go, however, and got ready for our longtime ritual.

When the *change* first started, in puberty, Gram had watched over me. I'd get undressed to make it easier, although it wasn't hard to slip out of loose-fitting clothes after the *change*. Gram would make me a bed on the floor, covering me with a quilt while we waited out the full sequence.

As I got older, I became uncomfortable with that, growing shy and self-conscious of the in-between stages, where you're most like the monkey-dog portrayals of werewolves in the movies. So I'd started retiring to the barn for the *change*. One of the benefits was that Gram was able to run interference if any unexpected citizens arrived, like someone who'd lost their way, or an unplanned delivery. Nosy neighbors weren't a problem, because there were stories of paranormal sightings in our valley on full moons, and even the scoffers managed to find an excuse to stay inside, superstition or not.

The sunset colors had long faded behind the mountains to the west when Gram kissed me on the cheek, scratched behind my ear for fun, and I went to the barn. Starlight was sparkling on the crisp snow and the sky was growing lighter in the east.

We'd made a nice little bed of straw, earlier, and I stripped off my clothes and lay down on the quilt Gram had sent out with me. I wouldn't have needed the quilt, because the fur had already been growing on my body, and the flush of the *change* itself always warmed me. Even in human form, I wasn't one to feel the cold much. The *change* was gradual unless I was stressed or angry or felt threatened in some way. Then it happened in seconds...probably the extra adrenalin.

As Mother Moon rose higher in the east, I felt the *change* surge through me. A certain amount of discomfort occurs as the bone structure reforms——kinda like banging your shin and hitting your funny bone and getting a charley horse cramp all in rapid succession. However, the wolf nature takes over and my human consciousness recedes somewhat, so I don't notice the pain after the first few seconds, and I'd become accustomed to what I did feel.

Animals in the wild are tough. They don't feel pain in the complaining way that humans do——who are always so aware of their bodies. But there is a mechanism left over in a human that is similar. When a major traumatic injury occurs, our bodies go into shock and we don't feel pain as much. We feel a pinprick much more, because that is useful...you react and pull away to avoid further injury. With major trauma, like a broken bone for instance, massive pain has no value and in fact would be counter-productive, so your body short-circuits it.

Take me Mother Moon, take me.

I felt my body changing, like evolution fast-forwarded, only in reverse. It's the change in attitude, emotions, awareness that I most notice...I say notice, but that doesn't really describe it. One moment I am a thoughtful self-analyzing, self-aware creature, and the next I am immersed in the world around me. Harley is still there, waiting in the wings, so to speak, but Wolf strides out into the argent spotlight on center stage, a powerful creature, assured, focused and very, very aware.

The change complete, we move outside, look up at the full Mother Moon rising above the mountains, and howl. We are wolf, the top of the food chain. Yet more, existing on a plane above even man, for we are werewolf...we are Harley Wolf, and we run free.

TEN

As Wolf trots out into the snowy field, Harley is along for the ride, like riding bareback. Wolf is my swift mount and I am holding fast to the thick fur on the back of his/my neck. I trust Wolf in the wild and there is no need to direct him. I feel what he feels, sense what he senses, and Wolf senses me...Wolf knows I am here. I am like another sense to Wolf, a super-instinct...he is like another body to me. We are the better part of two...one duality perfectly tuned. My body is wolf and part of my mind, but I am still Harley. I am we and we are me.

As I lope into the woods, I am nose down, separating scents like colors, now head up, ears perked, hearing each instrument in the night's symphony, both in totality and individually. I stop, aware of others like me, lurking far off the trail, scenting and hearing me as I do them.

I could chase them...it might be fun...but they are not alpha and are no match. They would quiver belly up before me, and there would be no fun in that. We move on.

Wolf and I are wary, this night. The thrill of running free is there, but diminished. Once again I am resisting that part of my wolf nature, which would have me go and fight for Helene.

I am restless and unsure of what I want or where I wish to go. The pack is here, but not close. I growl, and feel confused. I am not mated to Helene...she/her, but I feel...sense her presence, her need, the confusion/danger of the pack. More than she/her, Helene is, she/her/them.

I lope along my boundaries, marking territory. If they cross *over, if they challenge, I must fight. I cannot defeat the pack, but I know Helene will not willingly lead them into my terrain. I sense Silver's presence, and know that if we meet up he might force a challenge.*

I would willingly fight Silver, but he runs with the pack, he is of the pack, and although Helene leads it and has no mate, the pack might still decide to finish me or even turn on Helene. Silver is cunning, and we are werewolves, part human even now. He has following of his own within the pack.

I shrink back into Wolf. Human thoughts are not worthy of the moonlight. What might be is of no concern to a wolf, and we run on, ignoring the distant howls and yips of the pack called to the hunt as Helene leads them away.

Marking territory is my favorite ritual. No awkward clothes, no lifting and lowering of lids, no dribbles staining clothes, no elaborate aiming, no fear of zipper teeth or forgetting to zip up. As male humans we can write our names in the snow or make clumsy unfinished designs. But that is nothing like the purity of wolf marking territory. Perhaps the closest human experience is to see your name on a beautifully designed trophy, recognizing some hard-won endeavor, but even that is a piss poor substitute.

The boundaries of my territory align with those of the ranch, and it takes hours to complete the circuit. I hear the occasional howls and hunting calls of the pack, but Helene is leading them away from the ranch, and I relax, enjoying the run, the moonbeams sparkling on snow like diamond glitter scattered in celebration of our special night— the Night of the Wolf Moon.

And yet, beneath the thrill of the run, there is unease, a wolfish wariness that all is not right, like approaching a mantrap with instinct screaming, "Go back!"

I finish marking territory and make my way to the howling place, the wolf-sacred mountain ledge where my grandfather had howled his goodbye to Gram, and where I sing my moon-song to celebrate the change. But even this pure song of the night holds no true joy for me as I sing. It is a sorrowful howl tinged with loneliness and that most human of emotions...regret. Like the death song at the loss of a mate, it summons nothing but a soundless echo of emptiness.

After a few half-hearted, dismal howls, I give up. This is no alpha song, proud and strong, calling to a mate. Helene cannot answer such a piteous cry, and Silver must be pleased. The pack will be hard for her to control, feeling bloodlust, wanting to claim the territory of such a woeful defender.

Beneath these cares lies a hidden fear of other danger, unseen, unheard, unscented...gnawing at Wolf and me. Is the horrible nightmare killing of Gram I keep remembering, weighing on even Wolf, like an instinctual warning? Or is it some real danger that Wolf has sensed? As hard as I try, I cannot retreat far enough into Wolf, and the duality lingers between us. Trying betrays the need to try. For the first time ever in a Wolf Moon, we cannot run free as one.

It is still before dawn, but we make our way down the mountainside, heading for home. The moonlight reflecting off the glistening white snow is still as bright as a silvered day.

Only one danger exists that I cannot face, one terrible event I cannot endure, and that is harm to Gram. I have to know she is all right, that this insidious fear does not involve her. I know of no reason for anyone to harm her, but I cannot shake the growing premonition that she is in danger.

Running full-speed now, almost panicked, leaping ob-stacles, our body chemistry pumping every available aid through my veins. I am more than a mile away when I hear the screams, and incredibly, we find some reserve of speed, bounding along in great leaps of supernatural werewolf strength. I close the remaining distance in eye-blink time.

As Wolf races through the snowy field, approaching the back side of the barn, I can see there are two werewolves in the corral, where the mare fights a losing battle. My wolf side takes in the horrid, bloody scene with slow-motion intensity: the dying and mangled sheep in the next pen being finished off by a lone wolf—the stench of blood and entrails every-where, like in my dream—the fearful screams of the young colt and the fearsome neighing of its mother fighting desperately, but going down under the two-pronged attack of a pair of werewolves. I approach in fury, unseen.

There is no sign of other than these three, and I can only hope they had not yet reached the house. The split-second decision made, I approach the fence, leaping into the corral in a desperate attempt to save the mare and her young.

The enemy has taken the mare down—one wolf shaking and biting into her haunch while the second tears at her soft underbelly, ripping and clawing as it fights for greater purchase.

They do not see or sense me, and I hit them nearly simultaneously, a fury of lightning swift attacks with savage jaws and ripping teeth.

One of them whimpers, turning belly up, and we recognize the cowardly piss-scent of those hiding in the woods earlier. There is no time for regret that I had passed them by, only the instantaneous awareness. Although the one goes belly up, peeing and marking itself with fear, the second turns, fighting furiously, sensing I will give no quarter.

If they had fought like wolves, working together, it would have been a tougher fight, but the one fighting for his life is no match for me. I am all over him, snarling and biting furiously.

Then the third werewolf, the one in the sheep pen, leaps the fence, landing on me with full force, knocking me over and revealing my underside. The one we'd been fighting sees the opportunity and dives for my belly. I sense rather than feel its teeth rip, but with renewed fury I slash in every direction, while finding my feet beneath me once more.

The second werewolf, badly injured, loses heart at my renewed attack, breaking off to circle, waiting for an opening, giving me the opportunity to focus on the new sheep-bloodied enemy. He loses his balance as I press a furious attack and lunge for his throat.

The first bite is mostly fur and skin as he tries to pull away, but we throw our weight into the attack, pushing him back against the fence, tasting the blood of vengeance and digging deeper and deeper into his neck, going for the kill.

"Harley! No! Harley!" I hear Gram scream through the bloodlust mist. I hesitate a fraction of an instant, not relinquishing the neck hold, then press on, shaking, snarling, and still fighting for a death grip.

"Ka-rack"...and some mechanical sound..."Ka-rack"...again. "Harley, let it go," I hear Gram yelling.

Suddenly the fight goes out of all of us. The shock of the rifle's retorts freezes the enemy werewolves, and Gram's voice commands Wolf and I. The cowardly killers scramble out of the corral as fast as they are able, dragging themselves, leaving dark trails of blood across the bright snow field toward the woods, and for a few beats of my heart, my human side is both captivated and repulsed by the horrible beauty of the moment, like a battle scene from a Kurosawa samurai flick. Wolf is a kind of primal samurai, bound by rules of wild honor, and satisfied by having defended it.

Watching them go, I see movement in the moonlit shadows of the woods beyond, and I have a brief sense of Helene's pack, standing there, watching...but then they are gone. Was the pack really there? Could they possibly have been a part of this cowardly attack? My human side wonders: Is this senseless violence Silver's doing? Silver, the barista killer?

I turn to Gram as she leans the gun against the fence and lets herself in through the gate. "Thanks, Harley," she says, patting me on the head. "It would have done no good to kill the wicked beasts, and I know you wouldn't want that memory if it weren't necessary. Neither would I. I shot into the air. You had already defeated them. Killing them wouldn't bring back the other animals. Are you hurt bad, son?"

I sniff at Gram as she tries to look me over, and am reassured that she is unharmed. Considering the reactions of those three cowardly enemies, she probably hadn't been the target. They attacked the defenseless animals to hurt me, or to warn me. I had recognized them as three of the biggest sniveling losers in Silver's pack. "Looks like you will be okay," she says, checking out my wounds. "The worst bite glanced off your *ribs."*

I pull away from Gram to look at the poor mare, bleeding badly and whimpering between futile attempts to get up. I want to help somehow, but she whinnies in renewed panic as I approach.

Gram pushes me out of the way, kneeling beside the mare, examining her wounds, while the young colt huddles shaking in the corner beyond its mother. I realize I am Wolf to the mare and its young, like those who had attacked her, and sadly, guiltily, I limp to a snowdrift outside the corral to lick my wounds.

Leaving the mare, Gram takes a bridle from a nail by the gate, puts it on the colt and leads it out of the corral and around the barn. I limp along behind and wait outside the barn door, feeling helpless. The moon has disappeared beyond the mountains in the west and the sun will soon be rising.

Gram puts the colt in a small pen in the barn and then comes to me, kneeling down and hugging me while petting my head, her tears falling onto my wolf coat. She wipes them away and says, "She won't make it, Harley...too badly injured. I...I have to put her down...she's in a lot of pain."

We can hear the mare whimpering in the corral, still trying bravely to get up...to save her offspring, somehow.

"You go lay down, Harley. The change will be soon. I'll take care of this, and then I'll look after you. It's not your fault you know."

Gram walks to the fence to retrieve her old Winchester, as I walk into the barn to lie down on my straw bed. I feel the beginning of the change upon me and I am eager for it, anxious for the end of this Wolf Moon, disgusted with my own kind, and myself. They violated my territory in the worst way and I am sorry that I let them go.

The sound of the rifle's "Ka-rack" startles me, as Wolf begins to recede into the dark shadows of my mind, and the mare's whimpering distress is ended. A sick feeling of human anguish overcomes me. For the first time in my life I have to admit that humans aren't the only creatures capable of mon-

strosities, although we werewolves are more human than not. Before this night, as I personally resisted my predator urges, I had believed werewolves could rise above our human emotions and weak instincts too...that the war always raging within humans to control the animal within, to believe themselves above nature, could be overcome by recognizing the purity of instinct, the law of the wild, the strict rules and unwavering justice in nature— the terrible beauty of it all...to bloom and die and bloom again.

Humans, in believing themselves above and beyond nature, hound and kill indiscriminately that which they cannot control and those who are different, denying in an ironically perverse way that it is in our differences that the beauty and magic and unique possibilities of our species lies...the reincarnation of all nature within us. It is humanity's warped desire to clone itself, to force others to be like themselves, which has given rise to the senseless violence of war while rationalizing and thereby excusing the killing of innocents.

I am monster, I think, as the pure, innocent part of my werewolf nature recedes to leave me alone in my human form once more, lying there, shivering and wounded on a bed of straw. Who better to take down monsters preying on their own kind?

Keep it simple Harley. Forget the angst of living in a sometimes-monstrous world. Do what you can...what you do best. Use a monster to catch a monster. Be the monster in all its lonely, single-minded oneness, and hound the murdering bastards. Therein lies the circle of justice and redemption for you.

Eleven

The phone rang...and rang...and rang. I shut it down without looking to see who the caller was.

Arriving back in Seattle last night I had fallen into bed, and after a troubled, nightmare-filled few hours, I was trying to enjoy my coffee and my soymilk-drenched cereal and honey, before dealing with the persistent, demanding realities of my city life. That is, if I had a life here anymore. I did have a job to do though. In spite of being kicked off the barista case, working on my own I still intended to do what I could to catch the killer.

I knew Helene might be trying to call me. I'd left my cell phone turned off at Grams, so Helene had called and talked to Gram on her landline phone, telling her how bad she felt about what had happened, and that she hoped Gram knew she had nothing to do with the attacks. Gram had assured her she did know that, and not to worry. She didn't ask how Helene knew about it, and when Gram tried to hand me the phone I refused.

The first thing on my schedule was a visit to my friend and doctor, Sharon Dobie, at the University Family Clinic, to get the bandages changed or removed entirely. It'd been a week since the Wolf Moon...a week of licking my mental and physical wounds at Gram's ranch. The bites I'd received in the fight were healing well. Something in the werewolf genes speeds the healing process, and I wouldn't normally see the doctor except Gram made me promise to go.

The mental wounds, however, were still open and festering and needed attention too. I knew I had to talk to Helene and maybe confront Silver, and it was the conjunction of those two upsetting tasks that overwhelmed me.

I knew such a confrontation would happen in the course of the next day or two, whether I wanted it to or not, but I was in no hurry to move things along. The stitches were well healed and ready to be removed, and the bruised ribs better to the point that if I could find something to laugh about the pain would be minimal.

I made another large cup of coffee in the French press, and then I picked up the dreaded cell phone to call...my fingers hesitating—like mentally burned fingers tend to do—between the numbers I punched most often.

It rang three times and then the familiar voice answered. "Detective Larry Meyers, Homicide."

It took a beat before I could speak, my mind distracted by the decision not to call Helene first.

"Hello..." Larry said, patiently. Homicide investigations involve many reluctant participants so he is used to dead air on the phone.

"Larry, it's Harley," I replied, stating the obvious, as he will have recognized my voice as soon as I spoke.

"Harley, where the heck have you been? I've been trying to get hold of you for nearly a week."

"Sorry. I've been over in Eastern Washington, on my Gram's ranch, trying to get my head on straight."

"The thing is——"

"No, I understand. I just want to tell you I'll help in any way I can, free, no charge. I know I acted like a very unprofessional idiot and I want to try to make it up to you in whatever way I can. I'm going to keep working on the case, but I'll be less than a shadow and no one needs to know."

"Harley, will you listen to me for a minute? There is no problem. Silver told his lawyer to drop the whole thing while we were up at Harborview Hospital. He said it was his fault, that he'd threatened you earlier and insulted your girlfriend.

Said he had it coming and took a swing at you first...signed a paper to that effect, witnessed by his lawyer who couldn't stop spluttering."

"You're kidding? *Silver?*"

"Yep. If he's your enemy, you should have such friends."

Dead air again...much dead air. I was speechless.

"Harley, you still there?"

"Yeah...yeah, sorry Larry. You mean...?"

"Yep again. You're still on the payroll. Silver cooperated and seems to be clean on this. He had alibis, confirmed by several people, including your friend, Helene. It also turns out there were some mitigating circumstances in the complaint against him up in Everett. The woman had been heard making threats against him...a jealous girlfriend situation.

"We didn't go into it any further, because with the alibis we don't have a thing to connect him. Since he is in the espresso business himself, it makes sense he would be in contact with baristas and might frequent other businesses. Your friend up at the Second Cup said he had offered to buy her business, so it all makes sense. I can't really see him as the killer, Harley. He is pretty slick, the way he goaded you into hitting him, turning the whole situation around on you like that. But hey, slick is not a crime."

"So I'm still on the case?" I asked, stunned.

"Thank goodness. I need you Harley. This case is going nowhere, and if there is another killing all heck is going to break loose, not to mention the death of some innocent girl. I need all the help I can get, desperately. The chief keeps asking, 'What about Harley? Make sure he stays on this. Pull out all the stops'.

"So I'd really appreciate it if you'd get back to work, Harley. You stepped in it and came out smelling like you took a bath in some gol'durned rose cologne or something."

"Wow. That's fantastic. I thought my career was down the drain. I promise I'll make it up to you, Larry. I won't stop until we nail this guy, starting right now. Thanks. Thanks for everything."

"No prob, Harley. But hey, you ought to buy that guy, Silver, dinner or something, even if he is a slimeball. In fact, I'll chip in."

"I'll have to get used to the idea first. Silver and I have other issues."

"Hey, I didn't say you have to be buddies or anything. But he did both of us a huge favor he and didn't have to. In fact he could have sued us good. It may be awful hard to swallow, but you owe him big time."

"I guess you're right. I can't see any ulterior motive when he had me nailed."

"Well that's up to you, Harley. But we're batting zero with the Barista Basher, so if you can come up with something to help out, we sure need a break."

"It won't take me long to get my head back into the case, Larry. I'm on it hard as of right now. Anything new I should know about? Did you get the personnel report on Sunny Brown from McBucks Coffee?"

"Not yet. The Human Resources person up in Everett told me she would have to talk to her boss at headquarters. I sent them an official request, but I haven't heard back. I'll call them...and get a court order if I have to."

"I'll give that Rodriguez guy at McBucks a call...you remember? Sunny Brown's former boss?"

"Sounds good. I'll get on that personnel file. We need something soon, before this case gets any colder."

"I'll do my best, Larry. I won't let you down this time."

"I know you will. I'm glad you're back."

"I'll be in touch soon, and thanks a lot."

"Later, Harley."

I flipped the phone closed, laid it down on the table and sat back in my chair, drained, my head whirling at the sudden changes in my reality. It was way too much to try to understand and react to. Silver as my hero was way, way more than I could deal with, and if anything I was even more suspicious of his motives. This was like trying to play grandmaster chess after learning only the moves in checkers.

I felt manipulated and outmaneuvered, and guilty that I felt that way. Was I that wrong about the guy? Was it jealousy and envy on my part, as Helene seemed to suspect? Was *I* the bad guy?

I didn't know. I had no answers and no idea how to find any. It was all too confusing and emotional and I hadn't a clue as to how to resolve any of it. That associates of Silver had attacked my Gram's ranch there was no doubt, and they had to answer for it.

But I believed Gram was safe now, so that could wait. I had a job to do and it was time I concentrated on catching a killer. That was something I did know for sure and that I had done in the past. I'd never worked on a case of this magnitude, with the incredibly high stakes of another potential victim...a young woman's life hanging in the balance, maybe even someone I knew personally. Thinking about catching the Barista Basher put everything else back into perspective.

My personal life was on hold, as of now. I was back on the hunt, and this time nothing would stop me until I caught the killer or someone else did. In a way, I was relieved that Larry had dropped Silver from the list of suspects. More than anything, I didn't want the murderer to be a werewolf. But I couldn't quite cross Silver off the list myself. Maybe it was personal enmity.

However, if I got all convoluted with it, maybe his sucking up to the police and appearing to cooperate was the smart thing for a suspect to do. Dropping the charges against me and taking the blame so he couldn't sue us did make him look clean. It got the police out of his hair, and there was no real evidence against him anyway. It had sure changed Larry's opinion of him.

On the other hand, I didn't seriously think Silver was the Basher either. He didn't fit the profile and he didn't smoke Marlboros. At this point there were a lot of suspects I had no reason to suspect...practically every male Marlboro smoker in Seattle and anyone who had been in contact with the victims. And that was leaving out the random-victim possibility.

I'd been concentrating on Sunny Brown, the last victim, because that trail was the warmest. Now I'd have to work my way back to the beginning and talk to everyone involved with either of the previous victims.

But first I decided to call Arlene Fisher to try to get an appointment with her boss, George Rodriguez. I looked through my contact list and hit the number.

"McBucks Coffee...George Rodriguez's office. How may we help you?"

"Hi, Ms. Fisher?"

"Yes, may I help you?"

"I hope so. Are you ready to take that motorcycle ride?"

There was a pause...then... "The Harley guy. Are you really going to take me for a ride? I thought you were just kidding."

"Nope, I promised...the next time I got up that way. I've got to come up to talk to your boss. That's why I'm calling. Is he back in town? You said you'd call me when he got back."

Another pause, and then, "Yes, Mr. Rodriguez has returned from the buying trip, but as I told you before, he is a very busy man."

Her voice had gone cold and business-like, which I guess is natural...trying to protect your boss from unnecessary interruptions. Except this was a necessary interruption by an exceptionally nosy detective. "If Mr. Rodriguez is there in the office, I'd like to speak to him." It wasn't a question.

"Well, let me see if he has a moment. What was your name again?"

"Harley Wolf, Seattle Police Consultant. You know, on second thought, I think I'll come up there and talk to him in person."

There was a long dead space before Ms. Fisher replied, "Is that really necessary, Mr. Wolf?"

"Yes, I think it is. Tell him I'll be there in about forty minutes, and if he isn't there, the next time we meet will be with a police escort."

"I'm not going to tell him that," she said coldly. It seemed the ice age had arrived early, skipping right past global warming.

"That's up to you, Ms. Fisher. Tell him it shouldn't take long if he cooperates in our investigation. Oh, and tell him a double espresso and a cranberry scone would be nice."

I flipped the phone shut, got my stuff together and hit the road.

I was in luck. It was overcast, but not raining, and I got up there before the I-5 traffic through Everett had begun to jam up as it does every day after 3 p.m. I actually made it in twenty-three minutes.

I told the receptionist in the lobby, as I passed through, that George Rodriguez was expecting me, and I received the ritual smile.

My reception from Arlene Fisher in Rodriguez's outer office was not quite so warm. Well, not warm at all. She had an Ice Queen demeanor. But I am northern wolf and I can handle the cold. There are times I even prefer it.

"Hi Arlene," I said, flashing my toothy Red Riding Hood's grandmother grin. "I'm here to see Mr. Rodriguez...no need to get up," I breezed right by. It helps to make people uncomfortable in these situations.

"Wait! Hey!" she said to my back as she chased after me into the office, where George Rodriguez sat behind a huge desk with a view and tropical coffee plantation pictures on the walls. His first reaction had been to reach for the phone, probably to look like an oh-so-busy executive, but my end run ruined the effect. Arlene Fisher was trying to do her *I'm-sorry-boss* routine behind me, but I just played right over it.

"Hi Mr. Rodriguez...I'm Harley Wolf." I didn't give him time to stand up, or shake hands. I could play the busy man game too. Without pausing or waiting for him to respond, I gave him the whole official rigmarole. "Murder investigation," etc, etc. "I understand one of the victims...Sunny Brown...she worked for you?"

"Uh, Brown, you say?"

"Yes, Sunny Brown. She worked for you in quality control, I understand...as a tester?"

"A lot of people have worked here, Mr. Uhm...?"

"Wolf...Harley Wolf. It's an unusual name so it shouldn't be that hard to remember."

"Well, sorry, but we have only just met and..."

"I'm talking about your former employee. Sunny Brown. Sunny is an unusual name also. I'd think you'd remember if you worked with someone by the name of Sunny."

"I certainly did not work with Ms. Brown. But now that you've reminded me, I think I do remember someone like that working in the Department. But I don't see how I could be of any help to...I mean, we have a rather large turnover at that...you know...at the entry level." He said 'entry level' through his nose like it was some kind of road kill to be avoided at all costs.

"I'd think you'd remember this one, Jorge. Jorge...that's the Spanish pronunciation of George, isn't it?"

"Yes," he said, with some anger or indignation coming through in his voice. "But my name is George...spelled like the Presidents...if you don't mind?"

"Oh, sure...George Rodriguez. Like the President's. I've seen your file." I was purposely being rude. Guys like that, with a lot of employees working under them, they are used to getting special treatment. Anything that would shake him up a bit...get him down off his high horse...I got right into it.

"Sunny Brown was brutally murdered recently. You mean to tell me you haven't even heard about the Barista Basher killings in Seattle? You work in the coffee business. I can't believe that anyone working here at McBucks would be unaware that one of your former employees was beaten to death. You didn't even send flowers?"

"Uh, well sure, of course, now I do remember the incident. I'm sorry, I've only recently returned from an overseas—"

"Incident? You call the Barista Basher serial killings an *incident?*"

"Well, no...no...of course not. That's not what I meant."

"Look, George, if you don't wish to cooperate in a murder investigation that has the entire Seattle area in an uproar—with three innocent young murder victims who worked in your coffee industry— then I'm afraid we will be forced to compel you to—"

"No, wait, I didn't mean that. Of course I'll cooperate in any way I can."

"That's good George, because I wouldn't want to cause you or your company the embarrassment of a court order. The news media would have a field day with that."

"That surely won't be necessary, Mr. Wolf. I'm more than happy to help you in any way I can."

"Well that's good. Thank you Mr. Rodriguez," I said, turning on the charm. "We certainly appreciate your cooperation. What can you tell me about Sunny Brown?"

"I do remember her now, of course," he said, exhibiting a miraculous recovery from temporary amnesia that would confound the experts. "She had a difficult time with our dress code, as I remember."

"In what way?"

"Well, she changed hair colors often. Not the usual hairdresser thing. I mean orange...purple...like that. We're a fairly liberal company as far as our dress code goes, but we had some complaints, as I remember. Inappropriate clothing for an office environment. It was okay, down on the floor...what we call the factory. But when we gave her an opportunity for advancement...well, she didn't make the adjustment. You know what I mean?"

"You mean she dressed too sexily?"

"Uhm, well...yes...that and too many...uhm...body piercings...stuff like that."

"Like the tattoo?"

He actually blushed. "Well yes. That too."

"What kind of a snake was it?"

"Huh? I don't know, I'm sure. I didn't—"

"Like a Cobra or something? You know those hooded kind, like from India?"

"Well, possibly. I don't know."

"You mean to say you never looked? You didn't, you know...sneak a peek at the snake? C'mon...I find that hard to believe. Good-looking girl like her?"

"We have to be very careful these days you know. Sexual harassment in the work place...your career can be over like that. And it doesn't have to be anything. Someone gets upset with you...it's her word against yours."

"Did she threaten you, Mr. Rodriguez?"

"Huh? No, of course not. Ask anybody. I'm very careful about stuff like that. Anyway, I'm away on business a lot, and she was working in the lab. She just didn't come in one day."

"So she quit...without giving any notice?"

"It's not unusual for that type, you know, with drugs and everything."

"She was on drugs?"

"No, no, I didn't say that. I have no idea. I'm just saying her appearance...the way she dressed... made you think that maybe that was why...and ah...uhm...she was moody. You know...she dressed like a barista in one of those little independent stands, and for whatever reason, she just didn't come in one day. It's disappointing when you give someone a chance for advancement and...you know...they don't take advantage of it."

"I understand. We appreciate your cooperation, Mr. Rodriguez." I stood up and offered my hand, masking my distaste for the gesture.

"I'm more than happy to do anything I can to help you solve this terrible crime," he said, popping up and shaking my hand too eagerly. He didn't seem upset to see me go, but I get that a lot in this business. His sweaty palm was disgusting.

As I turned to leave, he said to my back, "If there is anything else I can do, just ask."

I turned back to him. "Well, you know, there is one thing. I wonder if you could get me Sunny Brown's personnel file from Human Resources? We can get a subpoena if we need to, of course."

"I don't know why not," he said. It was his turn to surprise me. "If you don't mind signing for it, I can call down and have it brought to the front desk. You can get it on your way out."

"That's great," I said, surprised and at a loss for words. I'd thought for sure he would put up a fight.

"All right," he said. "I'll call down now. If you need anything more, please let Ms. Fisher, my secretary, know."

"Thanks," I said, obviously dismissed, as he sat down and picked up the telephone receiver. Nice recovery. I had to hand it to him. "Oh," I said, stopping short of the doorway and turning back to face him again. "There is one more thing...pretty important too...good thing I remembered or I would have had to come back."

"Yes?" he said, holding the phone in the air.

"I need to know where you were on the nights the baristas were murdered in Seattle."

"Huh?" he said, still frozen with the telephone receiver in the air. "Wh...wh...wh...why do——?"

"Aw, you know what they say about murder..." I said breezily, flashing my *ain't-it-ridiculous* look. "Everyone is a suspect."

"But I...I don't see how...I mean I travel a lot and I probably wasn't even here when..."

"That'll be great then. We can get that out of the way and look for the real killers."

"But I have no idea...when they were...and I'd...uh...have to go back over my records and——"

"Of course, I understand. I'll tell you what...if you want to give a call to...got a pen?"

"Uhm..." He laid down the phone and picked up a pen. I gave him Larry Meyers' name and phone number. "He can give you the dates we're concerned with, and then you can get back to him with your information. Would that work for you?"

"Uh, I suppose I can——"

"And if you can get me that file on Sunny Brown?"

He let out a huge sigh. "All right."

"Thank you for your cooperation Mr. Rodriguez," I said,

turning and walking out.

Arlene Fisher looked up, nervously, as I came out of the inner office. "Is there anything else?" she asked, coldly, then hissed in a whisper, "You could get me fired you know." I was sure she had been listening to me verbally roughing up her boss.

"I think that's all I need for now," I said, flashing her what I thought of as a sympathetic smile. "Thanks. Thanks for everything, Ms. Fisher." Which wasn't much. It was my second time in the McBucks Coffee empire offices, and I still hadn't had a cup of coffee, let alone a cranberry scone. These people did not have the bribery thing down at all.

I had to wait a couple of minutes while the receptionist called Human Resources about the file, but it showed up before she could hang up the phone. It had been on the way after all. The HR secretary had me sign a sheet of paper with some legalese on it, and I scribbled my signature and received the manila envelope.

I carried it outside to where my bike was parked. The rain was holding off, and I leaned against the seat, opening the envelope. I was curious if there were complaints about Sunny Brown, or if she had made any against Rodriguez.

I read a couple of evaluations by supervisors, not Rodriguez, that were excellent. There was some paperwork regarding her promotion and transfer, and then there was a notation about a telephoned complaint regarding inappropriate clothing, and a paper signed by Sunny Brown that she had read the company dress policy.

No complaints by Sunny Brown about any ill treatment, in any way. The final paperwork was a statement that Sunny Brown had been absent for three consecutive days without notifying her supervisor. The supervisor, a Ms. Anderson, was unable to contact Ms. Brown and she was terminated.

That was all. It was disappointing, but Rodriguez's reluctance to want to be questioned about an ex-employee's murder certainly didn't make him a suspect. Who would want to be involved in any way in a case like this? An overly loyal secretary wasn't evidence of a crime either or we'd be arrest-ing half the city's inflated-ego bosses.

There just didn't seem to be anything I could sink my teeth into in this case, and all evidence pointed toward some stereotypical white serial killer. Of course, the biggest part of this job was eliminating suspects, but that wasn't going well either. So far the only one in this city who wasn't a suspect was me. If you put a Phillip K. Dick twist on it, me being a werewolf and all, what if there actually were something to the mindless savage pillaging we werewolves were infamous for? Maybe my whole vegan thing was self-denial.

Okay. I put the file folder back in its envelope and slipped it into my saddlebag. I threw my leg over and was reaching for the ignition switch when I spotted a familiar figure walking head down out of the McBucks building's front door.

Arlene Fisher walked in the opposite direction from where I was parked, hurrying down the sidewalk to the street. She was holding something like a handkerchief to her face in the manner of someone crying and wanting no one to notice. She didn't seem to see me, probably assuming I had already left.

I watched for a couple of moments, to wait until she reached her car, but she walked past the other parking lot to the street, taking refuge in the corner of a bus stop shelter.

I fired up the Harley, feeling guilty and quite sure that the rough handling I'd given her boss had been passed down to her. I hoped that the hostile reception I was about to receive would be mitigated by her love of Harley motorcycles, and hating me would come in second.

I pulled out of the parking lot and rolled up to the bus stop. She was huddled into herself like a cornered animal, hiding in the refuge of the big down jacket and rain pants she was wearing against the winter cold and damp of bus stop commuting.

I revved the engine once and shut it off, pushing down the kickstand.

"Go away," she screamed. "Haven't you done enough? Are you really trying to get me fired?"

Nope, the Harley magic wasn't working. "I'm sorry," I said. "It's my job."

"You may have cost me *my* job. He blamed me for talking to you and if he sees us" ...more sobbing... "Oh please, please, won't you just go away and leave me alone?" Less defiance this time and a lot more hopeless misery.

"I don't want to leave you here like this...if you hop on I'll take you where you want to go...please...there are worse things than getting off work early and riding away with a good-looking guy on a Harley."

There was a momentary hint of a smile contradicting the tears in her eyes as she looked at the bike, at me, and then back at the bike. She looked over her shoulder through the clear plastic of the bus stop shelter, toward the McBucks building, and stood up. "You're a bastard," she said, as I took the extra helmet off its peg, handing it to her.

"Sometimes," I said, standing up to make room for her to throw her leg over. "Where are we going?"

"North. Marysville, exit two-oh-two." She sniffled. "I hope you know this doesn't change anything. You really are a bastard."

I smiled and fired up the bike. *Yeah, but a Harley-riding bastard...the best kind.*

She held herself back, stiff at first, but we hadn't gone a mile before she snuggled up with her arms around me and her head resting up against my back, probably eyes closed. I felt her take a deep breath, shudder and sigh, as we took the back road along the waterfront and across the slough. She wouldn't be the first woman to have an orgasm riding a Harley. They said it was something about the powerful feel of the deep rumbling vibration between their legs.

I turned it up a bit, twisting the throttle as we left the back road and entered onto I-5, and I felt her hug me closer. Nothing like a motorcycle ride to make you forget the stress of the work environment, and hey, it worked for me.

We passed the Sound Harley-Davidson dealership, north of Marysville, where I'd purchased my bike. I revved the pipes saluting them. It was the newest Harley-Davidson franchise in the Northwest. I wondered if they had any idea how many werewolves rode Harleys.

The afternoon sun broke through the stranglehold of winter cloud cover, in places, and we rode right on past her exit without a protest. I felt her look up, then she laid her head back against me, and I imagined her pretty smile. She was dressed warm and I owed her more than a quick ride home. Besides, I was hungry.

I kept going another fifteen miles before exiting the freeway. Jogging around the little S-turn and across the railroad tracks into the little, granary train-stop, country village of Conway. Perched like an old Blue Heron on the edge of the beautiful Skagit Valley's fertile tulip fields, the Conway Tavern was a famous motorcycle touring rest stop, with their microbrews, great burgers and fresh-daily oysters.

I angled the bike into a parking space in front, idled for a couple of beats and shut her down. For a moment Arlene didn't release me from her bear hug, resting her chin on my back, like a lover in a spoon. "Oh, you bastard," she sighed.

She let go finally, and I made room for her to dismount. I followed, and we removed our helmets. Her hazel eyes were smiling, as she shook out her pixie-like, light brown, highlighted hair, and handed me the helmet. Like a librarian outside of the library, she had transformed from an ice princess to a ready-for-anything cowgirl, with one kiss of a Harley.

As I put away the helmets Arlene made room, backing up next to a pickup parked beside us. A dog, snarling with teeth bared, crashed against the inside of the pickup's passenger window.

She screamed and fell forward against the bike, panicking, rolling along the side of it in a desperate need to escape. I steadied the bike, and she didn't stop until she hit the center of the street, where she twirled around three times, stamping her feet as the realization overcame her that she was in no real danger.

"Damnit, damnit, damnit, I hate dogs," she said to the

universe in general as she stamped both feet one final time.

I decided this wouldn't be a good time to tell her I was a werewolf, so I went and put my arm around her. "They can be scary, jumping at you unexpectedly like that."

"It's not right that someone would have a vicious animal like that out in public. Both of them should be shot...the owner and the damn dog. I still have nightmares about them all the time...it's not fair."

I didn't say anything, because this subject would take a long, long monologue for me to even begin to explain my views on man and their captive beasts, and that would only scare her more. So I stood there waiting for her emotions to calm down. Finally, they did and she said, "I'm sorry. I'm scared to death of dogs. I had a bad experience as a child."

"Well," I said, "what is needed at a time like this is a drink to calm the nerves, and I just happen to know where we can get one. C'mon." I didn't mention the old "hair of the dog that bit you" thing that hard drinkers say.

We found a booth inside, sat down and ordered a pint each of Moose Drool micro-brew; I ordered a veggie burger and salad, and Arlene ordered the pan-fried oysters.

We both decided to ignore and forget the incident with the dog and she once again changed her volatile mood, like flipping a switch. Maybe it was my charm. "Been here before Arlene?"

"No," she said. "Is this where you bring all the gals you pick up by offering them a ride home on your motorcycle?"

"No, you're a special case. I felt bad about getting you in trouble with your boss, and I knew you liked Harleys. I'd have taken you directly home if you had insisted, but you seemed to be enjoying the ride...and the sun came out."

"The ride was fabulous," she said, smiling warmly. "It did help get the job off my mind."

"It usually works for me too. I hated to see you crying, and I'm sorry for causing you problems. However, a woman was killed, one of Rodriguez's former employees, and it is naïve of him to think we wouldn't be investigating her background.

Is he always so touchy?"

She studied me for a moment, unsure of how much she should trust me. "He can be difficult at times, but we're a very well-known and growing public company, in the news a lot, so he does have to be careful. If the press picks up on it...well, you can see it would not be good publicity to be connected in any way with a murder investigation. That would make any-one nervous."

"Yes, it usually does, so we're careful about protecting the privacy of witnesses. In this case, it's surprising the press isn't all over you already. Probably because she didn't work here last, and at the moment they're focusing more on what the police department hasn't done...like catching a killer. By the way, do you and George Rodriguez have a relationship outside of work?" I had to ask it sometime.

Her eyes flashed like heat lightning. "That's none of your business," she said angrily. There went the mood switch again. I was taking advantage of the situation, but having a killer on the loose seemed to override considerations of etiquette.

"I'm sorry," I said, "but taking his anger at me out on you seems to indicate something more than a boss/secretary rela-tionship."

"Our company is very strict about sexual harassment is-sues."

"So, as far as you know, he didn't have a relationship with Sunny Brown either?"

"I wouldn't think so," she said, coldly. "She wasn't the type."

Hmmm...but was he? She had left that door open.

"As long as we're getting personal," she said, looking me in the eyes, "how about you? Did you sleep with Sunny Brown?"

"No, I never met her in real life."

"So, do you have a girlfriend?"

"Uhmm..." She got me that time. I didn't know what to say.

"Either you do or you don't. It's not fun being asked personal questions by someone you barely know, is it?"

"Okay, well I'll do my best. Yes, I do have a long-running relationship, but we're...uhmm... temporarily on a sidetrack." That was weird, using a train metaphor to describe our relationship. It was probably from hearing the train a couple of minutes ago as it went through Conway, a block from the tavern. A train wreck would have been a better description of my relationship with Helene at the moment.

"What's her name?"

"Helene."

"Rhymes with Arlene. What does she do?"

"About what?"

"Very funny? You know...for a living?"

"She's in the coffee business."

"Isn't everyone in Seattle?"

"Seems like it sometimes...that and software. She owns a coffee stand."

"Oh, that's nice. Where is it? Maybe I've heard of it."

"It's the Espresso Passion, on Capitol Hill."

"No, I haven't heard of it."

I figured we'd gone far enough down this track. She was right though. I was pushing a bit hard with the personal questions. It really wasn't fair to interrogate her under these circumstances. Of course murder was never fair and investigators had to be especially ruthless when there was a chance of a possible future victim being added to the list.

"I'm sorry about the personal questions. They're rude and I don't like upsetting you, but they have to be asked if we're to prevent more killings. There's a killer out there who might strike again at any time, and so far we don't have much."

"I understand I guess," she said. "I mean I know it's your job. I shouldn't say this, but I'm mad at Sunny and that's not fair, because she's dead and all, but with Sunny you always expected trouble. I don't know what they were thinking when they promoted her. She hated multi-national companies. She was very political, if you know what I mean."

"Do you think her death might have had any connection

to her political views?"

"I haven't a clue," she said. "She was almost like a street person, with her weird art and everything. That kind of crowd, and the way she came on to guys...it certainly was no shock that she died violently."

Our food came and we dropped discussing Sunny for more immediate concerns. After the waitress left, Arlene said, "Mmmm. These oysters look good...would you like a couple?"

"I'm a vegan," I said, although I wasn't sure oysters would ever have been high on my list of edible foods, even if I'd been a carnivore.

"Really?" she said, surprised. "Like a vegetarian?"

"They say that vegan is an Indian word meaning, "bad hunter".

She laughed.

"Actually, a vegan is someone who doesn't consume any animal products."

"Yikes, that must be difficult," she said. "I don't think I could do that. Is it your religion or something? I mean, how did you...you know...?"

"No, it wasn't part of my religion—nothing like that. I just made up my mind at a young age that I didn't want to hurt innocent creatures. So it wasn't that hard, really. It becomes a habit you get into."

"Didn't other kids make fun of you? You know how they are with anyone who is different?"

"Yes, I know, and they did. Some. I was different and still am I guess...like Sunny Brown was."

She blushed.

"I had a couple of fights and then they left me alone. Bullies are not innocent, and I'm not exactly non-violent. I will fight back, and to protect those who can't." This was uncomfortable ground for me, since I couldn't very well explain about being a werewolf. Of course I'd invaded her comfort zone, so it was only fair. "How about you?" I asked, turning the question around. "Ever think about becoming a vegetarian?"

She looked at the oyster on her fork. "No. I'll eat any-thing," she said, with a smile. "I think it's cool you decided to do that...become a vegan," she said, like she was trying out a new word. "But if God didn't want oysters to be eaten he shouldn't have made them so delicious...and maybe he should have given them teeth," she said, laughing at her own joke. "I'm not non-violent either. As far as defending myself, I'm all over that. I have a black belt in Karate."

I laughed. "Thanks for the warning."

"It's only fair," she said, without a smile and looking me in the eye. It sounded like a threat. "If Sunny had made an effort to learn self-defense maybe she'd still be alive. They should teach self-defense to girls, starting in grade school, and maybe there wouldn't be such a thing as battered-women syn-drome."

"You're right," I said. There were certainly layers to this gal. Layers and edges. I wondered how someone like that would let herself be browbeaten by a puffed up egomaniac like George Rodriguez.

We were busy eating for a few minutes, and the conver-sation between bites drifted from self-defense techniques to Harley-Davidson motorcycles and touring, the excellent vari-eties of Washington wineries, and our favorite microbrews. We never even got around to comparing coffee beans and roast-ers. By the time we finished eating and left the restaurant it was dark, but we felt comfortable with each other, staying away for the rest of the meal from contentious topics like murder and McBucks coffee. The few clouds had dissipated, leaving a glowing second quarter moon and stars sparkling like snowflakes.

Out of Conway the headlights lit the back road through the fertile Skagit valley farmland to Stanwood—there is some-thing mystical about riding a motorcycle at night—and on to Goodwin Lake where she directed me into a short driveway and circular parking space. She'd explained earlier that she lived in a cottage she'd inherited. It was built on two levels on the hillside next to the lakeshore, and looked like a cozy refuge.

As I stood up to let her off the bike, I was wondering how she got from this rural spot to a bus that would get her to Everett. I shut the engine off and dismounted. As we took our helmets off and she shook out her hair again, she said, "I'm so embarrassed."

"About what?" I said.

"Well...I was going to invite you in for coffee or something, but I just remembered...when I saw my car wasn't here...it's so embarrassing..."

"What?" I said. "Where is your car?"

"I got so excited and lost and spaced out with what happened...and the motorcycle ride...and you...I totally forgot that my car is in the I-5 freeway Park and Ride over by Marysville."

I laughed and in the light of the motion-control spotlights mounted on her house, I saw her embarrassment turn to the first real laughter I'd seen from her. It was giggly stuff and reacting to each other we were soon laughing so hard we had to hold each other up.

Finally gaining control, but cross-legged and doing the gotta-go dance, she said, "Oh, do you mind? I won't make it all the way there and back. I've really got to go."

"No problem," I said. "If you don't mind, I'll find a bush here myself while you run inside?" Like most of Western Washington, the place was heavily wooded with the usual conifers.

"Help yourself," she said, bent over and barely able to keep from holding herself as she ran toward the house.

I found a spot behind a tree. From this moment we would probably never again feel like strangers with each other. There seemed to be a lot she wasn't revealing, but at least our surface reserve had melted away, and we had become real people with each other. It's always nice when that happens in this busy, stress-filled modern world, especially for a loner like me.

Should I worry that I had more women friends than men?

Nah. Way better than the other way around. And it was nice to have a new woman friend without all the tension-filled issues that had developed lately between Helene and me. While there was a bit of sexual tension, it wasn't something I intended to act on, and she wasn't coming on to me. We might become friends, and that was enough. We had Harley-Davidson motorcycles in common.

I was sitting astride the bike when she came back out, laughing again when she saw me. "I still can't believe I totally forgot my car," she said, taking the helmet from me and strapping it on.

"Well, it's a good thing you remembered it before I left."

"Yes," she said, climbing aboard, "but at least the Harley ride isn't over yet."

When we reached the Park and Ride and she dismounted again, she removed her helmet, handing it to me reluctantly. "You're not," she said.

"What's that?"

"You're not a bastard. I'm sorry I called you that. At least you're not a total bastard." She smiled and reached up, putting her hand on the back of my neck, pulling me to her and kissing me. It was a quick kiss, as kisses go, but a nice, friendly one. "You're a very nice man, Harley. I'm sorry I was so difficult. I...I'm...it's..."

There were lots of unspoken words there, which she decided to swallow. "Thanks so much," she said instead, "for one of the best times I've ever had." She turned and walked away.

I waited until she got her car door open. She gave me a little wave as she got in, then I pulled ahead and made a u-turn and stopped to wait as she started up the car and backed out. She rolled down her window and waved again as I followed her out of the parking lot. We turned opposite ways, and I checked out her taillights in my rear view mirror while imagining her doing the same, in a kind of Escher vision of infinity...me looking back at her looking back at me looking back sort of thing...all done with mirrors. And that's how I felt about her...that I was only getting some kind of reflected surface version.

I made my way back onto the freeway, heading south toward the city and all that.

At home, I wiped down the bike and went inside the houseboat where I discovered the cell phone I'd left on the kitchen table. I hadn't even missed it, but there were three missed calls from Helene. Damn. She probably thought I was avoiding her. I'd never set up the message capability, since I figured it was enough that I knew who had called. It would have been nice this time, to know what Helene had to say.

I put off the call I should have made, and called Larry to give him a report. It wasn't much, but I told him about instructing George Rodriguez to call in with his whereabouts on the days and times of the three murders. Larry said he hadn't called yet, and he told me they hadn't made any progress either.

I hung up...disconnected I mean, since hanging up is no part of cell phone use, unless it was the gallows-like feeling I had in the pit of my stomach contemplating the next call I had to make. Helene.

It rang several times and I was beginning to hope I'd delayed the long fall through the gallows trapdoor. Maybe she wouldn't ans—

"Hello...?" There was dead air as I found myself unable to speak.

"Harley, are you there?"

"Yeah Helene, I'm here," I said finally.

"Oh Harley, I've been calling you forever. We have to talk...please."

My cold heart melted. "All right, Helene."

"Harley, listen, you have to know I had nothing to do with what happened, don't you?"

"Yes, I guess I do...but..."

"Harley, listen, it was three from Silver's pack, and they're taken care of. You tore them up pretty badly. Silver wanted to finish them, but I didn't think you'd want that or you would have done it yourself."

"Actually, Gram stopped me or I might have. That would have been wolf justice, but now I'm glad she did."

"If they are ever seen in the Northwest again, they will be. I know you think Silver was responsible, Harley, but it didn't seem like it. He really tore into them."

"It doesn't matter. They were his, so he is responsible as far as I'm concerned. You're a pack leader...you know what that means."

"Of course I do. I meant...I don't think he knew about it, but Silver and his group are out of the pack, Harley. Like you said, it's still his responsibility. It wasn't working anyway. And they were a part of my pack so it was also partly my fault. I knew I didn't have their full allegiance so I should have dealt with it sooner."

I didn't answer. What could I say...I told you so?

"Harley...?"

"I'm sorry, Helene, but I don't know what to say. This is too hard over the phone."

"Can we get together then?"

"Sure...that would be nice," I said. In my heart I knew I wasn't being fair with her. She felt worse than me, I could tell, and I felt miserable and confused about everything. Even Gram had said I wasn't being fair to blame Helene for what had happened. "I'm sorry, Helene, about not talking to you sooner. It was confusing and I was upset and afraid I would say something I shouldn't."

"Thanks Harley. The truth is I do feel responsible in some ways, and like I said, I should have cut Silver's group out of the pack sooner. I knew that, but we practically grew up together, and he looked out for me. I've changed though, and so has he I guess. It's not just you Harley. I realized during the run that as long as he was there I'd never be the pack's true leader. Then after the terrible thing at your Gram's, I knew it was time. I really don't believe he knew about the attack, but I'm sure they thought he would approve, and that is nearly as bad. And I am just as guilty because I'm..."

I heard the tears in her voice. "Gram doesn't think so and neither do I. Like she said, it's over and done with. Let's get together soon, okay? I can't right now, because I have to concentrate on this case. The only lead we have is this Marlboro Man, and I have to find him, somehow, so tonight I am going to be busy with that. Maybe tomorrow...we'll see how it goes. I do love you, Helene. I know that...and it's been hell..."

"Me too...thanks Harley...thanks for forgiving me."

"Nothing to forgive really. We both had to work some things out. Nothing new for us werewolves."

"All right, Harley. Maybe tomorrow. Stop by if you get a chance. I love you."

"I love you too. Bye."

"Be careful out there...please."

"I will. Talk to you tomorrow." I hung up and sighed with relief, happy to be back to somewhere near square one. It's funny how real life can make the imaginary inner one seem small sometimes. Despite everything else, Helene was the best friend I had...well, after Gram, but that was different.

The rain was back, hard for a change, running off the boathouse roof into the black waters of Lake Union with a cascading rhythm. My blood was still thin with the Wolf Moon flow pounding in my ears in time to the beating rain. Rain that I knew would cleanse the night's streets of all but the players.

I dressed in my black, shadow-hugging Gore-tex ninja gear and headed downtown. I made another call as I loped down Eastlake Avenue, and after two rings heard the siren-like voice of Lovely Brown.

"Hello, this is Lovely," with an undertone threat daring you to poke fun at her name.

"Hi, this is Harley."

"Harley," she said, like a teacher to a ten-year-old boy late for school. "Where have you been?"

Déjà vu all over again. If you went a day without calling someone in the modern cell phone era, it was high crimes and misdemeanors. "I've been away," I said, leaving it purposely vague as I often did to annoy the addicted.

"I've been trying to call you for days," she said, her voice dripping with indignation.

"I'm here now," I said, refusing to give in to the underlying demand for an explanation.

"Well, you could have called," she said. "That guy was here."

"What guy, Lovely?"

"That guy...that big guy...the one who hit you...that guy who murdered my sister."

"When?" I said, suddenly all perked up ears.

"Five days ago."

"Did you call the police?"

"No, they're worse than you. Besides, I didn't even get a shot at him before he was gone. I'll call them when I want them to collect the body. They couldn't catch a cold in a day care."

"Whoa, wait a minute. You were going to shoot him?"

"Damn right, and hopefully just wound him with the first shot. I want him to suffer."

"Lovely! We're not even sure he is the killer. Breaking into an empty apartment isn't much of a crime."

"You said you thought it was the same guy."

"*Might* be. I said *might* be."

"I'll try not to kill him with the first shot. I'll make him confess before I finish him."

"Okay, calm down," I said. "I'm sorry I wasn't here, but you should have called Detective Meyers. He's a good cop. Tell me what happened." I was down to a slow walk. How people drive and talk on these things was beyond me. Especially those who can't drive in the first place, doing fifty and hogging the fast lane on their cell phones.

"I was sleeping...the first night I stayed here." Her voice was less assured now. In spite of the bravado she had been scared. "I heard a noise...I guess it was that big door out by the elevator. I grabbed the gun from the drawer in the stand next to my bed. I didn't turn the light on, because there is a lot of light that comes in from the street through those big windows. My eyes were used to the dark and I was hoping his weren't. Well, I didn't know for sure yet that it was him."

At least she wasn't going to shoot just anybody—I hoped. "You should have called 911," I said. "But I'm glad you had the gun at least, and that you weren't going to shoot just anyone who wandered in. So what happened?"

"Hey, if someone breaks in it's not some innocent sleep-walker."

"The door wasn't locked?"

"No, you can't lock that door from the inside. I called around, but I couldn't get anyone to install a lock before next week. I guess you're technically not supposed to lock those doors because they're fire doors or something. Everyone ignores that crap, but not just anyone will work on them. Anyway, I keep my lock in the drawer by the bed. It's spelled with a G...a Glock nine-millimeter."

"Your sister——"

"No, I told you she wouldn't have a gun," she said, mistakenly assuming she knew what I was about to say. Random assumptions were becoming a pattern with her. "And she used to let people off the street sleep in that outer room when it was cold or raining really hard like tonight."

"So it could have been one of those people?"

"Okay, well maybe. I wouldn't shoot just anyone unless they tried to attack me. Anyway...if you'll quit interrupting..."

"Go ahead..."

"Thank you," she said, sarcastically. "I got over to my door, you know...the one to the inner space. I started to open it slowly, because it creaks...but it creaked anyway, and I heard a noise like somebody scrambling...so I threw it open but I was barefoot and I stubbed my toe and it put me off balance, just enough that I saw him go through the door, but I couldn't get off a shot. It was him for sure...that same guy...big and wearing one of those cheap hooded sweatsuits."

"You're positive," I said.

"Yes, absolutely...well, I mean, it had to be him."

"You didn't see his face this time either?"

"No," she said. "That big door shut behind him and I was kind of hopping because of my toe. I heard the elevator starting down, but I got to that same window out there in time to catch a glimpse of him running up the street toward First Avenue. He looked back up at me, but he had that hood on and I couldn't make out his face. I don't care if you don't believe me. It was him, I know it."

"Hey, easy Lovely. I didn't say I didn't believe you about it being the same guy. He whacked me pretty hard on the head, so we know he is capable of violence. But we don't know if he murdered your sister or the other baristas."

"I don't care. If he comes in here again, I'm not waiting to see if he only wants to hit me over the head. Like that Dirty Harry guy said—it would make my day. And if he isn't the killer, well I've got lots of extra bullets."

Dirty Harry. That was funny, considering my background. My real first name had been Harry, before I'd changed it. I suppressed a smile. "Okay, well it would be a shame to see you be the one arrested for murder."

There was no snappy comeback this time, but I didn't think it changed anything. I needed to catch this guy soon, because in spite of what I said, it was strange that he kept showing up at Sunny's loft, and Lovely was in danger.

"Lovely, you still there?" I said into the dead air.

"Yes. So you're back from your vacation and working on the case again?" she said with angry sarcasm.

"Yes, I'm back, and the first thing I'm going to do is find that guy...the Marlboro Man."

"What are you talking about—Marlboro Man?"

"That's what I call that guy in the hooded sweatshirt. He smokes Marlboros." I'd neglected to tell her that bit, not wanting to widen the list of citizens she thought it okay to shoot.".

"Harley?" Her voice had softened suddenly.

"What?"

"I'm glad you're back. Will you stop over?"

"Well, it's late."

"What if I promise not to shoot you?"

"Okay, I'll try to check in to make sure you're okay."

"Better call first," she said, "I hate wasting ammo." Her voice sounded lighter and I was sure she was smiling.

"I'll try to remember that. If he shows up, just hold him for me and call, will you?"

"I don't know. Maybe."

Well, that was something. "Okay," I said. "Talk to you later."

"Be careful, Harley."

I hung up without replying. Being careful wasn't something I was good at. Neither was she.

I was on Fairview Avenue, a couple of blocks north of the Seattle Times building. The rain had let up and was back to Seattle drizzle. I decided to stop in and see Angie, a street kid I had helped out from time to time.

She was sixteen now, and would be upset if I called her a kid. In many ways she had never been a kid. She wasn't a werewolf, but she was different, and like many young werewolves the lack of a loving home had driven her out onto the streets. She'd been dyslexic and hyperactive and her meth-addicted mother had left her with relatives, claiming she had, "a gig in California and would come back to get her in a month."

That was the last anyone had heard of Angie's mother, and the poor kid got shifted around and abused until she took off to make it on her own on the streets. Every so often she'd get picked up and put into the under-funded and barely su-pervised Washington State Social Services' wasteland of fos-ter homes. She missed out on the whole *read me a story before bedtime* bit of childhood, and was a prostitute by age twelve.

Angie was fourteen going on forty when I first met her. She'd been standing on a street corner in the rain as I walked by staring at her puffy black eye and the swollen left side of her face.

"What are you starin' at?" she'd said, trying to keep her good side toward me. Then she offered to *trick me out*.

"Okay," I said. "Twenty bucks."

She looked around furtively. "Where you from, Yakima? We don't talk money up front." She looked me over, like picking out a pair of shoes. "You don't look like a vice pig."

"I'll take that as a compliment."

"Walk down the street with me," she said, looking me over again, and glancing around once more. "You sure you got twenty bucks? Ain't you got no wheels?"

"Sure, but I'm walking today."

"Show me," she said.

"It's a long way to my place," I said, confused.

"The money...like the flick, y'know...show me the money," she said like she was disgusted with amateurs.

"Oh, yeah," I said. "That was a good movie."

"It was boring as all fuck," she said. "I didn't watch the whole thing. The guy was drunk and fell asleep so I watched some of his videos."

"How much did you get for them?" I said.

She looked up at me with a sly smile. "Ow, that hurts," she said, holding the side of her face. "Don't make me laugh. Come on, over here." We'd reached the corner and she was pulling me by the wrist, toward the alley.

"Okay, give me back the watch," I said, feeling my wrist where it had been.

"Hey, I was just playing with you," she said, handing it back and looking up at me nervously, moving away, probably ready to duck and run if I swung at her.

"That was slick. What's your name?"

"Buttercup. C'mon, hurry up...in the alley," she said walking ahead of me.

"No, wait," I said. "Let's get a cup of coffee instead."

She stopped and looked at me like she'd suddenly recognized me. "Oh, one of those kind, huh?"

"What do you mean?" I said.

"I've seen *Taxi*. Cool flick. I ain't got all night though. Talkin' don't come cheap."

"That's okay."

"Twenty up front. You're getting a deal anyways, on account'a I ain't so pretty right now. Ordinarily it'd be fifty."

I got out my wallet, pulled out a twenty and handed it to her. She grabbed the bill, glanced at my wallet and looked around for cops all in one smooth motion. "Okay, we're on the meter," she said. "Where we goin'?"

It was too late, even for McBucks. "How about Mary's, up at Fourth and Virginia?"

"Hey, it's your twenty," she said, stuffing the money inside her bra.

Mary's was an all night place frequented by taxi drivers, cops and the bar crowd. Lots of big booths. They served Tully's coffee though, instead of the greasy spoon kind. There weren't many places that could get by with Maxwell House in Seattle these days. Even the drunks could tell the difference.

She looked small and vulnerable sitting there across from me in the overstuffed booth.

She'd moved over to let me slide in with her, but I'd taken the seat across, and she shook her head like I was some sucker she'd seen before. "So, you want me to pretend I'm your daughter?" she'd said, before the waitress came by.

"I don't think so," I said. "You're way too old for that."

She looked at me, confused again, but only for a second, shrugging it off. "Okay, it's your dough," she said as the waitress showed up.

From the looks the waitress gave me...*child beater*... she'd probably have spit in my coffee or dumped it on me hot.

Angie, whose name I found out much later—after this had become a routine with us—was very quick. She said to the waitress, "I was trying to do a rail slide on my skateboard and crashed, and Mom got all mad at me so I snuck out and came downtown on the bus with my friends, but Dad came down lookin' for me."

The waitress looked skeptical, but seemed to unconsciously decide she'd rather think that than the other. She said, "You want to be careful comin' down here at night, darlin'. There's some bad people out there on the streets."

"I know," Angie said, playing the part of 'daddy's good little girl who was sorry and would never do it again'. "Dad told me. I said I was sorry, but I am kind of hungry."

After that, the waitress took our order and we became just another part of her *long-hard-night-on-her-feet* story. Angie ordered a big breakfast called the "working man," that included three eggs, bacon, sausage and ham, hash browns, pancakes and toast. I ordered oatmeal, but the fact that the order seemed to be backwards didn't faze our waitress. She'd already withdrawn into her sore feet. Angie kept calling her over for coffee refills for me, and then she'd pour mine into hers. She must have drunk half a dozen cups of coffee, the little speed freak.

We were halfway through our meal when a couple of cops I knew came in for their coffee break before the bar rush started. The younger officer looked us over but walked on by, not knowing what to say. Sergeant Perkins stopped though, looking over my suddenly defiant tablemate, and then me. "This your daughter, Harley?" he said, and after a quick pause, "Or your wife?"

"I picked her up out there soliciting on your beat, Sergeant. Somebody had to look out for her."

"Watch it Harley, we're old friends with your little girl here. We take her in and she's back the next day. It doesn't make much difference what you do with her," he said. "Nothing she ain't seen before. Take it easy, Harley."

"You wish I was your little girl," she said to his back as he moved on. Then she gave me a look of betrayal. "You are a cop, you bastard," she said, starting to slide out of the booth to leave.

"Nice talk for a little girl," I said. "Sit down, I'm not a cop, but I work with them sometimes. I'm a Private Investigator, and I don't want anything but to help you out."

She gave me a, *'Yeah, I've heard that before'* look, but she slid back into place and without another word began forking in the food, carefully chewing on the right side only. She was a tough kid, ready for anything and expecting only the worst.

At best she thought I might be one of those do-gooder suckers she could work for a few bucks every once in a while.

That had been about two years ago, a lifetime for a street person unless they got lucky. Angie had. These days she lived in the storage room of an old apartment building. She didn't work the streets anymore, but I can't take the credit for that. She'd ridden the long slide for another year after I met her.

Angie'd been on meth, like her mother before her. As a hyperactive kid, she'd been prescribed Ritalin in school, which is an amphetamine, so it isn't a big jump to meth and you can hardly convince those kids they're doing wrong after it was the authorities got them started on it. She'd looked so bad I'd pretty much given up on her. There are a lot of casualties on the streets and after awhile you get hardened to it.

She disappeared off and on, so I wasn't surprised when I didn't see her for days or weeks at a time. I'd ask around, but usually no one had seen her or had any idea where she might be. Or they wouldn't say. Then one day after I'd become worried again and had been asking around, she found me.

Something traumatic had happened to her. She never told me what it was, but it scared her and she had gotten off drugs and off the street. She told me where she was living, that she'd worked out a deal to live in a storage room in an old apartment building.

The manager, a sympathetic older woman who had once been on the streets herself, looked the other way as long as she didn't become a problem and there were no drugs. The tenants' storage lockers had been broken into many times, and the deal was that she could stay there to scare off anyone who tried to break in. Most of those were sneak thief types who would run off if someone made some noise, so it wasn't as dangerous as I thought at first. After all, Angie had survived on the streets for years. The manager had found her an RV porta-potty when she got tired of Angie asking to use her bathroom. She washed up in the laundry room, and made a few bucks on the side doing people's laundry.

That was the thing about Angie. Her freedom was everything. She'd been taken advantage of so many times by people who'd said they wanted to help her, that she wouldn't take anything for nothing. Even with me, she'd take some money occasionally to spend some time with me, but it was always like pretending it was a working relationship—we'd talk and I'd buy her something to eat, and slip her a few bucks. If I stepped over the line and started to act like a parent or authority figure, she'd bolt like a rabbit, and wouldn't talk to me again for a while.

She was a feral creature, and I understood, although it was hard to accept things on her terms, because life in the wild is dangerous. Things had been better for a while though. She was off the street, if barely, and she'd staked out a traffic jam corner on Mercer Street where she panhandled enough to get by.

I knocked on her door. "Angie, you here? It's Harley."

"Just a minute," she answered. The door opened and she gave me a big hug. "Hey Harley. Ain't seen you in a while."

"Yeah, I've been kind of busy. How you been?"

"Straight and narrow and boring as hell. Hey, I'm workin' to get my GED."

"Wow, that's fantastic, Angie. Way to go." We exchanged high fives.

"Bet'cha never thought you'd see that?"

"I wouldn't have put money on you being alive today. Now, I think the sky is the limit. If you can beat the street, you can do anything you put your mind to."

She went quiet as she fought back tears, not having the skill or experience to handle sincere compliments, even from me. There was an awkward silence, and then she said, "Hey, pull up a crate and get comfy." She laughed. Her furniture was mostly milk crates and a telephone cable spool. She cooked with a hot plate. "You want some tea? The only coffee I got is instant and I know you don't want none of that."

"No thanks, Angie. I can't stay. I'm working on the barista killer thing. You've heard of that haven't you?"

"Yeah, sure. I know quite a few baristas. They're mostly

good to us street gals. That's a bad deal, those deaths. It's like it's as bad as workin' the street. I hope you catch 'im. I been thinkin' about maybe tryin' out bein' a barista."

"Maybe you should wait until we catch this killer, but Helene's offer to train you still stands."

"That's nice...thanks. I'm way more worried about messin' up with you and her than I am about some killer"

"She wouldn't bother with you if she didn't think you'd do a good job. Angie, you know a lot of people. What's the word on the street? Anybody saying anything about who might be doing these killings?"

"There's lots'a weirdos out there, but I haven't heard about anything or anyone that sounds like the barista killer. I'll ask around though...see if anyone thinks there's someone for you to check out.

"I'm not out there much anymore. A lot of my old friends are dead or moved on. I'll put out the word though."

"Angie, don't do anything risky. This guy is dangerous so I don't want anyone to take any chances. If you hear or see something, stop right there and get ahold of me, okay?"

"Yeah sure. No problem." She said it dismissively, like she always did when I got too paternal. I wished I hadn't brought it up, because now that she had it in her head she might shine me on and do it anyway. Asking questions on the street could be dangerous, even for someone like Angie. Of course there wasn't anything about that life that wasn't dangerous.

"Anytime you want," I said, changing the subject, "go up and see Helene. You remember where her place is?"

"Sure. I'm kinda nervous about it. Never had a real job before."

"Don't worry, you'll be fine. I guarantee you, if Helene trains you, then right off you'll be better than half the baristas out there, so don't worry about that. Anyone who can survive like you have can handle a job if you want to. It's up to you what you make of it."

There was an embarrassed pause in the conversation so I

took my cue. "Okay, I better get going," I said, standing up from my seat on the blue plastic milk crate.

"Thanks for stopping by." She gave me another big hug, her arms wrapped around my waist. The hug thing was recent in our relationship. "You'll never know how much of a help you were to me, Harley," she blurted out without looking up at me. "You're the only one ever believed in me."

I didn't know what to say. This routine was all new. She was definitely growing up. I bent down and kissed the top of her head. "The most important thing is that you believe in yourself, Angie. You're a remarkable person."

She released me and turned away. Maybe so I couldn't see the welling of tears I could hear in her voice. "Thanks Harley. And thanks for letting me try to help"

"See ya Angie," I walked out and heard the door locks click behind me. I sighed. It looked like she was going to make it after all.

TWELVE

After I left Angie's, I continued downtown. The rain had let up to a fine mist by the time I neared Pioneer Square, walking along First Avenue. This misty kind of rain was what we got the most of in Seattle. Walking in it at night always touched my wild side, like in those old horror movies on the English moors. I wanted to howl. It was cleansing as it closed in around me, making me feel alone in the world. In a city, the feeling of extra space was nice. I felt I could jump through time.

Even though the moon was waning and my werewolf senses were weaker, the scents of a rainy Seattle night enveloped me. The seaweed and other saltwater aromas drifting on the light, swirling wind from the waterfront, permeated the freshly cleaned air, giving it an ageless smell and feeling of primal life.

Seattle has changed constantly since the first white-man settlements arrived to take the name of the Chief of a small tribe of fishing and hunting gatherers, modifying the name of Chief Sealth to fit more comfortably the combination of languages and accents the settlers brought with them.

The indigenous people were soon marginalized. The streets I walked had begun as a settlement for logging the nearby hills, with the huge trees cut down, stripped, and skidded down the muddy slopes to the salty waterway, where they were shipped south to supply the rapidly growing population of California. This part of the city was a muddy mess back then.

I walked along with the ghosts of those days taking form like a schizophrenic's dream, visualizing in a video-like collage the passing of Seattle's youth from its rough and muddy skid road beginnings, with wood frame buildings built on oozy dreams of drunks, the silt of tide flats covered in long winding lines of plank board sidewalks. Then came the great fire that reduced that mad idea of progress to ashes and ruins.

Seattle was rebuilt atop the ruins, literally, but more substantially with these brick buildings, which were slowly being replaced with glass and steel. From mud to lumber to brick to glass and steel, the whole history of Seattle rots here in Pioneer Square in midden layers, all the refuse of the building of what we call civilization.

Tourists were taken on daytime tours of the underground remnants of Seattle's wooden past lying below the modern city like the bad conscious of a reformed alcoholic turned evangelist. For the tourists it was a Disneyesque walk through a haunted past, with some actual storefronts stocked with artifacts of the time.

Most of the old underground city has become part of the modern city's infrastructure. But at night, when the tourists had gone, ghosts roamed the old underground streets and building remnants. Sometimes street people gained access to these underground ruins for shelter. I had been going to investigate some of these places, to search and ask the denizens about the Marlboro Man.

I stopped in my tracks, my hackles rising, sniffing the air, turning slowly, trying to capture the undertone scent on the swirling breeze that had alerted me. *Damn my human-diluted senses.* I rose up on the balls of my feet, my nose in the air, tiptoeing around in crazy eight circles, desperate to recapture what I was sure had been the scent of the Marlboro Man—a scent I had stored away in my memory cells with care, like it had been the scent of the finest Cuban cigar.

If someone had seen me they would have kept their distance, with me prancing around like an overwrought ninja in a community theatre production of some edgy modern dance ballet. Being a werewolf detective was not always pretty.

Those thoughts passed my mind in the kind of giggly mania that underlies the beginning of the hunt. I increased the circles starting to think I'd lost it...then I caught it again. The first scent I'd picked up may have been brought to me by one of those restless spirits that roamed down here. They had helped me in that way before.

He had to be close. With my waning werewolf senses and the rain, I couldn't have picked up his scent from far away. Still, it came and went like wisps of fog, and each time I picked up the scent I could go no more than a hundred paces before losing it again. Yet it grew stronger each time, so that finally I knew the direction, since the canyons of city streets channeled the prey, the scent of prey...and me.

I realized I was tracking it toward Sunny Brown's loft, now occupied by her sister, Lovely. Would he be going back there again? Why? It made no sense, but I quickened my pace, not daring to take the chance of losing him by going directly to the apartment.

I lost it once more, but kept moving forward and picked it up again. Now I was at the corner, turning toward the building the loft was in a half block away.

The scent strengthened and I ran, not daring to stop and take the time to call Lovely to warn her, and not sure I could trust her not to shoot on sight. If I could get to him before he got in the elevator...there were no stairs in this end of the old grandfathered warehouse building. The elevator had been built for freight.

I raced up to the building's glass doorway and yanked it open, thankful he'd left it like he'd probably found it, propped open with a stick. His scent was powerful in the lobby, but I was too late to stop him. I heard the elevator creak and groan to a halt overhead. If he was smart he'd flip the switch and prevent the elevator from coming back down, but I hit the button several frantic times and heard it start to return. I shut off my cell phone to keep it from ringing at the wrong moment.

Would he panic now, when he heard the elevator ascend again? I hoped not. He had no reason to think anyone knew he was there. The elevator served the two upper floors of artist lofts and this time of night, nearing midnight now, there would be lots of comings and goings by the relatively young party crowd who lived in the building.

The elevator wobbled to a stop and the door opened slowly. I jumped in and punched the third floor button several times, like the action would make it go faster. Instead it was the slowest ride I've ever had, slower than freeway traffic through downtown Seattle during rush hour. Slower than January during a bad winter. In contrast the elevator crept to a stop as stealthily as a caffeinated marching band. The door opened a crack and I forced it wide enough to squeeze through, my patience exhausted.

Charging in was the only way. I pulled the heavy sliding door back and there stood the Marlboro Man in the center of the darkened room, halfway between me and Lovely, who was standing with her feet spread apart in a shooting stance, holding a gun on him in the classic two-handed grip.

He looked back at me, but even at the end I couldn't make out his face, hidden in the dark depths of the sweatshirt hood like some bad horror movie slayer. Then he turned back toward Lovely and stepped forward, saying in a halting, ghoulish, deep voice, "I won't hurt you. Your sister——"

I hollered, "No!!!" barely preceding the sound of the gun's retort, deafening in the empty room, and I'm not sure I even heard myself. The Marlboro Man spun half around, falling hard, and I rushed to him. I quickly checked him for weapons and finding nothing, I checked the wound. She'd shot him through the chest near his right shoulder. I know basic first aid, but I'm in no way a medic. The blood was bright and he was having difficulty breathing, so she had at least nicked a lung. It could be ugly with a smashed bullet and bone fragments.

I helped turn him on his good side so any blood coughed up could drain. He was choking and Lovely was screaming,

"Why did you kill my sister?" When I glanced back at her she was still holding the gun on him.

"Lovely!" I shouted, laying his head down as I stood up between her and the Marlboro Man.

"Get out of the way, Harley!" she screamed. The gun was now pointed at me.

"Give me the gun, Lovely," I said, softly but firmly as I stepped closer to her.

I saw her eyes flick sideways with the idea of getting around me for a better shot, and I lunged forward, grabbing at the hand holding the gun, pushing it away and down, hoping the force of the motion wouldn't cause her to pull the trigger. Wrong! The gun's recoil knocked her hand back into mine. I seized the gun with my other hand, and she let me take it. I'd felt splinters and a whoosh of air on my ankle from the bullet's passage into the wooden floor. I wriggled my toes to make sure everything still worked. It couldn't have missed me by much.

"Damn you Harley," she said in a kind of zombie-like voice. "I should have shot to kill the bastard. You heard what he said about my sister. It's him. He murdered her. How could you protect someone like that?"

"I'm not an executioner, Lovely, and neither are you. You stopped him, and now it's up to the law. You'd better call 911, and tell them to send an ambulance."

"No," she said. "I hope he dies."

"All right. Go inside. I'll take care of it." I knew she was in shock herself, in spite of her bravado. She would need medical attention too.

I dialed 911, gave them the information and then called Larry.

"Detective Meyers," he said.

"Hello, Larry, it's Harley. I'm over here at Sunny Brown's loft. Lovely Brown, the barista victim's sister, just shot someone. He may be our man. I already called it in on 911. He needs an ambulance."

"Is he dead?"

"No, I think he'll make it."

"I'll be right there."

He hung up. I pocketed Lovely's gun after putting it on safety, and went to see what I could do for our suspect. I didn't blame Lovely for shooting him, under the circumstances, and I was sure Larry wouldn't either. In fact she might be in for the reward. He was definitely the Marlboro Man I'd scented as being at the scene of the crime. That wouldn't do much to convince a jury that he was a killer, though, and I really had nothing else. There was no doubt he had some connection to the crime, and if he was the killer, a bullet wound was the least he had coming.

He had passed out or something, but now he moved, sobbed and groaned, regaining consciousness.

"Take it easy," I said, kneeling down beside him and using a corner of his jacket to apply pressure to the entrance wound. There didn't seem to be an exit wound, at least none that I could see without moving him much. Could be a lot more internal damage than was apparent. "The medics will be here any minute, so the best thing is to stay as quiet as possible."

"I didn't want to hurt her," he said, along with some mumbled words I couldn't make out.

I pushed back his hood to get a look at his face. He had short brown hair and otherwise ordinary features. He wasn't ugly but he wasn't especially good-looking either. His clothes were thrift store street clothes that hung on him like he might have slept in them regularly. There was no strong body odor and he seemed clean enough...just very rumpled looking.

I heard the elevator going down, and then returning on its begrudging climb back up with the medics. As they arrived I gave them a brief description of his wound, and after identifying myself and informing them that he was a possible murder suspect, I moved out of the way.

Larry Meyers arrived shortly after the medics, while they were still stabilizing the suspect and preparing him for transport.

"Hi Harley," he said. "How bad is he?"

"I don't know. They say he'll live."

"What happened?"

"He came back one time too many. When I got up here, Lovely had thrown down on him...she has a Glock nine millimeter. He turned around when he heard me, and then he stepped toward Lovely, and she shot him. She's a good shot so she wasn't shooting to kill or he'd be dead. As he stepped toward her he said, 'I won't hurt you. Your sister—' Then she shot him. Considering her frame of mind, I'd say it was self-defense. He's a big guy and I'm sure he's the one who hit me over the head. And he'd been prowling around up here again last week. It seems likely he's been stalking her. He was unarmed though." I didn't need to point out that he was a big guy, and the Barista Basher had killed all three women with his bare hands.

"How'd you happen to be here, Harley?"

"I'd talked to her earlier, by phone, and that's when she told me about him being here a few days ago, right after she moved in. I said I'd stop by and check up on her."

"Where's she at? Inside?"

"Yeah. She may be in shock too. One of the medics is going to check her out after they stabilize the suspect. Here's her gun. She also put a round in the floor, accidentally as I was taking the gun from her." I took it out of my pocket and handed it over.

He gave me a questioning look.

"Accidental discharge," I said firmly.

He nodded. "You okay, Harley?"

"Yeah, sure. Mind if I hang around while you talk to her?"

"No problem. Just stay in the background while I try to get her story, okay?"

"Sure. She's probably pretty shook up. She's tough, but it's not every day you face off with someone you think murdered your sister...let alone shooting someone."

"I'll go easy, but I need to get her story. I don't think there is any question of charges."

We went inside and found Lovely leaning against a window with her back to us. "Lovely," I said. "Detective Meyers from the SPD would like to talk to you...if you're up to it?"

She turned toward us, and I could see some of the tough exterior had melted away. She was crying silently, and she had her arms crossed. She raised her right hand to wipe at the tears, but continued to clutch herself with the other. This person was different from the one who'd fired the gun. She seemed to be imploding. There was no telling what to expect. She had been through a lot of trauma, even before this violent encounter with a person she believed had brutally murdered her sister.

She stared at us as Larry said, "I'm sorry to bother you after what you went through. It's best if I can get a statement now. Can you tell me what happened here tonight?"

"I shot the bastard who killed my sister," she said, looking from me to him like we were idiots. "I wish I'd killed him."

"Are you sure this is the same guy who attacked Harley, and was up here before?"

"Yes," she said. "He even said something about my sister."

"What did he say?"

"He said he didn't mean to hurt her," she said. The tears flowed again, and she turned away, back to the position she'd been in when we entered. She sniffled and said, "I'm not sorry I shot him...only that I didn't shoot to kill."

"That wouldn't bring your sister back," Larry said.

"No...no it wouldn't," she said, angrily, without turning around.

"I'm sorry you had to go through all this," Larry said. "Do you want us to give you a ride somewhere? The medics are going——"

One of the medics poked her head through the door. "Excuse me. Do you want me to——?"

"Yes," Larry said. "Ms. Brown has been through a traumatic experience. Maybe you could take a look at her." It wasn't a question, and Larry directed me to accompany him outside.

"If you don't need me," I said when we were back in the outer room, "I'll stick around and make sure she is all right."

"That's fine, Harley." He paused. "How sure are we that this is our guy?" he said.

I knew he meant evidence-wise. "Well, there isn't much hard evidence so far. Sarah, the owner of the café where the victim, Sunny Brown, worked, described someone like him lurking outside the café on the night Sunny was killed, but didn't get a look at his face, so that's not much in the way of a positive ID. And Lovely saw him twice, including when I got whacked on the head...but again the darn hood hid his face. I guess we'll have to hope forensics shows something. And maybe we can connect him to Sunny Brown some way."

"Yes, that's not much to go on, but it doesn't look like he's going anywhere for a while, so we'll see if we can tie him in."

"Before the medics arrived he did say something. Most of it was mumbling, but I did hear him say, 'I didn't want to hurt her,' but that could mean anything."

"Well, you both said he mentioned Lovely's sister, before she shot him, so it's pretty evident he's involved in some way. I think we've got enough to put a hold on him so we can post a guard outside his room over at Harborview."

"I'll get you a report as soon as possible," I said.

"Yes, that would help. The brass are going to want as much as we can give them. At least we've got a suspect...should take some of the heat off. See you later, buddy," he said, clapping me on the shoulder. "Tell the gal in there I may need to get a statement from her when she feels better...but not to worry."

"Okay, thanks Larry."

I went back inside as the medic walked out. I stopped her and asked, "How's she doing?"

"Well, she should see a doctor, but she refuses. With some rest though, she'll probably be okay. You family?"

"Friend," I said, stretching the definition. I didn't want to get into the longer explanation, and I was trying to be one.

"Okay, well, I've got to go. It's probably good if someone keeps an eye on her, but the most important thing is rest."

"All right, thanks."

"No problem, it's my job."

She left, and I went over to Lovely, who was still staring out the window, but at least she was sitting down now.

"Lovely," I said, not wanting to sneak up on her. "You okay? You want me to get you anything?"

"I'm okay," she said in a monotone.

"The medic said you should see a doctor. I'd be happy to take you to one."

"I'll be all right."

"You should try to get some sleep."

"I'll be fine," she said, testily. "Sunny left all kinds of medication in the cupboard over there so I don't need to see a doctor if you don't mind. I'd rather everyone just left me alone."

"You sure you wouldn't like me to stay? I could sleep out in the other room if you like?"

She turned on me. "Why? They've got the bastard. Why are you protecting him? If I'd killed him it would all be over. I let my little sister down and it's all your fault. I wish you'd just go. I don't want you here."

"All right...I'll go. If you change your mind, you can call."

She turned away again, and I left. I seemed to be upsetting her more than helping. It was too much to expect her to be rational after everything she'd been through. I'd done as much as I could. Some day she'd understand...or not.

I walked out and punched the down button for the world's slowest elevator, and waited.

❧❧

I was nearly asleep when I felt a body with contrasting warm bits and cold ones slip under the covers and spoon up behind me. "Mmmm," I murmured, reaching back to pull a leg over me. "Who is this?"

A knuckle dug hard into my ribs. "Ouch. Oh...it's you, Helene."

Earlier, after I'd emailed a statement to Larry, I called Helene, but she hadn't answered so I left a message for her to stop by if she wanted to. I was tired and feeling low after the Lovely shooting episode, and it was one of those times I hadn't felt like being alone. "Thanks for coming," I said.

"Not yet," she whispered, nibbling at my ear as her hand caressed my chest and explored southward toward my tropical polar region. "But it's a great idea, which I was thinking hard on...all...the way here."

"Mmmm," was all I could say, wanting to turn over and do a bit of exploration myself, but Helene resisted...enjoying the moment...which flowed into another and another as Helene slid over me, sitting up and pinning me on my back as she positioned the two of us.

I cupped her breasts in my hands, caressing her nipples with those opposable thumbs Mother Nature created for moments like this. There were some evolutionary advantages to being a human. Savoring her wild beauty in the dim light of the windows, I wanted to prolong the dance.

"Ohhh," she moaned, moving slowly, like melting chocolate dancing a tango. Metaphors mixed and flowed through us, one to another until language couldn't keep up, our words slipping into the sweet primordial liquid of our origins.

Afterwards, in those warm and languid moments when all that expended energy collapses in upon itself, she leaned down and kissed me, her shoulder-length red hair tickling my face and filtering the urban glow reflected off scudding clouds through the sliding glass door to the deck.

I tasted her salty tears and cuddled her close as she stretched full length beside me. We didn't need to say anything. We were beyond words, in that place where being together in each other's arms said all that need be.

❧ ❧

It was nearly noon when I awoke and slipped out of bed. I showered and then carried my electric razor downstairs to shave. I was late, wanting to get up to Haborview Hospital as soon as possible, to be there when the Marlboro Man was finally able to answer some questions.

I blended up a breakfast smoothie of soymilk, carrots and bananas, with cayenne and cinnamon for spice. I chugged it down, then washed the residue off my face and rinsed out the blender.

I went back upstairs and looked in on Helene. She looked so sweet, curled up and sleeping, the comforter outlining her basic curves, but hiding the intimate ones I'd shared not long ago. I wanted to forget the world outside and climb back in with her...way back into the burrow we shared in the deeper recesses of our werewolf minds...way back in a place where humans and the disruptions we cause in the natural world were no more than the scent of prey on the wind...way back beyond the mutant genes that bound us forever.

Even during the moon run, I never felt more wolfish than when I was with Helene, and I couldn't resist tiptoeing closer to be enveloped by her scent. I bent down and kissed her on the cheek.

"Hey, big guy," she whispered, half yawn, half moan. "Were you going to leave without waking me?" She grabbed my arm and pulled me down to her. "Don'cha think a gal could at least get a cup of coffee after that romp we had?"

"Uhm...sure. It's just that you didn't get much sleep, and I was afraid that if I woke you I wouldn't be able to resist climbing back in there with you. The trouble is, we have a suspect in the barista murders. Last night he went back to Sunny Brown's place, and her sister, Lovely, is living there now and she shot him. He's under guard up at Harborview."

"Oh," she said, awake now. Grabbing my pillow she put it with hers and sat up against them. "You were there?" she asked with a hint of jealousy.

"Yeah," I said, ignoring the lurking green monster. "I'd picked up the Marlboro Man's scent on the street and I was following it. I got there just as she shot him."

"Are you sure he's the guy?"

"No, not for certain. We don't have much hard evidence against him, but he fit a description we had, and I had picked up his scent at the scene. I also think he's the guy who hit me over the head, but I didn't get a look at him then...just his scent again. Hey, since you're awake now, let me make you some coffee. I guess the guy isn't going anywhere."

"Okay. I need to get into the bathroom too. I probably look like a stray dog."

"If they looked that good, I'd definitely get one. Probably be a lot less trouble—"

"Watch it mister big bad Wolf," she said, pushing me away. "You have no idea how much trouble I can be."

"You're wrong there," I said, retreating. "I take it all back...I'll get the coffee...no trouble...none at all."

When I got back with our coffee, a bran muffin and the fruit smoothie I'd whipped up for her, all on a tray, she was back from the bathroom and sitting up in bed. She'd brushed out her hair and was wearing one of my long-sleeved shirts that she wore around my place sometimes. It wasn't buttoned and I nearly tripped with the tray.

"Whoa, easy guy, watch where you're watching." she said. "Never seen a naked lady before?"

"Can't see enough of this one. I better set this down before I make a mess."

She settled the tray onto her lap, and I pulled up a chair.

"This looks good," she said. "I'm hungry."

While she ate, I sipped my coffee and filled her in on the latest developments, including the trip up to the McBucks roasting plant in Everett, and the motorcycle ride with Arlene Fisher. She raised one of those flaming eyebrows and I knew I was on melting ice.

"So, I suppose this Arlene is beautiful too?"

"Compared to you, not even close."

"Quite an interrogation technique you have...letting pretty girls ride around on the bike. Do you use that on male suspects too? Is that why you're in such a hurry this morning? You going up to give the Marlboro Man a ride?" She smiled at the end, letting me off with a warning.

"No, I don't think he's in much shape to ride a motorcycle. Arlene, on the other hand, loves Harley motorcycles and

I thought maybe she'd open up...uh, I mean...that she'd relax enough to talk a bit about the victim, who was supposed to have been her friend. I also needed to find out more about her boss."

She laughed. "First you bring Lovely up to the club, and then you pick up some woman to ride around on your bike. Nice work if you can get them, but wait...the Barista Basher still hasn't been caught. I haven't heard anyone suggest the killer is a woman. Don't you think you might want to be talking to some *male* suspects?"

"Hey...I told you, I went up to Everett to talk to Rodriguez. He's a guy. And the guy in the hospital...he's a guy too."

"Okay, but it does seem like there hasn't been much progress so far. It's not just me. Everyone in the business, including our customers, is starting to get real nervous that the police haven't done much. He could kill again and it could be any one of us next." She was serious now, and I understood how she felt. Baristas were competitive, but beyond that they were like a big family.

I sighed. "It's been a tough case with not a lot to go on, except this Marlboro Man. I hope he is the one, and I need to get up there."

"I know you'll get him," she said, "because I know you. But the others...they're scared...really scared. A few have quit and there has been a big drop-off in applicants. Ordinarily we get gals coming by every week, wanting to apply. My gals are great...very loyal...you know. But some places are working short-handed. I hope that guy in the hospital is the one you've been looking for."

My cell phone started ringing downstairs. "Oh, sorry." I took the tray and went down.

"Harley here," I said, while I rinsed the dishes with my free hand.

"Hi Harley...Larry here. You free to talk?"

"Yeah, I'm at home. What's up? Is he talking?" I asked, hoping the case was solved and Helene and everyone else could relax.

"Nope. He's barely conscious, but a friend got to him and advised him not to talk until he's got a lawyer. He's drugged up anyway and sleeping a lot."

"Oh, damn," I said. "Sorry Larry." I tried not to swear around him, because he didn't. "I was hoping we'd get something out of him that would help."

"Well, that's why I called, Harley. His friend...she asked for you."

"What? Really? What's the friend's name?"

"I don't know. She wouldn't tell us that either. She said she would only talk to you. Funny thing is, she looks kinda familiar, but then lots of people do."

"Did you find out anything about the suspect?"

"Nope. No luck there either. He had no ID on him, and they took him in to operate early this morning, so he's still kind of in and out of consciousness...very doped up. One thing though...I don't know for sure...he was just mumbling mostly...but he...he sounded like he might be...you know...mentally challenged."

"Really?" I said, surprised.

"Well I'm not sure. Harley, how soon can you get up there? The other detectives are out on that gang shootout in the south end and I'm stuck here at the shop. They're all over me here to give them something. They may go ahead with a press release anyway, and I'd sure hate to get too far down the wrong road, you know what I mean?"

"Sure. What do you want me to do? I mean if he's awake and talking, it won't be admissible now that he's asked..."

"Well, nothing he says will be usable anyway with him under the influence of morphine or whatever. Don't worry about all that now. We need some info on the guy. If you can, find out who he is...stuff like that...that will help get the brass off my back. We've got an officer on the floor, but it's just for looks at this point since we don't have a lot on him. Even being in the apartment...he was allegedly friends with Lovely's sister. He's not going anywhere in his condition, but we're going to have to fingerprint the guy. So if I get the okay we'll go

ahead and arrest him soon...for something. We can't just turn
a possible serial killer out on the street. And it won't be long
before the press will be all over it. I'd like to know a little more
before that happens."

"I'll get right up there. Where are you going to be?"

"I've got to be here, so let me know as soon as you can,
okay?"

"Gotcha." I flipped the phone closed.

I ran up the stairs. "Sorry, Helene," I said, trying to control my urge to crawl back into her den. "I've got to run. Larry
wants me to get right up to Harborview."

"Okay, I may go back to sleep for a while," she said, half
sitting up, pulling me close and kissing me. My willpower was
crumbling, but I really did have to get going. The comforter
fell below her breasts and my knees weakened, sitting me down
on the bedside while my hands dropped for one more caress,
and her grape-like nipples reminded me of the sweet vine-
yard below.

"Harley," she said, her voice dropping an octave. "While
you were downstairs, I remembered something. Seems like a
strange coincidence. You were talking about McBucks and it
reminded me. Silver told me he's been buying bags of coffee
beans at a low price."

Silver. Not a topic I wanted to get into right now. I reluctantly disengaged, the spell broken by that one word. What
was she thinking? "Yeah, it sounds like Silver to try to get away
with selling a lower grade product," I said, standing up and
moving toward the door.

"No, that's the thing, they're the best...Arabica grade
beans, but he's buying them at way below wholesale prices."

"Do you know who the seller is?" I didn't understand
why she was telling me this now. I didn't want to talk about
Silver and I was impatient to get going. "Not that it matters
much to me. I wouldn't stop at a Silver-owned stand if he was
serving iced mochas in Hell."

"It's not about Silver, Harley. He wouldn't tell me where
he was getting them, but I stopped by his stand in Ballard. I

know the gals there. They made me an espresso and let me look at the beans."

"So?" I said, getting more impatient with the subject.

"So, Harley," she said, covering my sarcasm with some of her own. "I recognize the blend. They're McBucks, I'm sure of it."

Now my ears perked up. "You mean someone is selling McBucks beans out the back door?"

"Considering the low price Silver was bragging about, that's what it looks like to me."

"That's interesting, but why are you telling me?" I said, curious now, pushing aside my dislike of anything connected with Silver. "You want to hire me? I really should be paid for the professional quality of services I perform for you, like last night for instance."

"In your dreams, Wolfboy. I thought you might be interested, since you're so tight with that hot little bike-hopping bitch up at McBucks. Maybe you could find out something. It's not fair competition if the price of beans is being undercut by stolen product. One of my friends has a stand over there, and it would be just like Silver to try to drive her out of business so he can take it over. I know how he works."

"Okay, I'll bring it up the next time I take Arlene for a ride." I smiled.

"Great," she said, with a wicked smile of her own. "And I'll continue my undercover work with Silver."

Damn...checkmated again, but I wasn't going to let on, even though I knew she knew she'd got me. "I'll see what I can find out...no extra charge. Maybe I can get Silver busted for receiving stolen property."

"You don't have to take it that far. I just want to stop whoever is selling to him at deep discount."

"No promises, but I'll look into it, Helene," I said, taking the time for another hug and kiss. "Sorry. I'm still touchy about Silver. Forgive me?"

"I guess...sure. You better get going." She pulled up the covers and lay back down.

"I'll call you later, okay?" I said, turning to leave.

"That would be nice. Good luck with the case," she hollered after me as I started down the stairs.

Thirteen

At the hospital I found a safe place to park the bike at an attended parking lot and threw a cover over it even though the rain seemed to be holding off. I went directly to the intensive care ward, and located the SPD officer. Larry had notified him that I'd be coming, so once I introduced myself he pointed out the room and told me the suspect's friend was in there with him. Eager to find out which of my friends also knew the Marlboro Man, I walked into the room and stepped around the privacy curtain. "Angie!" I said, surprised.

"Hi Harley," she said, turning from the window next to the bedside. "Sure took you long enough."

"How the heck...? You know this guy?"

"Sure. Everybody knows Big. He's like my little brother."

"Kind of big for a little brother, isn't he?"

"Nah, I don't mean for real, dude. I kinda look after him sometimes...like that."

"You mean he's on the street too?"

"Well, lately he's been staying in a shelter sometimes. We all try to look after him. I heard right away he was shot so I busted up here."

I looked the big guy over. He was sleeping peacefully, with one of those clear plastic oxygen masks over his mouth and nose. He was at least six-foot-five and his feet were right up against the foot of the bed. He looked a bit overweight, which seemed strange since he was living on the street. High carbs in those shelter meals, probably. He had brown hair and regular features that seemed angelic in his sleep. Although he looked strong enough, he didn't seem like the serial killer type, whatever that is.

"Angie, how did you know he'd been shot?"

"Another dude saw him being carried out of Sunny's place an' word travels fast on the street."

"Wait a minute. You knew Sunny Brown?"

"No, not personally. I seen her a couple times an' I knew her name 'cause she let Big Mike...that's his name, but everyone jus' calls him Big...she let him stay up in there sometimes...when it was cold or raining."

Damn. I couldn't believe I hadn't thought to give her a description of the Marlboro Man. Guess it wouldn't have made any difference though, unless I'd gone to see her sooner. Still, it was a huge mistake on my part, and it was no excuse that I'd been distracted by personal stuff.

"Harley," Angie said impatiently. "Why'd they shoot him? Big wouldn't harm a street dog flea an' he's not smart enough to be doin' no crime."

"He broke into Sunny Brown's place. Her sister is living there now and she shot him."

"What the hell...? Why'd she go an' do that? I tol' you, Big stayed up in there sometimes. Sunny even left a key out for him. If Sunny's sister shot Big, she must be some kind of superbitch."

"Well, there's more to it, Angie. He's a suspect in the barista murders."

"Fuck...that's jus' plain ignorant. Big never hurt no one...wouldn't know how. He's a bit short in the brains department, but he wouldn't hurt no one. An' how's he supposed to have outsmarted all you know-it-all cops anyway? Someone's jus' makin' up 'scuses to get that bitch off."

"Angie, he was at the scene where Sunny Brown's body was found...that's for sure."

"Oh, and bein' on the street's a crime huh? They can go aroun' shootin' people for that, but child rapin's okay? When's the last time they shot someone for abusin' kids? Besides," she said, slapping away a tear like it was some kind of bug, "Big took care of Sunny as much as she took care of him. He was like her shadow, makin' sure she got home okay at night. Everyone had been kiddin' him 'bout how he had a girlfriend. If he was there it was 'cause he was tryin' to protect her."

Jeez, Angie had knocked the whole Marlboro Man theory to bits. Of course, no one was going to believe a runaway child prostitute. "Does Big have any family, Angie?"

She didn't answer, just stood there looking at her friend Big.

"You gonna help him Harley?" she asked, looking up into my eyes.

I hesitated. "I'll do what I can," I said, knowing it was going to be hard to turn back a city hungering for a suspect. A lynch mob mentality existed out there right now, and I felt like the one who'd been holding the rope.

"If I'm going to be able to help him I need to know something about him. Does he have family, Angie?"

"You got to have a mother and a father to get born, they tell me," she said bitterly. "But family? If it wasn't for us street trash lookin' out for each other best we can, none of us would know what that word means. I'm his family, and so was Sunny Brown. She may not have been one of us, but she cared, and none of us would'a harmed her. 'Specially Big."

"Okay Angie, but I'd like to know why he hit me over the head. Has he been able to talk much yet?"

"I talked to him some, but he was pretty out of it. The nurse said they were cuttin' back on the drugs an' he should be comin' aroun' by tonight. I gotta go home and take care of the manager's stuff. She's gone for a couple'a days. But then I'll come back and stay with him."

"All right, look, they're going to come in and officially arrest him at some point...fingerprints, the works, but probably not until tomorrow when he's more alert. You were right in asking for a lawyer for him. That means they can't question him now without a lawyer present. You should tell them everything you've told me though. They'll ask you to make a statement and you should cooperate with them."

"If you say so, Harley."

"They don't really have much against him, but you can't withhold evidence, okay? Since you have a juvenile record, they'll be hard on you if you're not straight with them."

"Harley, if there's one thing I know, it's cops."

"All right. Do you know Big's full name?"

"Nope. Nobody uses their right name on the street. And no one asks either."

"You said he isn't very smart?"

"Hey, he's not stupid or nothin'. He's jus' a little slow. He's more like an angel than some mean bastard that'd go around killin' people."

"You said he was like a bodyguard for Sunny?"

"Yeah, I guess...sorta."

"So if someone tried to hurt her, or you, he'd try to stop them?"

"I guess so, but it would more likely be me helpin' him. I still don' believe he was the one who whacked you. It's not like him."

"But he could be violent if it was necessary?"

She saw where I was going. "Hey, whose side you on?"

"Others are going to ask you the same thing."

"Well I never saw him get violent. People teased him a lot an' I never seen him hit someone. He's a big guy, and if people didn't know him they wouldn't bother him. Jus' cuz of his size, you know?"

"Someone dressed like him hit me over the head up at Sunny Brown's place, after she was killed."

"I dunno but I don't think it was Big. I can't see him doin' that."

"Even if he was scared? What if he thought I was the murderer?"

"Uhm...well, maybe. I dunno'...I still don' think so. He was really, really upset 'bout Sunny gettin' killed that way, but more confus't 'bout it that anythin'"

"All right, Angie. It's nice you're here looking out for him.

What do the doctors say? Is he going to be all right?"

"Aw fuck," she said looking past me.

"So! Just as I thought!" said a woman's voice behind me.

I whirled around and found myself staring down the barrel of a Glock 9mm. "Lovely, what are you doing?" I asked. Stupid question.

"I knew you were protecting him," she said, her face twisted in anger...not a good look for her. "I'm going to make sure there is justice for my sister's murderer."

"He didn't murder nobody, bitch," Angie said. "Big was her friend, and if you was her friend you'd know that."

Lovely pointed the gun at Angie now. "I'm her sister and he killed her. That's all I need to know." She panned the gun over to point at Big. She looked at me. "He could have killed you too, that night when he hit you over the head."

"What if you're wrong, Lovely? You don't have to believe me, but I don't think he's the killer. If you're wrong you'll be the one arrested for murder. This guy was a friend of your sister's, and she let him stay up there sometimes. But the police are on their way here with an arrest warrant for him, so either way he's not going anywhere. If you kill him we may never find out the truth."

She started to lower the gun, wavered, then raised it again and looked at me as I moved in front of her. I looked into her eyes as she lowered the gun and let me take it.

"You sonofabitch," she said. But it was halfhearted and technically incorrect since my mother wasn't a werewolf. I'd put enough doubt in her mind to weaken her resolve, and maybe down deep she hadn't really wanted to go through with it. Maybe it was guilt that had brought her this far. Guilt that she hadn't done enough or been close enough to her sister.

"You'd better leave, Lovely. I'll hang on to the Glock for a while," I said, putting the gun behind my back in the waistband of my pants. My jacket would hide it.

"You're not going to arrest..." she said, tears welling up in her eyes.

"No," I said. "No harm done. And whether you believe

me or not, I intend to find the killer, whoever it is. I don't think it's this guy, but if it is I'll find enough evidence to convict him."

She backed away, then turned and left.

"Wow," Angie said. "You're somethin' else. Never saw you in action before. That was cool, dude."

"I'm glad someone thinks so." It seemed like I'd been called bad names a lot lately...by women too. That's not good for your self-esteem.

"You sure you should'a let her go? What if she comes back?"

"I don't think she will, and I don't believe she really wanted to do it in the first place. If she were serious she would have shot him right away when she came in. She was trying to convince herself and I think she wanted to be talked out of it. That doesn't mean things couldn't have gone bad."

"I hope yer right 'bout her, for Big's sake."

"Besides, this is the second gun I've taken away from her in two days." I'd bet anything this was one she bought for her sister. "Okay, I'd better call in. By the way, Angie, you never told me what the doctors said."

"They didn't want to talk to me at first, thinkin' I was a kid. But I said I was his sister and our parents were dead, so they finally tol' me. They said the operation went okay...he had a collapsed lung an' somethin' else I don' remember, an' he was lucky they said. I was real shook up an' jus' glad he was gonna be all right. Sunny's sister is lucky too. If she'd killed him, she would'a had me to deal with."

"She'd have had her hands full all right. See you later, Angie. Thanks for your help."

"Okay. Remember you promised."

"I know," I said, hoping I wasn't going to regret it.

I'd promised to help clear the SPD's only suspect, which was kind of working backwards, if you looked at it from a police perspective.

Then I'd told Angie to give the SPD information that tied Big to one of the barista victims. He was a compelling suspect, being a street person with no known income who broke into, technically, the victim's former residence and her sister's present one.

It was weak considering what Angie had told me, but if they found anything in his past, or anything else at all such as a connection to the other baristas, the circumstantial evidence might be enough to try him. And he had whacked me over the head evidently. Although Lovely's description was sketchy, it did match Big's, and Lovely would be sure to claim it was him. She believed it enough to want to kill him.

However it was possible the real killer knew the description of the person we were looking for and had copied the look to set him up. We had asked half the city's baristas about someone like that, and the papers had picked up on it. It could have been anyone who hit me. It's hard to judge size just getting a glimpse in the dark at a distance, and other than the clothes that's all we had.

Once I got outside the hospital, I used my cell phone to call in my report to Larry. I left out the Lovely incident. I was gambling big-time that she was through trying to kill Big, for the time being at least.

"So you don't think this is our guy, Harley?"

"No. But I haven't any more evidence that he isn't the Barista Basher than I do that he is. My friend Angie doesn't think he is and she's known him for awhile."

"Yes, but you said she is a prostitute?"

"Was a prostitute, Larry."

"Still and all...we're going to have to arrest him. The Lovely gal, she still thinks it was this guy who whacked you?"

"Yes, but...I don't want to press charges."

"Doesn't matter, Harley. It's all part of the shooting case now. He broke into a private residence at least twice that we know of, and perpetrated a felony assault. I have orders to arrest him. We'll hold off on the murder charge, but we have to consider him a major suspect in the case."

I was hearing all the code words that meant a three-ring media circus. "The guy may be mentally deficient to some degree. I'd proceed as cautiously as possible, Larry. My instinct says this isn't our guy."

"Well, if it were me I'd take your advice, but we have to answer to the public in the end, and considering the circumstances——"

"Considering the evidence, I'd go slow. It would be great if you can keep me out of it, too, so I can go on working on this without running the gauntlet."

"All right Harley, but if this is not our guy, we'd better come up with a better candidate, soon."

"Now that you mention it, did Rodriguez...from McBucks...did he come up with an alibi?"

"Looks like he's not a candidate, at first glance anyway. His secretary sent a bunch of stuff showing he was out of the country on business on at least two of the dates, including the Sunny Brown murder. We're checking it out."

"Darn!"

"Unless you've got something else...this guy...Big, you called him?"

"Yeah, Big Mike...I don't have a last name for him. You guys will have to come up with that."

"Yes well, maybe we should call him Big Trouble because it looks like he is in trouble big-time."

Cop humor. "Talk to you later, Larry."

"Stay in touch, in case the brass wants you in on this."

I groaned.

"I hate to say this, Harley, but it goes with the territory."

"Later Larry," I said, flipping the phone shut in disgust. Larry was big with the clichés.

I'd asked Larry if he could set it up so I could see all the evidence, especially from the earlier murders, and he said he'd get it scheduled for me. I didn't know what to do other than go back to square one.

I got the bike, fired it up and rode down from the area informally known as Pill Hill—— because of the numerous hospitals and clinics located there——and headed for home, my thoughts rumbling in harmony with the Harley.

Where was this case going? We had caught our strongest suspect, the Marlboro Man, who we now knew as Big, but he didn't seem to me to be the killer type. He was connected to Sunny Brown, and a crime of passion made him a strong suspect. That didn't make him a suspect in the earlier murders though, and that's where the case against him seemed to break down. Of course there could be more than one killer, but the similarities made a strong case for one killer. Of course there were always copycats who tried to give a get a serial killer blamed for their own dark deeds. Big Mike definitely didn't seem that complicated.

I knew the police department and politicians would work hard to make a case against Big. He was a street person. He had connections to one or more victims. He had attacked me. And his size and alleged mental deficiencies made him an easy mark.

But the actual evidence against him was circumstantial. Being different or poor should not be a crime, but many innocents had been convicted for just that reason, combined with circumstantial evidence, as the recent use of DNA to solve old cases has shown. If it were revealed that I was a werewolf, I might be considered a prime suspect, vegan or not.

There isn't much tolerance for people who don't fit into one of the accepted slots for playing a role in our society, especially in the work place. Even at Microsoft—a corporation known for breaking the mold with such things as a relaxed dress code and flexible work schedules—the acceptance of socially inept nerds as role models is a myth. In actual fact, a preppy type who is liked by everyone is more highly valued there than a highly talented person who doesn't do well in popularity contests.

Big was a likely suspect, but he had a tough former prostitute friend and a werewolf on his side so maybe all was not lost.

I needed to go over the physical evidence collected at the earlier murders to see if there was any trace of the Marlboro Man. If I found nothing I could be pretty certain Big wasn't the Basher.

I had some time to kill before going downtown to check over the evidence. I didn't want to get there until after the brass and the press had left for the day, so the Harley took me home. Sometimes it seemed to have a mind of its own. It didn't like public parking lots where frantic or careless drivers could back over it.

Of course the thought that Helene might still be lying there all warm and snug in bed might have had something to do with it too. Since my conscious brain was concentrating on the case, some lower, more elemental force had been driving the bike. That mythical Harley motorcycle vibration again.

I stashed Lovely's gun, on the run, and I had already removed and discarded most of my clothes by the time I reached the bed. Maybe Helene had heard me coming, but she kept quiet, lying with her back to my side of the bed as I slipped in.

That pretense didn't last long though. "Oh damn, grand-mother, what cold hands you have," she said.

"All the better to feel you with my dear," I said, my grand-mother voice cracking in my excitement.

"Uhm, grandmother...uhm...why you're not my grand-mother at all, are you?" she said, turning over to face me. Her hands were very soft and warm, and I was heating up fast.

"Uh-oh, the jig's up," I said.

"And that's not all, Mr. Wolf."

❧❧

A long, long romp in the woods later, we collapsed spoon fashion into each other and lay there, her back to me once more.

After a few moments, Helene said, "What a wonderful beginning to another day."

"Some beginning," I said, "It's seven p.m."

"Omigosh," she said, jumping up. "I had no idea it was that late."

"Were you supposed to work a shift?"

"No, it's covered, but I do have things to do. I should get

up there," she said, disappearing into the bathroom.

I lounged around in bed, my strength temporarily sapped, enjoying the moment and waiting for her to come out of the shower. She was singing a medley of parts of songs, and ended with, "Who's afraid of the big bad wolf...the big bad wolf...the big bad wolf...?" as she came out of the bathroom, smiling, naked and toweling her hair dry. Jeez, she was so beautiful. At the moment I couldn't think of anything but howling.

I watched her dress in the extra clothes she usually brought when she visited me, and she did a good job of it. After she had finished and was ready to leave, she came over and sat down on the bed, kissing me on the forehead and running her fingers through my hair.

"Uhm, Harley, remember I told you about the McBucks coffee Silver is buying?"

"Sure, why?"

"I decided I'm going to find out who it's coming from."

"Hey, I'm the detective."

"Well of course you are. But it looks like so much fun I thought I'd try it. Besides, you're busy trying to solve the barista murders."

"I don't know...it might be dangerous. There might be a lot of money involved."

"Hey, I'm a werewolf and a pack leader and I've taken care of myself most of my life. I didn't grow up being babied on a big ranch by my grandmother. Are you saying I can't—?"

"I didn't say that," I said, knowing the more I protested the more resolved she would be to do it. "I meant that if you do find out anything, you can tell me and I'll get the police department involved, as well as telling the company they've got a huge theft problem. Okay?"

"That's my guy," she said. "You shouldn't complain about me having fun with a little undercover work."

"There's under cover work and there's undercover work," I said, holding up the sheet in an invitation for her to get back in bed with me.

"Oh no you don't," she said, jumping up. "As hard as it is

to leave you like this, I really do have to run." She was all aglow and laughing as she left the room.

I looked at my watch—seven-thirty—then jumped up and hit the shower. It was getting late and I had a lot to do myself. I was starting at the beginning all over again.

❧❧

After checking in at the cop shop, they gave me a cubicle in the evidence room where I could look over the gathered items of evidence from each of the three crime scenes.

I worked my way backwards, starting with the Sunny Brown evidence. Like most murders, a large part of the physical evidence was the clothing the victim had been wearing. I didn't expect to find anything that couldn't be discovered with the usual forensic methods. The Seattle Police forensics work was as good as any.

What I wanted to find out was if there was any trace of Big's scent, the Marlboro Man traces I'd picked up at the Sunny Brown scene. If there were, I could accept that he was our killer, but if not then I'd have to work fast to find the real murderer, or the injustice would be compounded.

The mixed odors of a violent death are not pleasant, but beneath the overlay of blood and the fear-spiced, adrenalin-laden sweat and other bodily emissions, I could still pick out the strong scent of the Marlboro Man, as well as the distinctive scent of the Mukilteo Coffee used at the Second Cup, where Sunny Brown had worked.

There was also the reeking Dumpster garbage collage of odors...spilled beer and coffee, pizza and other food from the neighboring restaurants and taverns that used the trash receptacle. I didn't need to spend a lot of time on that evidence since it was all still filed in my brain.

I moved on to the evidence collected at the scene of one of the earlier victims. Up until now, all I knew of the earlier crimes was what I'd read in the reports. Not having been at the earlier crime scenes or having examined the physical evidence, this was all new to me. Being part human, even I make mistakes.

Now I took my time, working my way with light sniffs similar to the way wine tasters work, but with much more detail, following scents down through the layers, meticulously separating them into pure elements, for comparison with the endless olfactory bits a werewolf's brain stores.

I could find no Marlboro Man traces, but the unmistakable brand of coffee I encountered struck me like someone putting smelling salts in front of my sensitive nostrils, and I gasped for air. McBucks! That was an unexpected shock, since I didn't remember that either of the two earlier victims had worked for the McBucks Coffee Company.

I searched my memory. This victim, Tiffany Fredericks, had worked for Cupa Java, a drive-through stand on Queen Anne. There was no record of her ever working for McBucks. She got her start at a stand way out in Marysville, called the Buzz On. I'd never been into the Cupa Java, so I didn't know which brand of espresso beans they used, but I knew it couldn't be McBucks. They only supplied their own establishments under the McBucks name.

The first victim's name was Sheryl Calico, and she worked at a stand in Ballard, called Coffee Time. I opened the evidence carefully, working my way down through the olfactory complexities, and there it was again. McBucks! Unmistakable. I couldn't believe it, and again, there was no known connection between the victim and the McBucks Coffee Company.

I turned away from the evidence for a moment to clear my senses, and then started back down through the layers of scent, searching carefully for a trace of the Marlboro Man. It took no more than a moment this time to separate the bits and compare them. There was no Marlboro Man. I was absolutely positive.

Were there two killers? No Marlboro Man traces on the first two victims, but definitely McBucks Coffee, while I had detected only Mukilteo Coffee at the last crime scene and in the Sunny Brown evidence. Mukilteo Coffee and the Marlboro Man.

I thought back to the Sunny Brown crime scene...there was something...that spilled cup of McBucks coffee. It had been in the Dumpster before the body, but what if I'd discounted something because of it?

I needed to go back over the Sunny Brown evidence once more, to be sure. I put away the Sheryl Calico victim evidence, and was about to reopen Sunny Brown's, when my phone rang. For a moment I considered ignoring it and letting it ring, but whoever it was knew me well and was persistent.

I flipped it open. "Hello," I said in my unenthusiastic cell phone voice.

"Harley, it's Larry. Big Bird has flown the coop."

"Huh?"

"Our murder suspect, Big Mikey...he skipped out."

"What? You kidding me? He wasn't even conscious the last I saw him. What about Angie...?"

"She's gone too...must've helped him."

"I don't believe it. I didn't think he could even walk."

"Well, the nurse said he was awake and alert. He wouldn't be running any hundred-yard dashes. Going slow he would be all right for a while, especially with help. She said that without the morphine drip he was going to be in a lot of pain, and moving around could kill him."

"What about the officer on—?"

"He wasn't official. We hadn't arrested Big...so far as they knew he was the victim of a shooting and maybe a B&E perp...anyway, the uniform was posted on the floor, but he could leave the floor for coffee or to get something to eat. We didn't think he would be able to get out of there in his condition. My fault."

"Damn...I mean darn-it all..."

"You were right the first time. This is a damned mess and the Captain is going to have my hide. Looks like he's our perp though. If your little friend helped him, she's going to be in *Big trouble* too."

He emphasized the *Big trouble*. I could almost hear him smirk at his clever wordplay.

"A nurse saw someone in a hooded sweatshirt who was being pushed into the elevator. The one pushing had a hooded sweatshirt on also, so she couldn't ID who it was, but it sure sounds like your gal. They've outlawed hooded sweatshirts in London I hear...not a bad idea. Too many young punks wearing them to commit crimes so as no one can ID them. This guy might be slicker than we've given him credit for...might be pretending to be a dimwit. Got any idea where to look for them?"

Larry sounded frustrated and upset. "I don't know...yeah maybe. At least I know where she has been living."

"See what you can do, will you? If we get them back before we have to tell the press..."

"Yeah, I know. This is so stupid. We didn't have much on him. Now it really looks bad...at least for the Sunny Brown murder."

"I like him for them all. Seems he hung out around stands a lot. Did odd jobs for lattes and stuff."

"I don't know, Larry. I better get on it. The guy could croak if he falls or something and starts bleeding internally."

"Save us a lot of—"

"I'll call you back," I said, flipping off the phone.

FOURTEEN

"Angie," I shouted, knocking while standing at the door of the storage room where she stayed. "Angie, are you in there?"

"Harley, somethin' happen to Big?" she said, yanking the door open. "Is Big all right?"

For a moment I was stopped in my tracks. She seemed genuinely surprised and worried. "He left the hospital. You didn't know?"

"He left?" she said, backing away from the door.

"Yeah, the police think maybe you helped him."

"How could he? He's bad hurt. He was sleepin' when I left. I had to do some stuff here an' I was jus' gettin' ready to go back to the hospital. Are they sure he's really gone?"

"Looks like it. A nurse saw someone pushing him out in a wheelchair. They think it was you. I don't think anybody could lift him or force him to go if he didn't cooperate."

"But who would do that? I'm the only real friend he's got."

"I don't know, Angie. Even I thought it had to be you. It makes him look really guilty to take off like that."

"But he could die if he's not in the hospital?"

"He'll probably be all right," I said, trying to reassure her. "But we need to get him back there. Do you have any idea—?"

"I've got to get out there and find him, 'fore the cops shoot him or somethin'."

She had grabbed her jacket and was out the door and

past me in a flash. "Angie, wait," I said. "Lock your door. Do you still remember my cell phone number?"

"Yeah," she said, coming back to lock the door.

"Tell everyone you know on the streets to watch out for him, and give them my cell phone number and tell them to call me right away if they see him. They can ask any pedestrian on the street if they can use their cell phone for an emergency."

She gave me one of those "duh" looks, as if I was wasting her time. "Do you want a ride somewhere?"

"Nope. People on the street don' stay all up in one place," she said over her shoulder as she hurried off down the sidewalk and into the mist.

With the police and Angie's gang looking for Big, there wasn't anything more I could do along those lines that wasn't already being done. There was the possibility he might go back to Lovely's place so I gave her a call, but there was no answer. In my mind it was possible that she was the one who got Big out of the hospital, since I knew now it hadn't been Angie.

Would he have gone with her? Maybe. She did shoot him, but she was beautiful and smart and she was Sunny Brown's sister. He might go along, but I found it hard to believe she would be that stupid.

I opened the secret compartment and took out the .38 Police Special and clip-on belt holster I kept there. I didn't have any real reason to think I'd need it, but intuition or whatever similar werewolf senses I had, told me that things were heating up, so I clipped it on my belt at the back, with my jacket hiding it. Then I fired up the bike. I didn't really like carrying a gun, but with so many of them turning up in this case, I decided it was best to be prepared. I was getting tired of looking down the wrong end of the barrels.

With the bike idling, I called Larry and told him Angie wasn't the one who'd helped Big out of the hospital, and that she was going to help us try to find him, so they shouldn't pick her up.

I rode down to Lovely's place in Pioneer Square. The streets were slick, the air heavy and damp with ground fog, and the scent of the sea was strong as I parked the bike. I looked up at Lovely's loft windows...the place was dark.

I decided that as long as I was there I might as well go up to make sure nothing was amiss with her. If Lovely wasn't involved with Big's disappearance, and he was wandering around the streets on his own, there was a slim chance he might come here. I had to check, for both their sakes.

The old elevator ambled slowly upward, like an elderly person shuffling in front of you in the checkout line at the grocery store. At last the door opened into darkness. I knew where the switch was located, but being in the dark was no problem for a werewolf.

I switched it on and off anyway, flipping it back and forth a few times, like that would make it work. I didn't hear or feel any glass crunching underfoot.

The light fixture was at least twelve feet overhead, so the old trick of intruders unscrewing the bulb didn't seem likely. It was probably burned out—GE's contribution to the planned obsolescence our economy depends on. Making things that would last was as unlikely for the modern corporate world as tying the salaries of its grossly overpaid executives to the company's productivity.

I pulled back the sliding fire door. With all that had happened in this place recently my senses were on high alert, but I detected nothing out of the ordinary.

I called out, "Lovely...are you here?"

No answer. I decided to go on in and make sure everything was okay. I crept across the big outer room where I'd been clobbered over the head, and where Sunny Brown had put up street people during bad weather. It seemed to me the better of the two Brown sisters had died, but the best often do. Not that I wished anything bad for Lovely, but the down-on-their-luck poor would definitely miss Sunny.

Looking in through the door of the living quarters bathed in the reflected glow of street level neon, it appeared to be empty and orderly.

I turned on a lamp and searched for paper to leave a note for Lovely. It was important that she know Big had left the hospital...escaped, Larry would say. That was assuming she knew nothing about it.

I explained as much as I could of my view of the situation...that Big was seriously injured and in danger of dying if we didn't find him...that he had been helped to leave by someone unknown...and that I didn't think he was guilty of anything other than being in the wrong places at the wrong times. And I asked her to call me when she returned.

He might find his way here at some point, wounded and confused and thinking of this place as a refuge where he had been befriended in the past. Of course he had been shot here, but I'd bet the Harley he didn't have a clue as to what had happened. Bad luck was like a shadow for those on the street, especially for the mentally challenged.

On the other hand, it was quite possible Lovely had spirited Big out of the hospital, and if that was true it didn't look good for the big guy's survival. It would be tragic to have to arrest Lovely for murder.

As I made my way back to the street, I desperately longed for an espresso. I thought of McBucks, not far away, and that made me think of the McBucks scent I had earlier discovered on the first two barista victims' clothes, back in the evidence room.

With all the excitement, I'd temporarily filed it, but now it popped up. The McBucks connections kept coming back, like bats to the dark recesses of a cave.

Warming up the bike, I mused about thoughts being like bats, but then there was all that guano to shovel...layers of guano. Like Rodriguez. The McBucks' employee didn't smell like a rose, and I wasn't all that impressed with alibis by Arlene, who seemed to be in love with her demanding boss. Rodriguez claimed he was careful about sexual harassment issues, but then what else would he say? Liars always lie about lying. Maybe he was just careful about getting caught. I couldn't escape the strong feeling that Rodriguez had played a bigger part in this mess than it seemed on the surface. If he wasn't the killer, I was sure he knew something about it. There was also the matter of Helene's discovery of black-market McBucks coffee beans. My predator instincts told me it was all connected somehow.

I'd written down Rodriguez' address after an earlier conversation with Larry, thinking it might be good to talk to him outside his work domain, where he felt so secure and superior. This seemed like the time to make that call. It would be kind of late when I arrived, but it would be no social call and interrogating him in his pajamas would make him feel that much smaller.

First though, I'd pay a visit to Silver at The Den to see what I could get out of him about the source of those black market McBucks coffee beans. Maybe I could use that information to jack up Rodriguez, by threatening to take the whole mess and dumping it in his bosses' laps, like discarded McBucks-labeled garbage littering the Northwest.

⌇⌇

I walked into The Den half expecting to find Helene there, but relieved that she wasn't. Silver looked up from his place at the end of the bar, where he stood chatting up a pretty customer.

"Well, what do you know," he said with a slick, toothy grin. Without taking his eyes off me, he said, "Babe, let me introduce you to Seattle's dysfunctional detective." The woman seated next to him, turned and gave me the once-over as she exhaled cigarette smoke my way. She wasn't as pretty as I'd thought from the side view, but I'm biased against smokers, automatically deducting points from their IQ's.

"Yes," Silver went on, "this is the guy who hasn't solved any of the barista murders, but then he couldn't even protect his own grandmother."

Well, it looked like Silver had forgotten his apology for that incident and was back to being his old obnoxious self. I ignored the jabs though, not really caring what his smoking girlfriend thought. "I'd like to talk to you Silver," I said. "Alone, if you don't mind."

He looked me over, disappointed that I hadn't taken the cheap-shot bait. "All right," he said, reluctantly. He stepped behind the bar and poured a drink, then picked up his own and led me over to a booth. "Here, try this," he said, turning on the charm end of his mercurial personality, like he hadn't just insulted me.

I sniffed the brandy's fruity bouquet from where it swirled, glowing in the snifter. I'd rather have had a good espresso, but the brandy was probably a better choice for sealing my psyche from the pervasive dampening effects of Silver's company.

I sipped the brandy's silky warmth, and took a moment to appraise its origins. Not the best, I decided, but not far down the spectrum. I looked at Silver, wondering why the guy's pride in his liquor didn't apply to the espresso he served. "I hear you're serving bootlegged McBucks coffee at your stands. It's a step up from what you generally serve, but I imagine the McBucks people wouldn't be too happy to find out some of their product is going out the back door."

Silver looked surprised, but then understanding crept over his slick but handsome features. "Helene's got a big mouth sometimes. I told her I have no idea where those beans come from and I don't care. They're good and the price is right. If someone is stealing from McBucks...well, hey, they can afford it. Spreading the wealth is a good thing. A do-gooder like you should be able to appreciate that."

I took another sip of the brandy, its descending glow coating Silver's remarks. After a pause, I said, "Unfortunately, it's beginning to look like there might be a connection between the barista murders and the stolen McBucks beans, which would put you right back in the middle of it." That was all a stretch as far as any evidence went, but saying it aloud made the suggestion suddenly seem more likely than all the tie-ins being mere coincidence.

"That's ridiculous," Silver said. "The barista murders

you're supposed to be investigating have nothing to do with me."

"It does if you're withholding evidence from a murder investigation," I said. "I want to know where you're getting the McBucks beans."

Silver hesitated for a few beats, contemplating the situation. "Why didn't your bitch girlfriend tell you?" he snarled, calling my bluff. "Get your fucking buddies in the police department to hassle her if you want to know where the beans come from. Otherwise, talk to my lawyer."

I was stunned. "What makes you think Helene knows?"

"Because she asked me about it so I told her. I also told her not to tell anyone. She had the nerve to say, 'That depends.' I practically raised that girl from a pup, but I'm getting tired of having you always sniffing around after her. She deserves better and so do I." He stood up, grabbed my glass and threw it into the gas fireplace, breaking it against the fake logs. "Now get out of my place," he said, pulling a Glock 9mm from beneath his black leather jacket. Somebody must have had a real fire sale on those automatics. They seemed to be the glam choice in gun-wear.

I contemplated taking it away from him, just for fun, but you never know for sure how those ploys will work out. Besides, I was already one or two up on him and that was enough payback for his remarks about Helene. His reaction proved that she had hurt his pride by siding with me. In macho alpha werewolf language, that was a huge win for me. I knew I shouldn't be so smug about it, but I couldn't resist.

I gave Silver my own cat-chasing grin, and turned my back on him and his gun's inadequate phallic replacement.

Outside, the grin melted into concern. I punched in Helene's number, but it switched to the phone voice saying that number was unavailable.

If the black market McBucks beans and the barista murders were connected, then Helene could be putting herself in danger by snooping around to find out who was selling the beans. Her unanswered cell phone became an insistent alarm in my head, and I had to fight back a sense of panic. I needed to find her before I did anything else. The unanswered cell phone was probably just a dead battery or something. It had happened before, because she used it so much.

I tried to tell myself that was the reason, but after firing the bike up I carelessly spun out on the wet street, a bit out of control as I rode for Helene's espresso stand.

I could see the flashing blue lights before I got there and my heart sank. I roared up to the stand, skidded to a halt, pegged the bike stand and jumped off.

One of the patrol officers was standing in the doorway shining a flashlight inside, and the other was in the car talking on the radio. I said I was a friend of the owner and pushed past, hollering for Helene.

"Hold it a minute buddy," the cop in the doorway said. "We just arrived, but there's no one here. Looks like a burglary. You want to call the owner?"

"That's why I'm here. She hasn't been answering her cell phone." I reached for the light switch and flipped it on. "Damn," I said, shocked at the mess. It looked like a large animal had torn the place apart. The espresso machine looked like it had blown up and there was water everywhere. I introduced myself to the officer and asked if I could look around.

"Yeah, sure, I've heard of you. Go ahead. You don't think this is another of those barista—?"

He didn't finish what he had started to say, probably remembering I had said the owner was a friend. I went all the way to the back where the little office was, and the shock hit me hard. There was money all over the floor, scattered around. I staggered back, feeling dizzy with dread. It wasn't a burglary or a robbery, so something very bad had happened.

The cop in the doorway had followed me back, and he reached out and steadied me. I said, "Call Larry Meyers down in homicide will you?"

"You okay?" he said.

"No...hell no I'm not okay. This is my girlfriend, she's missing and we have a barista serial killer out there. Just make the call, will you?"

He left me, and I tried to pull myself together. I took a deep breath through my nose, gathering the scent, working through the layers. There was something out of place, but I couldn't make it out at first. Then it hit me...McBucks coffee...the unmistakable scent of the McBucks blend. It was as out of place here as the smell of pesticide in an organic garden.

Then I remembered the exploded espresso machine. Something had caused one of the boilers to blow. I picked through the pieces of stainless steel...and there it was...an entry hole where a bullet had penetrated.

I looked around again. There was a little blood and the scent was Helene's, but it didn't seem to be enough for a serious injury. Hopefully it wasn't anything life-threatening. It looked like she had put up a good fight, at least until the gun came into play. The thing was, the barista killer didn't use a gun. Maybe there was a chance this was something else, but somehow, deep down in my werewolf senses, I didn't think so.

My cell phone rang and I answered, hoping...hoping... "Damn...not her," I mumbled after flipping the phone lid.

"Harley, hello, are you there?"

"Yeah, I'm here Larry. Somebody has Helene..."

"Your girlfriend?"

"Yes. I'm at her espresso stand, the Espresso Passion, on Capitol Hill."

"Okay Harley...they gave me the address and I'm on my way. Any ideas?"

"We'd discovered there are black market McBucks coffee beans being sold to some stands. Helene was going to check into it, because they've been undercutting the prices. Then I learned tonight that she might have found out who was selling them."

"So her disappearance doesn't seem to be connected to the Barista Basher cases?"

"I don't know Larry. I have a feeling there is a connection, but maybe not. There was a shot fired inside the stand, which doesn't fit. I don't know. Can you put out an alert for her?"

"Of course. Give me a description."

"She's twenty-seven, five foot-six, red hair, dark brown eyes, athletic build. Her name is Helene Star."

"Got it. Anything else?"

"Can't think of anything right now. Nothing on that guy, Big?"

"No, but if he's our guy he's one tough dude. You going to wait for me there?"

"No. I'm going to get everyone I can out looking for her, and I have a couple of things to look into."

"All right Harley, but keep it within the law. You understand?"

"Sure, I'll try, for your sake, but I can't promise...if anything has happened..."

"Keep me informed Harley. That's an order."

I flipped the phone shut and ran outside. I got down on all fours, sniffing the ground, getting a light scent of Helene even in the rain, but it ended, maybe where a car would have been parked. I jumped up and went for the bike.

I heard the cop calling, "Heyyy—" as I fired it up, but the roar drowned him out. I didn't care much what he wanted from me. I was heading back to Silver's hole.

❧❧

I walked into The Den and went straight for Silver, who had been talking with a couple of the goons beside him at his usual place at the end of the bar. I threw the two aside in quick succession, with one falling backwards over a nearby table. The other recovered his balance and tried to grab me, so I stomped hard on his right foot and drove my forearm into the side of his head.

I turned and caught Silver's wrist as he reached inside his jacket for his gun, twisting it as I pulled him around, pushing his face down on the bar. "Okay, Silver, someone has kidnapped Helene," I growled into his ear, feeling the adrenalin surge taking me very close to the *change*. I lifted his head up by the hair and slammed the side of his head back down into the bar.

"Ow, damn you," he said. "I don't have any idea who would do that. I don't give a fuck what you think, she's like family to me. We've had our differences, but that is because of you. I would never hurt Helene."

I slammed his head down again. "Then tell me who you're getting the McBucks beans from."

"Fuck you, you dog-sniffing bastard," he mumbled through the blood trickling from his mouth. "I'm not telling you anything...but if you think there might be a connection...I'll check it out myself. Let me up and I'll get the pack out looking for her. Bashing me around is doing nothing——" I let him up. "Except make you feel like a piss-assed hero."

"All right Silver, we'll do it your way. You're just stubborn enough to get her killed thinking this is all some alpha contest between you and me. If anything happens to her though, you're going to need more than that gun to protect you...a lot more."

I turned and walked toward the door, heard a round rack into a gun, and felt the bullet graze my right ear, splintering a hole through the door in front of me. "That's your warning, Wolf. You're the one who got Helene rooting around in other people's business. If anything happens to her, you are the one who is going to pay."

I pushed on through the door, relieved to find there was no dead body on the other side. I found it hard to believe someone had risked kidnapping Helene over a few stolen coffee beans, but this was Seattle. Anyway, Silver had convinced me he would spare no effort looking into that angle. Getting in the last word meant he had to back it up.

There was one angle that had been bothering me. My werewolf intuition told me there was something not right about Rodriguez, but I hadn't been able to get back to him. I had sensed he was lying about something when I'd talked to him, and the image of Arlene, his assistant, crying as she left the office that day, meant her boss had come down hard on her for something unusual.

I checked his address on the paper in my wallet. He lived in Lake Forrest Park. I knew the area well and could nearly visualize the address. I had a friend who once lived close to Rodriguez's address, so I thought I could find it. If not, I could find it with the Garmin GPS unit I carried on the bike.

Fifteen minutes of riding through heavy rain got me to the right street. It was a dead-end with nice houses on big lots. I parked the bike a block away and walked. The bass rumble of a Harley always attracted a lot of attention and I wanted to surprise Rodriguez.

The houses were on a wooded ridge, and I found the right numbers on one of the two mailboxes marking a drive at the very end of the cul-de-sac. There were two houses on the long, curving drive, probably built when the property had been sub-divided. An eight-foot high cedar fence surrounded the prop-erty, and had what looked like an electric sliding gate as well as a cedar pedestrian gate. The setback from the next house was a good forty feet. The neighbors on this side had a hedge that ran along the fenced property line. These people liked their privacy and probably only knew each other by the make of their expensive SUV's.

The house itself was a low ranch type with a wrap around deck facing the ridge. There was a late-model VW Beetle sit-ting in front of one of the three garage doors. Did he have a guest?

I quietly let myself through the gate. The lights in the house were low. I assumed the master bedroom was in one corner of the main floor. I checked my watch...twelve twenty-seven.

As I made my way along the side of the house it looked like there might be a daylight basement with a covered patio protecting it from rain and any run-off from the deck above. I saw a flickering light shining on the trees, and I heard a low moaning...maybe a man's voice...and a strange whacking sound. Could it be Big? Somewhere in the distance, a police siren went off and coyotes down in the ravine gave an answering call, the dumb mutts.

Something strange was happening inside. I crept to the corner and looked around. I don't know what I expected to find there, but it wasn't what I saw through the sliding glass doors. There were candles everywhere, and a couple of red lava lamps lighting the depraved scene.

A tall, blonde woman dressed in black leather chaps, black boots and nothing else was standing behind a man kneeling on the floor with his head and his wrists sticking through what appeared to be one of those wooden stock things they used for public punishment back in the Colonial days. The guy was dressed in black chaps also, with his bare butt facing me. The woman was standing behind him, whipping him with a short cat o' nine tails as she pushed a dildo up his ass.

Jeez! I couldn't see the guy's face, but I recognized his voice as he moaned and begged for more. Rodriguez. Cute. Of course he was in what he probably thought of as the privacy of his own home, and if it weren't for being desperate for some clue to Helene's whereabouts, I would have turned and left.

Instead, I stepped up and slid the sliding glass door open. "Excuse me," I said. "Is this the Rodriguez residence?"

The moaning stopped, the whipping stopped, and there was an awkward silence. Then the woman faced me without embarrassment and said, in a calm, officious voice, "Who the hell are you?"

"I'm a consultant with the police, investigating the murders of three baristas in Seattle." I was on shaky ground but this wasn't the time to worry about little things like that. "Are you a professional?"

"No, I'm his fucking grandmother and I caught him being a bad boy."

"You're trespassing on private property," Rodriguez whined. "You have no right to come in here like that. Bitch, take that thing out of my ass."

"You don't call me bitch, little boy," the woman said, whipping his naked buttocks furiously, with Rodriguez screaming in pain. "The safe word is definitely not bitch."

I waited a few beats, then I put my hand on her shoulder and said, "That's enough. Get rid of that thing, will you?" She gave me a fierce look...like, did I want some? I put my hands up and said, "Pretty please remove that object?"

She smiled a smile that made me shudder. I looked away and walked around to his front side, pulling up a nearby chair. I heard a sound that led me to believe the dildo had departed, and when I looked up, the dominatrix was standing there, smiling, her legs apart and with both hands on the whip handle, holding it in front of her. There were worse things in the night than werewolves, by far.

I took out my cell phone and held it up in front of Rodriguez. "Here's a phone. I'll dial 911 for you and then we'll all just sit here and wait for them...well, kneel in your case. I'm sure your friend here has an arrest record and it will all look swell on a police report. You might even make the TV. By the way, this is a camera phone. I wonder what your bosses will think when I send them some pictures of you like this."

I started dialing 911 and got to the last digit before he hollered, "All right, stop. What do you want? I haven't done anything."

"Not quite true, Rodriguez," I said, bluffing as I flipped the phone shut. "You withheld information in a homicide investigation. I want the truth this time. What was your relationship with Sunny Brown...and the other two murdered baristas?" Including the other two dead baristas in my question had just slipped out...a hunch.

"All right, all right, who told you? It was that bitch secretary of mine wasn't it? I dated both of those girls, but I happen to like baristas. I date a lot of them. Is that a crime?" I was surprised at his admission. He sagged sideways as far as the stocks would allow, looking about to cry. The dominatrix whipped him another good one and he straightened up, screaming, "Stop...stop...this isn't fun anymore."

"Well, pal," I said in my best cop voice, "Dating baristas is a crime if you murder them. You withheld information in a police investigation, and that's illegal. What about Sunny Brown? Were you doing her too?"

"Did Arlene tell you that? I don't care what she said, I never slept with that stuck-up little bitch. I just flirted with her some and she got all huffy. I had to pay her off to keep her from reporting me. What did she expect the way she dressed? She did it purposely to get money out of me. She didn't like working there so I gave her five hundred bucks to go away."

"That doesn't look good for you. Blackmail is a motive for murder. It's probably enough to arrest you on."

"I didn't do anything, I swear. I'm not a killer. Besides, I got even by screwing her sister."

"Lovely Brown?"

"Yes. Lovely ass too," He said sarcastically. The jerk couldn't resist bragging about it, even in that position.

I nodded to the blonde with the whip. She smiled and gave him a couple more hard whacks. They were not love taps this time.

"Ow, hey, damn, that's going to leave marks. I said to stop."

"Did you forget the safe word, you bad boy?" she said, raising the whip to strike again."

"Mommy, mommy," Rodriguez mumbled.

His hired whip stopped her arm in midair and grimaced, shaking her head with a look that said she thought he was pathetic. "Your mommy isn't going to get rid of me," I said, getting in his face "You're going from there to jail unless you answer my questions. Did Sunny know about you and her sister?"

"Okay, okay, I had my secretary tell her—they were friends, sort of—I mean I asked Arlene to get friendly with her so I could find out if she liked me...you know, what she said about me."

"You're a first-class slimeball, Rodriguez." I felt like going around behind him and giving him a swift kick...see if I couldn't score a goal.

"I can't help it if women are attracted to me. C'mon, let me out of here. I'll help you in any way I can."

"You've done enough, pond scum." I nodded to the woman in leather and said, "Let him out, and get dressed...you're giving me goosebumps."

She didn't budge an inch, saying eagerly, "Give me some time with him and I'll find out if he goes around killing innocent women."

I didn't answer for a moment. It was a tempting offer, but then I sighed and said, "No, I believe him. I don't think it was him. I wish he were the killer, but I'm afraid he's just an asshole."

I didn't know why, but I was becoming more and more convinced that it had to be the killer who had kidnapped Helene, and she wasn't here. I hoped the killer was holding her hostage somewhere. If he had wanted to kill her he could have done that at the stand. Somehow Big was involved, and maybe Lovely. She had neglected to tell me about her relationship with Rodriguez. Maybe she wanted Big dead because he knew something. Was it all a crime of passion, or a cover-up for a ring of coffee bean thieves? Maybe Sunny's death was a copycat murder to cover up other crimes. I knew I was getting close, but would it be in time to save Helene? I stood up and walked to the door where I'd come in. Then I turned back. "What do you know about the bootleg McBucks coffee beans being sold on the black market?"

"Fuck, you know about that too? What's that got to do with Sunny? I thought that investigation was all internal. Shit. They just told me last week. They said they were close to arresting the guys, but they think there is somebody higher up. Maybe they did take it to the police. It's a trucker and a couple of warehouse guys, so far as I know. They told me not to tell anyone until the investigation is over. I guess it's already out, but I had nothing to do with that or any other crime. Honest. Please let me out of here."

I didn't answer. Leaving it up to his hired help I walked

out, shutting the door behind me. I felt like I was going around in endless circles, like chasing my tail. I was halfway up to the gate when my cell phone rang. "Hello," I said.

"Hi Harley, it's Angie."

"Angie? Someone kidnapped Helene."

"No kiddin'? Damn Harley, I'm sorry. But I got some news for you. One of the guys searching for Big talked to some guy who told him that Big, a while back, useta' hang out in this old warehouse down First South...down pas' Safeco Field."

"What's the address?"

"That's just it, I don' know exactly. I jus' got directions. It's a couple of buildings across First Avenue South from Sears...well used to be Sears anyway."

"Jeez Angie, that's kinda vague."

"Yeah, I know. Sorry. He did say they stored coffee in there. Said Big let him stay up in there sometimes. Said those bags made good beds and he jus' had to get out before the workers came in the mornin'. I guess Big had permission from somebody long as he did'n get caught or tell anybody. Sorry I did'n fin' out—"

"You did fantastic, Angie," I said, suddenly excited. "Keep an eye out for Helene will you?"

"Sure...but—"

"Gotta go," I said, closing the phone and running back down the hill and around the corner, sliding the same glass door open. "Rodriguez," I shouted. "I'll try to keep you out of this if you answer one more question. Does McBucks have a coffee warehouse down on First Avenue South in Seattle?" He had a robe on, the woman was dressed, and he was handing her money.

"Yes, we do," he said.

"Give me the address."

～ ～

It seemed like a long ride to Seattle, although I've never ridden with more urgency. My mind was turning faster than the bike's black chrome wheels. I went back over everything that had happened, over and over it in a loop. There was a connecting trail and I knew the answer was there, like a rabbit hiding in underbrush, if I could just flush it out.

All the distractions kept it hidden from consciousness. Worry about Helene kept intruding—fear that I was already too late...if the Barista Basher had struck again...he had never kept a hostage before that we knew of. I tried not to go there. But then the loop in my mind would start all over again.

I was surprised when I realized I was getting close, riding along First Avenue South. The ride seemed like nightmare time, but the torturous wait was almost over, or so I hoped. I had no real reason to think I'd find Helene there, so maybe it was a werewolf thing between Helene and me, like that sense a wolf has of where its mate is...the silent howl.

I found the warehouse, next to the railroad tracks, and parked the bike. I could see two doors on the loading dock...one a freight door and the other routine access. The building looked deserted and dark, and my hopes sank. There were no vehicles in the small parking area.

I tried the regular pedestrian door—it was locked. I abandoned all pretense of stealth, slamming my shoulder into it. I could feel some give to the old door and I slammed against it again. A little more give so I hit it again and went crashing through into black space, tumbling and rolling to a stop on a cold concrete floor.

I got to my knees and reached for the gun I'd forgotten to draw, and the small flashlight I always carried, one of those little key chain lights sold at REI for hiking emergencies. It was too dark. Even werewolf eyes needed some illumination. I heard muffled noises as I clicked my little light on, my gun ready.

Huge burlap bags of green coffee beans, sixty-pounders on pallets, were piled high everywhere. I made my way down a walkway between the beans, toward the interior and heard sounds that sounded like a muffled human voice. I didn't look for a light switch, thinking the dark gave me cover, and my senses functioned better in the dark than that of pureblooded humans.

I moved toward the muffled sounds I heard, and suddenly, in the weak light, I saw Helene and rushed to her. She was slumped to the floor, her hands tied behind her back and around a structural post. The bluish-white beam of the flashlight revealed her left eye was swollen shut and there were other bruises on her face. Good-for-any-crime duct tape covered her mouth. The muffled sounds I had heard had come from her. She was trying to tell me something.

I hesitated before ripping the tape off as carefully as I could, hoping her other injuries would lessen any short burst of pain from the tape removal. And besides, I could tell that was what Helene wanted, desperately. She had been badly beaten. Blood still oozed from a cut above her swollen left eye, and when I removed the tape, she spat blood from her mouth. She was having a hard time holding her head up.

She spat again, then said, "I...I knew you...were coming. I'm...sorry I'm...such a...mess."

"You've never looked more beautiful...you're alive," I said, kissing her forehead. "Let me get you loose."

The look of momentary relief drained from her and she looked at me with sudden fear and panic. "No...she's liable to...be back any...she...she went...to...kill——" She choked, and spat blood again, then a coughing fit seized her.

"Lovely?" I asked, trying to help...to save her the pain. It seemed all she could do to speak at all. Like a flash in the dark, it suddenly made sense——the one answer that connected all of the dots...all of the victims...the coffee bean thing.

"Dizzy," Helene whispered. "Sorry."

With my sudden epiphany I felt a little disoriented myself. I holstered my gun, taking out my jackknife to cut her bonds.

"Quick," she said, looking confused. "You've...got to be careful...she——"

"Who?" I said again——like a stupid out-of-place rendition of that old "who's on first" routine of some long-dead comedians——wanting her to confirm what I already knew.

"I think she means me," I heard, as the warehouse lights came on, momentarily blinding me. I reached for my gun, but too late as my vision recovered enough to see she was holding a gun on us.

"Hold it," Arlene said, "Take it out and lay it down like a good boy."

I did as she ordered, while the rabid rabbit broke through the brambles in my mind. Arlene!

"Okay, now slide the gun away from you, but be careful...your girlfriend gets the first bullet, and that would be very upsetting. I'd rather finish the bitch the way I started."

As I slid the gun away, the anger that had been building inside boiled over. I guess it was the viciousness of her words that set it off. I tried to control it...a glance at Helene's battered face, still defiant in spite of it...the look in her eyes telling me to go for it...hold nothing back. We both knew she intended to kill us anyway.

Then I saw Big, tied to another post beyond Helene. He was slumped over, unconscious.

If she had shut up, I might have been able to stop it. But her psychotic mind wanted to gloat...to revel in the control of us...to make us feel as helpless and low as she felt in her daily life.

"You had to interfere, didn't you Mr. big-shot detective. He loves me, I know he does, deep down. Once I got rid of those floozy barista bitches who were always flinging themselves at him. I'm the one who loves him...*I'm the only one who really, really loves him*," she shouted. "Then you had to come along and upset him. He didn't mean to holler at me, I knew that. He's just weak."

"You're....the weak one," Helene spat out.

"We'll see about that bitch...see how you like watching me shoot your boyfriend. He's my special bonus baby. I think you'll be begging me to shoot you too, before I'm done with you. Then fat boy over there will shoot himself, and the cops will find their little barista mystery all solved for them."

While she was doing all her ranting, rage was rising in

me with a flood of adrenalin and whatever other special mix of chemicals I'd inherited that brings on the *change*. I couldn't stop it now. It was taking over and I fell, writhing on the floor, going with it. It doesn't take a silver bullet to stop an enraged werewolf—that's myth—but if you don't have one it does take quite a few of the ordinary lead kind. *Mother Moon, take me.*

I heard Arlene say, "What the heck?...stop that...I'm going to—"

The last part is blanked out as the change takes me with a rush, the fight or flight call of the wild speeded up by the urgency of the moment.

Wolf/I suddenly on four paws, shaking out of clothes, growling, fangs bared, stalking forward ready to spring at the enemy.

Arlene paralyzed with shock, screaming in horror. "No! No!" Backing away, she is barely able to look at Wolf, her nightmares becoming reality. "You know I hate dogs...no, no, nooo, stay back...this is some trick...you're trying to make me think I'm crazy aren't you?"

Suddenly she is remembering the gun in her paralyzed hand...staring at it for an instant...back and forth...looking from the gun to the snarling beast stalking her, poised to spring for her throat...she backs away, stumbling against the walls of coffee bean-filled burlap bags, trying desperately to make some sense of the creature before her eyes...denying this new external insanity...desperate to make it all disappear back into the dark corners of her mind.

She fires the gun, wildly, over and over, the blasts ringing in my ears as Wolf springs for her.

I barely notice the burn of a bullet, like some ionized, supersonic, steroidal mosquito. My front paws hit her chest as my jaws seize the gun, wrenching it from her as she falls backwards. She hits the concrete floor hard beneath me, making the dog-like sound of, "woof," as wind is knocked out of her. She gasps for breath, moans and is quiet—falling unconscious. The sound of coffee beans falling like waterfall from bags ripped open by wild bullets fills the sudden silence.

With a swing of my head I throw the gun across the floor and trot over to Helene. Her head is down and I am afraid a wild bullet has injured her.

I lick her face and she lifts her head. She spits out blood, and reading the worry in my eyes says, "Don't worry, she missed me. Good boy...you...magnificent creature. I...don't know how you did...that..." She tries a smile. "But you've got to...teach me."

I feel my tail wagging like some crazed bass drummer's thumping drumstick, feeling a little silly, but as happy as I've ever been. Then I remember Arlene and realize I'd better make sure she is incapacitated before I chew away Helene's bonds.

I look over and don't see her. I bound closer, but she is gone. The purse she'd been carrying is there on the ground, and when I look for the gun, it is still where I tossed it.

I pick up the black leather purse in my mouth and carry it back to Helene. I must hurry, but I'm afraid to leave her tied up.

She is weak, but she knows what is happening and she moves around so the knot tying her hands is facing me. I bite at the ropes, savagely, but it is awkward without hands and takes a couple of precious extra seconds.

When her hands are free, I pick up my gun from the pile of clothes strewn on the concrete floor, and give it to her. She is too weak to stand up, but she takes the gun from my muzzle, pats me on the head and says, "Go get her Harley."

I hesitate, afraid to leave her alone, but she reaches over and picks up my pseudo-leather jacket lying on the floor next to her where I'd shed it. She reaches in the right-hand pocket and pulls out my cell phone, smiling at me weakly. "Go..." she says, and Wolf bounds out the door in hot pursuit of the barista killer. On the loose, Arlene could kill again before she is caught.

Outside, I see her car is still parked there as I'd hoped it would be. The keys are in her abandoned purse. Habits die hard.

Maybe she has a concussion, or maybe she is faking injury, but fear and confusion are paralyzing her and she hasn't *gotten far. I see her out on the sidewalk, and a howl escapes my throat. Wolf leaps from the loading dock, bounding out into the street after her.*

She sees me and keeps trying to run but in her haste and fear, repeatedly falls down, unable to take her terrified eyes off the Wolf, stalking closer.

The railroad track barriers come down with the lights flashing red and the freight train's engineer blowing his horn.

Arlene looks at the approaching freight train, then back at me and she can't resist flashing a psychotic grin before turning to run. There is barely time for her to make it across, but she will make it, looking back at me one last time, her fear of Wolf greater than her fear of the roaring steel monster hurtling at her.

Tripping on the uneven footing of the railroad crossing as she turns to run, she falls forward.

Wolf's muscles tense to spring to save her— too late. The engine's locked-up screeching steel wheels accompany her rabbit-panic scream as the train runs over her.

With that horrible death-scream, all of the predator energy whooshes out of me, leaving a vacuum of sadness and sorrow. She really was a rabbit in life...a rabbit turned vicious...a rabbit infected with a rabies-like disease of the mind, but peculiar to humans. Obsessive, psychotic jealousy.

Turning to hurry back to Helene, I could already feel the change seeping out of me and I couldn't let that happen out here on the street.

Wolf/I find Helene, lick weakly at her wounds—then collapsing, I lie down, head on her lap.

She runs her fingers through the fur on my head and neck, whispering, "You're hurt Harley...easy boy, easy. Help is on the way."

Wolf departs from me, with my depression at the loss of him taking me stronger than usual as I change back, becoming, on the surface at least, a very weak human once again.

EPILOGUE

Wolf bounds through snowdrifts in the lightly wooded meadow. As the rabbit zigs left...zags right...then with all four lucky feet kicking up rooster-tails of snow in my face, it ducks into a tangled web of briars. I slide to a stop nearly nose to white furry tail as it turns and sits there laughing in my face. But it isn't a rabbit laugh, or it somehow morphs into an insane woman's laugh, and I spin my own four paws to get away from the crazed creature. I want to get far away, and the suddenly bright light on the white snow turns to gray...as I opened my eyes, looking out through a window at the gray clouds scudding across the sky.

"I'm sorry," a woman's voice said. I turned my head and saw a nurse, a wide smile lighting up her brown face, and it came back to me. Harborview hospital. Trapped in a bed. I frantically looked the other way and saw Helene, or at least the bit of her that showed through all the bandages.

"Yes, she's still there," the nurse said in a hushed voice, almost a whisper. "We usually don't do coed rooms, but you two fought like wild animals to stay together, so we figured you were mates of some kind, even with different names."

"Oh...sorry...I mean thanks...uhm..."

"Oh no, you're the one who deserves the thanks. You're a hero...caught that murdering Barista Basher. Who'd of thought it would turn out to be a woman? Those kind are usually depraved men, beg your pardon."

"Can you tell me what Helene's injuries are and how she

is doing?"

"She's doing good considering the concussion, the deep cuts and contusions about her head, the broken nose, the burn on her left arm, a couple of cracked ribs and a bunch of other bruises. She was beat-up bad, but she should recover quickly with no lasting damage. Sounds like you were both lucky to escape with your lives, bad as the killer was."

"What time is it?"

"It's two-fifteen in the afternoon. You slept well after you got out of the operating room where they fixed up that bullet wound in your shoulder. I'm sorry I woke you. When I came in you were sleeping, but you were thrashing all around and sort of yipping, almost like my little terrier Boomer does when he's sleeping. We always say he's dreaming of chasing rabbits. It made me laugh, but yours could have been a bad dream too considering what you went through, so I woke you up. Do you want to talk to the policeman waiting outside? He's pretty anxious to see you."

"Do you think it will bother Helene?"

"She's on a morphine drip so I don't think so as long as you keep your voices down."

"Is the cop's name Larry?"

"I think that was it...plainclothes."

"Okay, have him come in, and thanks."

The nurse smiled and left. I remembered I hadn't asked her name. I looked at Helene...the nurse was right...we had been lucky to escape with our lives.

I closed my eyes for a minute, thinking I needed to get out of the hospital. I did feel tired though.

"Hey Harley," a familiar voice said, whispering.

I opened my eyes. "Hi Larry."

"How you doing guy?"

"I'm okay. Helene is the one who took a real beating."

"Yes, I know. But the doctors say she is going to be all right. That guy Big is down the hall. He's going to live, but he lost a lot of blood. You've got quite a few people out there trying to get in to see you both, but the nurse is keeping them away until you get some rest."

"What about Lovely Brown? Arlene was after her too."

"Yes, but luckily Lovely was up in Everett helping out a sick friend with her espresso stand. I've talked to Big, and from what you all said, the perp intended to kill everyone, including Lovely, and blame it on Big. When Helene called her at work asking about the stolen coffee beans, she decided to get even with you too, but it wrecked her timetable. She had to kill Lovely before she killed Helene and Big, to make the tie-in with Big stronger. She knew Big from being friends with Sunny, and he thought Arlene was his friend as well. If you hadn't figured out where they were when you did, there would have been at least two more dead. She could have decided to leave Lovely for later."

"I have to thank Angie for that."

"She's been here ever since they brought you all in. I thanked her, and I'm putting her in for a commendation medal. We may get her juvie sheet cleared too."

"That's great, Larry. She's a good kid."

"The papers have picked up the whole story, and I wouldn't be surprised if her and Big come out of this with a good financial start. The city's baristas are taking up a collection for them, and the media boys tell me there are lots of offers coming in."

"Wow, that's fantastic. Maybe some good will come out of this. Sounds like you've got most of the loose ends tied up."

"This was one weird case, Harley. Who'd have guessed the Barista Basher would turn out to be a woman? She's not the first female serial killer, but the way it was done, beating them to death...turns out though she was a workout nut and a Karate black belt. Tough gal."

"And one consumed with hatred. I knew something wasn't right with her, but there are lots of people with problems who don't become serial killers. Her obsession with Rodriguez pushed her over the edge. What about him? I told him I'd keep him out of it."

"We could try to get him on obstruction charges, but since

we got the killer no one is too excited about that. Most of it came out in the papers though, so he'll undoubtedly lose his job. McBucks doesn't like that kind of publicity and the killer worked for him."

"That will be as hard on him as anything. He deserves whatever he gets. Not leveling with us almost got more people killed."

"You know, Harley, there is something else that's weird."

"What's that?"

"The engineer of the train that ran over the perp...he...this is going to sound weird, but he swears he saw a big dog or something chasing her, but he didn't see you. He said it might have been a wolf, which is ridiculous...a wolf in downtown Seattle...a coyote maybe, but not a wolf. You didn't see a big dog did you?"

"No, I didn't, but I was intent on catching Arlene. It was dark, and to tell you the truth, when you see a train about to run over someone, that's all you see. You know, the witness thing. When that engineer saw he was about to run over a woman, I doubt if he was looking around much. Maybe he saw a dog just before it happened. Even with the street lights it was pretty dark."

"Yes, that's what I think too. But he swore over and over that's what he saw. Of course he was a *trained* observer."

I shook my head as he laughed out loud at his pun, and then he put his finger to his lips, shushing himself. "I better get out of here and let you get some rest," he said in a loud whisper.

"I'd like to get out of here myself," I said, "but then Helene would insist on leaving too, so I guess I'll spend the night."

"Good idea, Harley. I'll check in with you tomorrow. Anything I can get you?"

"Hey, would you send Angie in so I can thank her? But that's all. I don't want anyone to bother Helene."

"Absolutely. Get some rest buddy."

I sighed. That was too close. It was very lucky that eyewitnesses are notorious for what they miss at a crime scene.

Larry didn't say anything, but usually they see different things, rather than hallucinating big dogs...or werewolves. It's a good thing people report seeing all kinds of strange stuff, like UFO's and Bigfoot. Witnesses who say they've seen things the ordinary person hasn't seen tend to get put in the wacko category.

I looked up and saw Angie standing in the doorway. She was trying to wipe away tears, as I motioned her over. She put an arm across my chest and lay her head on the bed beside me. She was too short to give me a hug. I stroked her hair with my free hand, and we stayed that way for a moment.

Then she lifted her head and tried to wipe the tears away. "I'm so glad you're all right," she said, through her sniffles. "Thanks for savin' Big."

"It was you who did it, Angie. I'd never have found them in time without you. You're a hero."

"No I'm not. I was just helpin' friends like anybody'd do."

"Well, you're my hero, and it sounds like most of the city of Seattle agrees with me."

"People've sure been swell," she said, her face beaming through her tears, like a rainbow after a storm.

"How's Big doing?"

"Los' a lot of blood they said, but he's feelin' better, 'specially since I tol' him we were both gonna get off the street. He don' understand a lot of what went down though."

"Yeah, he was already unconscious when I got there."

"That Arlene woman got him out of the hospital. He thought she was a friend, an' she tol' him she needed him to help her catch the person who killed Sunny. She tol' him it was your girlfriend there, Helene," she said, nodding over toward the next bed.

"It's not Big's fault," I assured her, "none of it. Like you said, Arlene knew Big because she was a friend of Sunny's. She took advantage of him being a gentle guy and that he was living rough. She knew everyone would believe it was a street person who was the Barista Basher, so she tried to set him up."

"We're not no more. Anythin' I could get you, Harley? I owe you a lot."

"Are you kidding? Helene wouldn't be alive if it weren't for you."

"Okay, well, we're even then. But don' you want a burger or somethin'?"

"I'd really love a soy latte," I said with a sigh.

"You got it babe," she said. "The java here is good, at least I think so."

"As long as it's not McBucks," I said with a shudder. "I never ever want to drink another McBucks."

ABOUT THE AUTHOR

Murdoch Hughes has lived his adult life along the West Coast of North America, from Mexico to Alaska's Aleutian Islands. However if he were to call a place home it would be Seattle, walking her misty streets at night with the ghosts of her past, while sipping

Photo by Chris Amonson

the dark espresso of her present, and scenting the seaweed and cedar dreams of the area's long Native American history.

He lived for six years on Unalaska Island, in the Aleutian Islands, working as a fisherman and a marine engineer. Then he sailed for two years with his wife Jan on their thirty-two foot sailboat, Hunter Star, down the Pacific Coast and into the Sea of Cortez, exploring the many islands and coves of Baja California Sur, Mexico.

Swallowing the anchor and moving ashore, they lived for four more years in the beautiful, peaceful city of La Paz, near the tip of the Baja peninsula. It was there he wrote his Baja and Mexico based Rick Sage Mysteries: *Murder In La Paz*, and *Death Mask of the Jaguar*.

Murdoch is presently living and writing in the Seattle area.

Printed in the United States
101337LV00001B/70/A

9 781594 264863